CALL OF THE SYRON

—Book One —

ALYSSA BUKOWSKI

FriesenPress
One Printers Way
Altona, MB R0G 0B0
Canada

www.friesenpress.com

First Edition — 2022

ISBN
978-1-03-912721-0 (Hardcover)
978-1-03-912720-3 (Paperback)
978-1-03-912722-7 (eBook)

1. FICTION, FANTASY, ACTION & ADVENTURE

Distributed to the trade by The Ingram Book Company

CHAPTER ONE

I pressed my hands into the sand, letting the grains slip between my fingers, the feeling calming my mind. I felt the roughness of each mote as they coated my skin. As the sand fell, I mentally prepared myself for the approaching challenge.

Kneeling down next to the pit, I evened out my breaths. My eyes were closed, leaving the world around me dark. Though, even with my sight gone, I could feel everything around me.

I listened for every little sound, building up the terrain in my mind. The fighting pit was right in front of me, my opponent shuffling a few feet ahead on the other side. Too my left another brawl was in full swing, grunts and curses leaving the competetors.

Focus.

I heard her voice clear as day, coming from behind me this time. The woman that seemed to always be in my left corner. She visited me mostly in my dreams but as the Darion invasion came closer, I started hearing her and seeing her in the real world.

She seemed to give me advice, an unbiased opinion, a voice of reason. She calmed my thoughts and leveled my head.

I opened my eyes, my vision sharp as my irises burned in the slightest. The sandy pits around me were filled with fighters, but her figure was to my right. I turned my head to see her standing there, on the edge of the training field, watching me—a ghost of a smile on her face.

As if my stare startled her, she suddenly turned, her paper-white hair flowing behind her, all the way down to her tailbone. The top layer adorned with braids and jewels, her hair was pulled into two soft buns above her ears towards the back of her head. The gold jewellery sparkling in the sun.

The impact of my opponent's body crashing into mine pulled me back to reality.

I sucked in a sharp breath and rolled through the sand, ducking under his arms and using the momentum to jump back up to my feet.

"You're not paying attention princess." Gallio said, bouncing back up to his own feet. "What's distracting you today?" He asked, a smirk pulling at his lips as he threw his fist towards me. I dodged, grabbing his wrist and pulling him towards me to land a jab to his side. A small huff left his lips as I made contact, but he was quick to spin in my hold and turn the fight back to his advantage.

"Nothing." I grumbled as he landed his own hit to the side of my thigh, a sting of pain spreading from the blow as I stumbled a few steps. I glanced back to where the woman had once stood, but she had vanished into thin air.

The mysterious woman was one of the strangest humanoids I had ever seen. She had the whitest of skin, like freshly fallen snow, with striking sapphire stripes falling down her face. They started at the top of her forehead and travelled over her eyes and down her cheeks. I had been seeing her more often lately. And she always looked the exact same.

Her birthmarks continued down her neck and chest before they were hidden by her white-gold chest plate, engraved with vines and petals across the entirety of the metal. Her white and blue skin was shown again down her stomach before being hidden by a white cloth that wrapped around her waist. Her thighs and legs could be seen as the fabric was so light it flowed in the slight breeze, unveiling her skin now and then. The same fabric covered her shoulders and arms, bunching at her elbows. Like me, she seemed to be barefoot yet she floated a few inches from the ground.

She was an anomaly. I wondered why I seemed to be the only one ever able to see her.

"Della," Gallio said from next to me, locking an arm around my shoulder and throwing me down into the sand again. The air left my lunges in a quick gasp, sand flying up from the impact.

"Stars, Gallio. What the hell?!" I said, laying on the ground a second longer to steady my head before attempting to get up.

"Sorry princess, I thought you saw that one coming." He said with a lopsided smile, offering me a hand. I shook off his help and pushed myself up to my feet, scratching the loose sand from my hair as it started to itch.

"Yea, well I didn't." I grumbled making the man laugh.

"Your head has been in the stars lately, Aladella. You could have blocked my attack easily, just a simple side step. What's got your mind all wrapped up and turned around?" He asked, snapping his fingers in front of my nose. I snorted out a laugh and pushed his hand away.

"I'm right here Gallio, and I've been right here. I've just had a few things on my mind." I said, reluctant to admit that my mind had been elsewhere in our sparring match.

"Well, rightly so. I do believe you are expected to see your mother shortly anyways. Might want to shake out the sand before tracking it through her palace." He noted, straightening his back and dusting sand from my shoulder. "I'll meet you there then?" He asked.

"Yea, yea, I won't keep you waiting." I said, puffing out my cheeks with a breath feeling the stress build between my shoulders again.

One of the side effects of an impending invasion.

The Darion had taken our sister planet, Diarna, almost six years ago. The entire invasion taking no longer than a few years. And now, they were headed for our planet. My home. Prytha.

"It will be fine, but I will need your help convincing your mother." Gallio said, placing a hand on my shoulder and squeezing it reassuringly. I gave him a tight-lipped smile in return, his words going in one ear and out the other.

With one last squeeze on my shoulder, Gallio left me in the training fields to attend to his actual position in the palace. The queen's right-hand man, her royal advisor. Discussions between my mother and the Darion's leader Darious would begin soon, and we had to devise a plan before he arrived.

* * *

I watched as worry took over my mother's face, her perfectly sculpted eyebrows creased in the middle, and a soft sigh escaping her lips. I reached across the table grabbing her jewel-adorned hand softly, giving her a comforting squeeze. Her golden-brown eyes lifted from where they had been glaring a hole into the table to meet my matching irises.

She gave me a soft smile, which looked more like a grimace than an actual smile. It did not make me feel better about our situation in the slightest. I wondered if the universe had planned out our unfolding of misfortunes as well.

"My Queen, you must understand, the survival of Prytha depends on your decision." Gallio said, trying once again to find an angle that would ensure the safety of my home world. We did not want a repeat of what had happened on Diarna.

That battle had lasted months and had been the most gruesome and devasting battle our corner of the galaxy had ever seen. It had been year and a half full of fear and uncertainty as the Darion took full control of our sister planet. The war ended with few Darion soldiers killed and the fall of Diarna's freedom.

The Darion has been infesting planets across the galaxy for the past five hundred years and had finally made it to the outskirts.

The Darion asked for loyalty and lodgings in exchange for protection. Funnily enough, the protection they were offering was from their army itself.

The Darion proved to be the biggest, and only, threat in our galaxy. The options they gave were to come to an agreement or be wiped off the face of existence. Sadly, when Diarna fell, few had been able to seek refuge on Prytha. My father and sister had gone to save as many as they could. Three of the ten transport ships had returned, my father and sister, not on them.

The past twenty generations of my family have been suffocated by the presence of the Darion empire. Starting with Emila and continuing with Darious.

Though, no one had seen the young lord in almost two hundred years. Unlike his mother, he preferred controlling the galaxy in private. Emila used to be on the battlefronts, slaughtering with her mindwiped soldiers on the front lines. Darious had tried his best for the first century after his mother died. But he hasn't been seen since. His symbol and soldiers did the work for him, whenever the emblem made an appearance in a city, the soldiers would arrive in the few days that followed.

I remember when I saw the emblem for the first time. I had been to Diarna with my sister and father. I had only been twelve or thirteen at the time, and my sister, who was two years older, was leading me through the market. We had gone on an adventure to find what the traders had brought from other worlds.

We had markets in Prytha but our planet was known for its nature, beauty, and pilots. Diarna was known for its culture and diversity. You could find anything you could dream of there. We had rounded one of the street corners and had seen someone burning the symbol into the side of the building. A dark triangle with a dark panther crawling around one of the peaks.

After that, all I remembered was my father pulling us off the planet as fast as he could. The invasion had come three days later.

"You know how I feel about this already, Gallio. I am not going to stand aside. This scum of a leader, Darious, cannot just expect control of the throne that I fought hard to keep." The fire in my mother's eyes raging as she glared at her advisor. They were seconds from falling into a very familiar argument.

I folded my hands in my lap and turned to face my mother, knowing this was as good of a time as ever to voice my thoughts. "Mum, I think you need to think about this," I started, noticing how both of their gazes turned to me rather quickly. The sharp turns of their necks making me wonder if it hurt.

"All I'm saying is we don't have to agree with them, and we don't have to enjoy them being here. But, isn't their nuisance of a presence on our planet better than losing souls in a war we cannot win. The emblem showed up this morning. We can't keep pushing off this meeting any longer."

As much as I didn't want to think about it, the emblem was here, we would either fall into a war or find peace. Glancing across the large throne room I couldn't help but look out the open windows, at the peace just beyond it. I could hear the birds from the forests just outside the castle, a light breeze carrying conversation from the town. Mountains stood proud in the distance, protecting the capital from the frozen desert beyond. But I couldn't help but notice how utterly silent it was, no children laughing or playing, not many people joking in the market or city square. The Darion had forced fear into our hearts, making my home fall silent.

If we brought war to our planet, the Prythian army wouldn't be made up of me or her, or any high-ranking officials. It would be made up of citizens fighting for their land and for a life they could live freely. We couldn't make that decision for them.

My mother watched me carefully before her lips turned up slightly into a proud smile. "I wish I had a mind like yours sometimes, ma belle," she said softly, running her fingers across the side of my face. It was rare we shared precious moments like this anymore. Since my sister's and father's deaths, we had been occupied with the Darion. Them settling on the planet they slaughtered meant they were always close; we didn't know when the infestation would begin.

Her hand left the side of my face after a few seconds and she stood from her seat at the head of the table, Gallio and I standing with her.

"Let me think. We will host a meeting here with Darious in three days to Negotiate. If he is to infest my planet then he will do so on my terms," she said, walking across the room to the main doors leading back to the castle.

I couldn't help the grin that pulled on my lips; my mother was a proud woman, Darious should be scared of how difficult she could be. As she left the room, I let out a soft breath I didn't realize I was holding, stepping down from my own seat. My heels clicking on the marble floors of the throne room.

"I should have invited you to a discussion days ago," Gallio joked, standing a little way away from me with his arms behind his back, feet shoulder-width apart. I rolled my eyes with a smile, walking to meet him in the middle of the hall, continuing in step with him towards the exit of the room.

"Well, you should know how persuasive my words can be, there's a reason I'm the Negotiator," I tell him with a wink. My princess responsibilities and persona dropping immediately as I was left alone with my friend.

"You keep telling yourself that, Princess." He said with a small laugh. With a small tip of his chin in farewell, he turned and headed down a separate hallway. Off to deal with more important things than the princess's social life.

The scariest part of the invasion was that everyone could see it coming. Literally and figuratively. The Darion had been destroying cultures and civilizations for half of a millennium, so we all knew it would happen to our home eventually. But seeing the dark outline of the Darion transports and carriers in the sky send a different kind of bone rattling chill down the spine.

However, my mother had kept moral high and hope in our hearts, encouraging us to believe in a better future. A stronger future. And we all believed her.

CHAPTER TWO

I dusted my hands on my pants softly as I stood up from where I knelt on the sand, my knee pressed against Gallio's back.

"And another win. You give up yet?" I asked the man still lying on his back on the ground, looking winded.

I offered him my hand, brushing away the loose hairs that fell in front of my eyes. He glared at it for a second before sighing and grabbed my wrist, allowing me to help him up. I knew it hurt his pride for me to beat him, having to go back to his training with the soldiers and be teased later. Anything to knock him down a few pegs.

"I don't get it. I clearly had the advantage there. I have no idea how you gained the upper hand, or where you learnt some of those moves, I mean I haven't seen anyone on this planet pull that," Gallio said, brushing the sand from his blonde hair with a rough shake.

"It just comes to me naturally," I said sarcastically with a teasing smirk.

If I was being honest, I didn't know how I pulled off the sparring match. He was right, he did have the advantage. In the one spot where I got stuck, I just stopped thinking and suddenly my body had pulled itself out of the situation. The only answer I had for the sudden burst of adrenaline, or whatever it was, was instinct. Pure instinct.

Gallio gave me a strange look when I said it came naturally and looked down at me as if contemplating something. I wondered if I should get his mind off of it and tell him he was just being a sore loser. But he would probably tackle me into another match, one I wouldn't win for a second time.

"What? Why are you looking at me like that?" I asked waving my hand in front of his face a bit to snap him out of it. He blinked a few times, furrowing his eyebrows as he looked down at me, his eyes slowly becoming clearer.

"Nothing, just had a thought." He muttered. I frowned at his answer but thought nothing of it.

"Okay," I say dragging it out, giving him a confused look. I had no idea why he was suddenly acting so strange and ... well, out of it. As soon as I muttered the few words it was almost like his gaze had faded over, and he was looking through me as he got lost in his train of thought. It was strange, I had never seen that look on his face.

"I need to get cleaned up before meeting with Mum again. I think she wanted to have the Marques' over for dinner so she could talk about the invasion after." I tell Gallio watching him nod his head, knowing about the dinner plans as well.

"Well then, a pleasure, as always, Princess," he said with a sickening dramatic bow making me roll my eyes at the gesture. I give him a ghost of a curtsy making him chuckle before I turned and headed into the palace once again. My sandy feet trailing a few grains onto the marble floors.

* * *

The sound of my heels as I walked down the hall was almost comforting. It was one of those things that you didn't realize you enjoyed till it caught you off guard. Yet, the sound gave me some sense of power, independence.

The dress I had picked was sure to impress our guests. The long, soft, yellow skirts and billowing sleeves wrapped my arms in clouds. A contrast from the tighter structured bodice. I couldn't explain it but as I walked into the hall, I couldn't keep the small smile off my face.

I was surprised as I entered the hall that the Marques family had already arrived. The three of them, standing next to the table and caught up in conversation with my mother and Gallio.

My mother's eyes caught mine over Lord Marques' shoulder. "Darling! Just in time!" she said with a kind smile.

Lord and Lady Marques turned their heads, eyes shining as they sent me a smile. And of course, I noticed their son Erick standing a little bit behind them. They were covered in their family colours, a deep rosy pink and dark green.

"Princess Aladella, how nice it is to see you," Lady Marques said as she stepped closer to me, her hand bracing my forearm as I held hers, a sign of greeting and respect with our people.

"And you as well, Lady Marques," I respond politely, giving the woman a dazzling smile. My eyes shifted to Lord Marques and he also looked down at me with a wide smile, bracing my arm in his in greeting.

"And of course, you, young lady, are looking as dazzling as ever," he complimented making me smile genuinely at the man.

"Thank you, Lord Marques, you are too kind. However, I think it is you dazzling us this evening," I respond gesturing to the new gold chains adorning his neck. The man smiled proudly at my compliment, letting me know I observed correctly.

"Yes! These were given to me by my son, Erick. A winning from his latest adventure you see, oh you must hear it all from him," the lord said, gesturing to his son. Erick stepped forward when his name was brought up and he approached me, with a smile just as striking as his father's.

They both shared many of the same features. Both had dark, raven hair, shiny smiles, and slightly crooked noses. Erick had not gotten his mother's pastel-pink locks but did get her deep magenta eyes. He was very striking.

"Princess," he greeted clasping his arm in mine.

"A pleasure, Erick. I can't wait to hear about your adventures, Maybe I can live through them. Pretend I'm out there on some daring quest as you were," I said grinning, knowing it was exactly what the group wanted to hear. The lord and lady chuckled with my mother at my words and smiled proudly. I was playing into her all too obvious plan, not that I minded, Erick was handsome.

"Well, let's not wait any longer. Let us take our seats," my mother said smiling.

I knew exactly what she was up to. I had a keen eye and was a very good observer, one of the reasons why Gallio called me the Negotiator. I knew what people wanted to hear, I could look at them and somehow say exactly what they wanted to hear so I could make them like me, trust me even.

I took my seat on the right of my mother since she took the head of the table, Lady Marques next to me. Across the table sat Erick, then next to him his father. Gallio seated next to Lady Marques. A clear indicator of what this was. A setup.

The only reason my mother placed Erick across from me was so he could see me, and I see him. It was easier to talk to someone sitting across from you. If he were to sit next to me, it wouldn't be natural to turn my body to look at him, so across the table was the perfect spot. I knew what my mother was up to. She was smart like that.

I caught her gaze for a quick second giving her a small almost teasing glare, telling her I knew what she was up to. She only responded with a sly wink and a smile.

I rolled my eyes softly at her response. Erick wouldn't be the worst match. But I was hoping I could meet someone on my own. I knew it wasn't likely I would since I barely left the palace and since the invasions started, parties were few to none. This wouldn't be the worst match, plus he had pretty eyes.

I glanced up across the table and my bright-gold irises automatically locked with his deep-magenta colour. I lost myself for a second in the shade. I was shocked from my trance when the doors to the kitchen opened and the room was filled with the smell of amazing food. Plates were placed on the table stacked with drool-worthy foods making me realize how hungry I actually was.

"Thank you," I said softly as a young girl filled my glass with sparkling blue wine. She gave me a kind smile before retreating to another serving girl around her age, maybe sixteen.

The table fell into easy conversation as we ate our meals. I contributed in some parts where I thought necessary but otherwise, I let my mind wander a bit.

I was shocked out of my current train of thought when I saw her. The lady with white and blue skin, stood across the room behind Erick, her face holding a panicked expression. And in the faintest of whispers, I heard her speak to me, her voice echoing around to room.

"*Run.*"

The moment passed slowly. Her voice echoed in my head as her figure retreated down one of the back corridors of the palace.

"Come quick."

I heard her voice again as she turned to look at me giving me a gesture to follow. This was the first time she ever interacted with me; I had thought she was a figment of my imagination. I thought I had conjured her out of stress and panic.

I turned to look at the table, no one noticed her. I placed my napkin on the table before excusing myself. My mother gave me a strange look and as I stood up, I leaned closer as if to kiss her on the cheek. "I have a bad feeling," I whispered quickly against her skin. I moved away and we locked eyes and she nodded.

I quickly moved from the hall to where the woman stood, almost transparent; I looked at her strangely. Just as I was about to ask her who she was, or more, how she wasn't just a figment of my dreams and imagination, a loud banging echoed through the palace.

The hall doors opened with a bang and two palace guards ran in.

"My Queen, the Darion is here. They wish to speak immediately," he said breathlessly. My mother glanced at me and we locked eyes, she gave me a subtle look to leave quickly so I wouldn't be involved. Somehow, I knew she would handle it.

"Very well, let Darious in, I hope he's hungry," my mother responded; her voice poised yet fierce as her eyes narrowed.

With that as my cue, I turned back to the ghostly lady, slipping my heels off and racing down the palace halls. My feet were silent as I ran.

"I didn't think you were real," I said to the woman once we were out of earshot.

"Of course, I'm real, you think your little brain could come up with something like me?" she said with a little bit of sass raising an eyebrow at me. I let out a small huff of laughter at her point. Despite all that was going on in the palace, I knew, had a feeling, it would somehow work out.

"Well, what are you, then? And how do you just appear? And why can only I seem to see and hear you?" I asked the questions I've had for a long time all bubbling to the surface immediately.

The ghost lady let out a sigh before stopping in front of my room door next to me.

"My name is Aisha, call me Aisha, not ghost lady," she said making me look at her a bit shocked and confused.

"You can read my mind too?" I asked, feeling violated all of a sudden.

"Really? I appear in your dreams and you think I can't read your mind? C'mon use your star-given brain," she mumbled. A chill ran through my body. Every time I had seen her observing, she had been looking into my mind, not only observing me but reading my every thought like an open book.

I closed my room door behind me and turned to face her quickly.

"Stars," she mumbled. "Listen, I talk a lot; you don't have to listen to every word I say. Now hurry up and hide I can hear them coming." Her tone suddenly became gentle as she pushed me farther into my room.

Did she talk a lot? She barely spoke a word to me throughout my childhood. My imaginary friend, who had just become a real being, could read my mind and walk through my dreams. On top of that, had decided now was a good time to show me the truth.

She clicked the small button on my wall opening it up to the hideaway cupboard. I was about to voice how she knew it was there but Aisha interrupted me before I said anything. "I read minds; I appear in your dreams. Of course, I know where your hidey-hole is. Now get in and keep quiet," she said, pushing me in and closing the door, leaving me utterly confused about the chain of events that led to this moment.

As soon as the door clicked closed, I let the confused curses leave my lips.

CHAPTER THREE

I held my breath as the door to my room was pushed open. I could hear a strange buzz, soft and muffling, like it was sucking out any other noise from the room. It seemed to be coming from whoever entered my room, their presence creating the suffocatingly silent energy. Not a single word was spoken as footfalls passed the entrance of my doorway. Their steps were perfectly in sync, making it hard to distinguish if it was a single person, or ten.

The room remained completely silent for a few moments, the intruders falling into an eerie stillness. I held my breath as if the sound of my exhale would alert them of my hiding spot.

Then there was a crash. Something had hit the wall just in front of me, right where I was hidden.

The sound was sudden enough to make me jump. My heart hammering against my chest. All I could do was sit and wait silently as whoever had entered my room began to tear it up. I could hear them open every cabinet and drawer, the humph of fabric making me realize they were tossing my belongings to the floor. Tearing apart the room in a frenzy as if searching for something, or someone.

By the sounds of their actions, I could tell they weren't looking for me. They seemed to be searching every inch of my room, including the nooks and corners where I wouldn't be able to fit. They were looking for something I had. The thought confused me since everything of value was locked up in the treasury, and I only had a few valuable pieces in my room.

I covered my mouth with my hand as I heard footsteps approach the wall I was hidden behind. I stayed as still as I could. Focusing on the musty smell of the cupboard. How my hands had grown clammy from nerves. My eyes burning holes into the panel of wood in front of me. As soon as there was a sign they had found where I was hidden, I would have to fight my way out. The gown I was in was not made for fighting.

After what seemed like an hour, but was probably only a few moments, the slight hum of silence left the room. Not trusting my ears completely, I stayed where I was for an additional moment. I wanted to be certain they were actually gone before stepping out of the hidey-hole.

I was right. As soon as I opened the crack in the wall, I could see the destruction. My room had been torn to pieces. It looked like a mountain storm had spun straight through it. Broken furniture and my belongings were thrown across the room, even my bed was shifted off the frame, the covers were torn off and my mattress cut down the middle, suggesting they had searched through its stuffing for whatever they were looking for.

I took a few careful steps, my bare feet stepping on small pieces of broken wood and cloth, being careful about the glass.

"Aisha?" I whispered out into the silence that enveloped my room. I waited a few minutes but there was no answer.

"Aisha!" I said again a bit louder this time wondering where my ghostly observer had gone. I could feel she was around, her presence becoming familiar, now that I could recognize it belonged to her. Either she wasn't around me as I thought, or she chose to remain invisible as I called to her. Whichever it was I softly cursed her out for leaving before I rummaged through the mess around my room.

I saw a glint in the covers of my bed that had been tossed across the clutter of my room. I knelt down getting closer and reached through the folds in the fabric.

My hand grasped a familiar hilt and I pulled out my father's dagger. It was a beautiful gold weapon adorned with a few striking jewels on the handle. Gold vines and leaves twisted from the base of the handle and up the blade a bit, shining in the light from my windows. If they had gone through my room looking for something valuable, why had they not taken this? The dagger of a king nonetheless should have impressed the soldier's lord.

As my hand grasped the dagger, I heard movement in the doorway of my room. I spun quickly holding the knife out in front of me at my attacker.

"Woah there, spitfire, no need to point that at me," Gallio said with a lopsided grin. He stood in the doorway looking the exact same as I had left him at the table. That was a good sign, it meant the Darion had not attacked. They were safe. For now.

I breathed a sigh of relief when I saw his familiar face and threw my arms around his shoulders. "Thank god, I thought they had come back," I said softly into his shoulder. He held me close for a comforting second before pulling away, looking me over to make sure I was alright.

"When your mother realized they were searching the palace while she and Darious spoke, she became livid, going off about how she was supposed to trust this leader while he was sneaking around her home. She sent me here before it got rough. But we need to go. Now," he said quickly moving from in front of me to glance out the door.

"And go where? I can't leave mum here by herself. Especially now that Darious has his disgusting, parasitic boots on my planet." I spit, standing my ground against his offer to leave, well more like order to leave. He turned to face me quickly, his eyes roaming across my features, a look of concentration across his features.

"Aladella, if I am right, you need to get as far away from this planet as possible," he said, his voice calm and low. The seriousness in his tone made me straighten up. The look of concern didn't seem to come from him looking out for the planet, my home, but for me specifically. But what would Darious need with me? Unless he planned to kill my mother, my home wouldn't need an heir for years. Even if he did, the planet would be run by the Marques in my absence. They would be in good hands.

"Right? What? Right about what, Gallio?" I ask utterly confused, his vague explanation annoying me slightly. It was almost as if he was speaking in tongues and I couldn't understand a single thing.

"I'll explain when we get out of here, but now we leave." A look of concern flashed across his features, but I could see what he was actually feeling. His eyes were clouded with fear. Something I had rarely seen on him; he was always calm in situations like this. The last time I had seen that look, I was fourteen and my family had been butchered a planet over.

"Fine." The concern and fear on his face urged me to heed his warning and follow him. When Gallio was scared, I should be too. He nodded his head and rounded the doorway from my room. I took a step to follow him but paused to look back to my room, getting the feeling that it would be a while until I saw it again.

I glanced down seeing my black corset lying dead in the mess across my floor. With I sigh, I picked it up, my corset in one hand and my father's dagger in the other.

"Alright," I muttered softly to myself, plucking the courage and focus I would need to pull this off. Turning the corner Gallio was already waiting for me, a strained smile on his face as if he knew we would not be coming back for a while.

We quickly made our way through the palace, my heels that were returned to my feet clicking lightly on the ground. A necessary evil since once we got outside my bare feet would have been ripped apart by rocks and debris.

Reaching the stables, I immediately gravitated towards Raya, she was the steed I usually rode when we went out racing. She chose me as a rider and I couldn't help but be thankful.

Raya was a tall, beautiful Rawahorn. A tall equestrian creature, native to the plains and forests of Prytha. She had eight long, powerful legs making them one of the fastest creatures on our planet. The high of her back was almost six feet making it hard to climb up to ride her, but once situated, incredibly hard to fall from. The ridge of her back dipped naturally giving the rider a grove, hard to be kicked from.

I jumped up on the fence of the stable before swinging my leg over her back. She made a soft purring sound of approval before stomping her hoof in the sand. She was excited. She knew nothing of the dangers we were running from, only that we were leaving the crammed stables for the open forest.

"Let's go," Gallio said from ahead of me, mounting his own teal stead. Without another word he sped out the door.

I leaned close to Raya, wrapping my hands through her bright-blue mane. "Catch up," I spoke softly to her. She responded right away, bursting out the same way Gallio had just escaped and racing after him. We caught up quickly, racing through the woods, side by side. I couldn't keep the smile off my face as my golden-brown hair flowed freely in the wind, sometimes whipping across my face.

My small moment of freedom was quickly ruined when the sound of a blast flew past my ear and exploded against the tree just in front of me. The black beam lit the tree up, the flames travelling across the bark as it burst into flames. I let out a small scream and Raya swerved past the tree. We had barely missed the flames, the heat warming up the side of my face as we passed.

I glanced at Gallio next to me whose features were furrowed in concentration as he glanced behind us. I followed his gaze and looked to see how many were trailing us.

Besides the sound of our Rawas' huffing and crunching the leaves under their hooves, the forest seemed to go silent. As if all life had just picked up and disappeared from our green surroundings. The usual hum of life was replaced with the suffocating buzz of silence.

Paired with the noise were two men on all-black speeder bikes, zipping around trees after us. The characters were dressed in basic soldier attire, chest plate, arm guards, utility belt and thick pants. Besides the outfit being all black they were dressed like casual warriors. What stood out was the fact that the men's eyes were covered.

A silver piece of technology wrapped around the Darion soldier's eyes. The tech shining under the sun peaking through the canopy of trees. Though, the black screen on their headpieces was so dark you couldn't see anything through the glass, the light being consumed by the deep colour.

I had never seen Darion soldiers before and couldn't help but wonder if they all had this feature soldered to their skulls.

My thoughts were once again interrupted as the Darion soldiers started shooting at us again. The dark laser blasts shot over Gallio's shoulder as he took a position between me and the soldiers. I glance back to look at him wondering what the hell he was doing.

"Keep going, don't turn around!" he yelled ahead of me before pulling a slick silver blaster from his coat, something I didn't know he carried with him. I nodded my head and turned to face forwards. I leaned forwards, closer to Raya and urged her faster as we bolted through the trees.

From behind me, I could hear blaster shots going back and forth, hitting trees, the ground. The small explosions echoing through the forest.

I heard a yell cry out and could only assume someone was shot down. I turned as fast as I could in my seat, hoping it wasn't Gallio. I turned around just as one of the Darion soldiers slid from the seat of his speeder bike to the forest floor, his bike crashing into a tree not more than two seconds later.

As I turned back to face forward, I was greeted with Aisha floating just ahead of me.

"Don't turn around," was all she said, a fierce look on her face. I nodded my head and looked dead in front of me as she disappeared again. I urged Raya through the trees, bounding over the short brush and ducking my head under the lower branched.

Then another cry echoed across the forest. Only this time it was a voice I recognized. I remembered Aisha's words but couldn't stop my body from turning at the sound of his yell.

Some part of me wished I had listened to Aisha's words and not turned around. However, I knew if I hadn't, I would have regretted it more.

I watched Gallio slump forward on his stead, a burn mark through his shoulder almost cutting straight through the limb, his bright red blood spilling over the side of his body and the creature he rode.

My heart stopped.

I heard a scream echo through the forest and it took me a second to realize it was my own. I sat up straighter to pull Raya in the direction Gallio's stead had fled. But before I could even grab Raya's mane to guide her, Aisha was once again in front of me.

"No, continue. There is nothing you can do, if you follow him, you'll be killed. Then would his death really be worth it?" she said sternly and pushed me forwards. I tried to tell her his death wouldn't be worth it, tried to pull Raya in his direction anyway. When I did try a soft white shimmer enveloped my hands, keeping them in Raya's hair, guiding me forwards.

"Go," she said.

I glanced at Gallio's retreating form and couldn't stop the tears from falling. I took a deep breath, realizing he wouldn't want me to risk myself in this situation. I bit down the words I wanted to curse at Aisha and nodded my head.

And I pushed forward.

I watched as Aisha above me moulded her hands together. Her eyes rolled back into her head and the whites started glowing a brilliant, clean, pearl colour. Her irises peeked from her eyelids, shivering as she pulled something from deep within. I saw her lips move as she muttered a few words and her hands began to glow much like her eyes.

With a fierce battle cry coming out of my ghostly friend's mouth, she pushed her hands forward. The energy she held in her hands formed into spheres of light and she threw one at the enemy still on our tail. The light hit the Darion soldier in the chest and with an ear-shattering scream, the light ate him whole. Turning him to dust on his speeder.

I glanced up at Aisha shocked at the sheer amount of power she seemed to possess. She looked down at me giving me a cheeky wink before vanishing into thin air again.

Once again on my own, I pushed forward. Gallio's death plaguing my mind as my journey continued to the closest town, almost an hour away.

CHAPTER FOUR

I hopped down from Raya's back in the tree line leading to the village, keeping under the canopy of leaves not wanting to draw any attention. I couldn't do much about the evening gown I was still dressed in since I had no other clothing options, but riding through town on a Rawa would most definitely make people stare.

I sighed looking down at the dress I was wearing, sad I would have to ruin my favourite gown. The thought was fleeting as I remembered my friend was laying somewhere on the forest floor. I just hoped someone from the palace had followed us and would find him.

I ripped the sleeves from my shoulders and pulled one off my arm. I tied off the sleeve and dropped my folded corset, dagger and heeled shoes into the makeshift bag, tying the open end to the side of my corset securely.

I didn't want to ruin the dress further so just grabbed a handful of the skirt and hiked it up as I walked. I needed to find something else to wear and preferably cover my head. If the Darion knew I was headed this way they would surely infest the town, if they weren't already crawling around the streets.

I ducked behind the tall stone buildings, hoping to keep myself hidden in the thin alleyways and routes around the town. I tried to stay as far away from the main trading street as possible knowing that's where most people would be and they would recognize me instantly. I made it a few blocks into the city where I knew the hangar would be. Hopefully, there I would be able buy passage to some other part of the planet. Hidden from the Darion I could wait out the invasion, at least wait until the Darious left the planet. I would wait out until my mother sent word about what the Darion would be doing with our planet, our home, then I would return.

I was about to duck through another building when a pair turned down the alley ahead of me, headed right in my direction. I stopped dead in my tracks. I ducked to my left; the crates stacked next to the corner of the alley providing the cover I desperately needed.

"No, you know what, Jude, I quit! They want us to run ... I can't do that." I heard, a male's voice, though he sounded young. At least younger than my twenty-year-old self.

"C'mon Lore, don't do this; they aren't running away, they're getting help," the other man, Jude, said.

"No, I don't care at this point," he mumbled. I flinched when the crate I hid behind moved a bit. He had placed something on top of the boxes. What it was, however, I couldn't tell.

I heard the other man sigh and dropped his own package, or belongings on the box. I couldn't really tell what it was from the thump. "I get it, our first mission isn't the one we wanted. But let's just think it over okay, I mean this was going to provide for us," the Jude character said, his voice a bit softer.

"Fine whatever."

I waited a bit as I heard their footsteps carry them away before standing from where I was hidden to look at what they placed. And it couldn't have been more perfect. Stacked on the boxes were two flight jumpsuits and matching helmets.

"Stars, thank you." I muttered before grabbing the smaller one and slipping into one of the empty doorways.

As fast as I could, I stripped from my yellow gown and white corset. Flinching a bit as I tightened my black corset on my bare skin knowing I would regret it later when it bruised and cut up my skin. I pulled on the jumpsuit as quick as I could, zipping it up all the way and pulling the velcro of the waist tight along with the small piece around my neck.

The outside of the jumpsuit was a bright-yellow amber colour, I guessed bright enough that pilots could see you walking around the hangar. The inside of the suit was a dark brown colour that could easily be mistaken as black. I rolled the sleeves up past my wrists and tucked my makeshift bag under my arm. I quickly pulled the helmet onto my head and bunched up my small bag before walking freely into the street.

The helmet didn't cover my entire head. It was completely black and strapped under my chin, something I didn't do up, with a black visor coming down to hide my eyes. It left the lower half of my face exposed.

"Hey!" I heard from behind me making me freeze. "Yeah, you, pilot!" the same voice said making me turn to look who was calling me, my hand hovering over my knife.

"You must be one of the new recruits," the man said shaking his head. "Well let's go, follow me," he said. I hesitated before playing along and following next to him. He was wearing the same kind of jumpsuit only had it tied around his waist, showing off the white tank that covered his chest. I wouldn't have said he was plain-looking; blonde hair was hard to find on Prytha since the folk usually had bright blues or soft pinks. His eyes, however, were a striking dark green, something I had only seen a few times.

"Where are your shoes?" he suddenly asked me with a huff of laughter escaping his lips.

A bit flustered I shoot my gaze down to my feet. Bare feet. "Umm ... someone took them," I said simply, it was a complete lie. The guy had walked away with his shoes.

"Alright then, recruit, let's get you that first," he said with a small smile. He led me into the hangar and over to a boot rack. I quickly grabbed a pair and sat on one of the blocks they had there, grabbing a pair of clean socks from a bin and began lacing them up.

"You're name recruit?" he asked as I pulled a boot on.

I paused for a second not sure what to say, I looked up at him seeing his questioning gaze and came up with something quickly. "Umm ... it's Ada," I said, offering him a slightly uncomfortable smile not really sure if he would believe my alias.

"Alright, Ada, by the numbers on your jumper, seems like you're apart of my squadron. Captain Nells," he said, offering a hand and a kind smile.

I had heard that name before. He didn't seem that much older than me but he had been one of the surviving pilots from the transports that went to Diarna. Out of the few that had returned, he had been one of them. A decent man, brave and an incredibly good pilot, from what I've heard. Though he must have been fresh from flight school when he had been called to the transport ships. Probably only eighteen or nineteen. I wonder what he had gone through? It must have been frightening to say the least.

I finished tying my boots up and took his forearm. "Very nice to meet you, Captain," I said with a smile.

"You as well, Ada. Now, let's get on that ship before she sails without us," he said with a cheeky grin. I nodded my head and followed him over to a group wearing the same bright-amber jumpsuits as myself. We slowly filed into the ship, everyone falling into whatever open seat was closest. I hopped into a seat next to the window and besides, seemingly, the only other girl on the ship.

Before I knew it, we had lifted into the air and we were leaving the atmosphere, I looked down at the fading planet I called home with a small sigh before shifting my attention across the recruits around me.

In an empty seat across from me sat Aisha, a sad smile on her face but a determined look in her eye. Letting me know this was only the beginning of our adventure.

CHAPTER FIVE

"Mama, tell us about the Syron again."

Little hands grabbed at the queen's sleeves as she tried to tuck in her youngest daughter. Her oldest moved from under her blankets to kneeling on her bed as she begged her mother to tell them her favourite story. The light of the moon cast soft shadows across the room, the soft candle next to the girl's beds lighting up their bright faces as they waited for their mother to settle in with them.

The queen only smiled back at her beautiful daughters, brushing her fingers through her youngest's hair as she moved to sit on the small bed with her. "Mama pleeeease?" her youngest, Aladella, pleaded. Her golden-brown eyes wide and begging as she met her mother's matching irises.

"As soon as your sister gets in bed, I will start," their mother said.

"Cerey, quick!" Aladella pleaded, bouncing under her covers as she rushed her sister. The blonde princess quickly scrambled to get under her own covers, pulling them taut to her chin as the two girls stared up at their mother expectantly. They had heard the same stories since the day they were born, surrounded by the mystical legends of the Syron, ancient protectors of the galaxy. But the story

never got old to the children, they would dream about the day the Syron would come back and rip a hole in the dark shadow the Darion had cast across the galaxy.

"A long, long time ago, before I was born, the galaxy was filled with an alluring unity. Everyone was friends with everyone, and elated peacefulness blanketed every planet. The galaxy only knew beautiful Song and friendly acquaintance." As the queen spoke to her children, she could see their minds turning behind their eyes, their wide imaginations stretching further than their small bodies and creating the beautiful world of the Syron. Something they had never experienced.

"A long time ago the worlds were protected by the Syron. The Syron were beautiful, enchanting, immortal creatures who were born from the last lights of a dying star. In those precious last moments of warmth and light before a star's life ended, she would send that special life-giving power into an exceptional child." The queen poked her youngest daughter's nose softly as she spoke of the extraordinary creatures. The two girls giggled, wanting nothing more than to have the magic of a Syron. "The child was born from the sun's lifeforce. And that baby's first cry into their world would echo the explosion of their bonded star."

"Mama, what does a star exploding sound like?" The queen smiled down at her curious daughter.

"Well, Cerelia, it sounds like this ..." The queen trailed before opening her mouth in a silent scream. The two girls couldn't help but fall into their own fits of giggles, rolling in their sheets as they faced each other and screamed silently at one another. The queen laughed with the two, tucking her youngest's brunette curls behind her ear as she settled them back into their blankets.

The queen hummed softly to pull the young girls' attention back to her, and the story she was just starting. "Now, what did the Syron represent? What was expected of a Syron child's behaviour as they grew up?"

"She would be kind, and smart, and light!" Cerelia responded, a proud smile on her face as she pulled her blankets tighter around her shoulders.

"That's right, she would have to be all those things. A beacon for those who didn't have hope. Do you know any other things a Syron might have to be Aladella?" the queen asked, turning to her quieter daughter. The smaller brunette's hair was a mess around her head from running around with her older sister, and her eyes were dropping as the excitement of the day was finally taking its toll on her small body.

Her small eyes widened a bit as the question was directed towards her. "They have to be brave, and funny, and smart." She answered, her slight childish lisp pulling the 'r' from her sentence.

"Della, I already said smart silly." Her sister giggled from across the small space between their beds.

"Oops," the youngest said, the innocent smiles stretching across their cheeks as they turned their attention back to their mother.

"A Syron's skin would shimmer as if kissed by stardust and they carried a very special gem with them. One that held all their powers. It was called their Song. The Syron would wield this mystery power only few know the true extent of. No one has seen the true power a Syron can possess, but it was said to be very magical. The Syron would keep these special stones on them at all times, either on their favourite weapon or in their fine jewellery. That stone held their lives."

"A Song would travel to the ends of the universe in search of their Syron. The Song would find that child through fate, since the connection between the two was always meant to be. Then, when the child grew up enough to leave her mother and father, they would be taken to a very special school where they would be taught how to use their very special magic."

Cerelia turned over again in her bed to face her mother, her own eyes drooping as she felt sleep start to pull at her mind. "Mama, can

I go to the special magic school?" She asked, her words a mumbled mess as they fell from her lips.

The queen only smiled, knowing the school had long since been disbanded. But, not wanting to step on her child's hopes of becoming something she was not, she nodded her head softly.

"You can go anywhere and be anything you'd like darling, as long as you take your little sister with you," the queen reasoned, knowing the sisters would have a hard life ahead of them and would need each other to get through it.

"Of course, I'll take Della, we do everything together. And she never leaves me alone," Cerelia said groaning as if complaining about her little sister always being around her.

"Hey, that's rude! Syron are kind," her little sister said, tossing one of her pillows across the gap between their beds at her sister. Cerelia only giggled and pulled the pillow into her chest, cuddling it as she settled in again.

"How well do you girls know the story of Faye?" the queen asked the girls. As if a bucket of cold water had been dumped on her youngest's head, Aladella shot up, roused entirely from her sleep knowing the story of Faye as if she had lived it herself.

"Mama can I tell the story, please?" the queen only nodded her head at the young girl's request, letting her sit up a bit as she got comfortable enough to tell her story. "Faye was the youngest Syron ever, and the last one ever," she started, her eyes sparkling as she retold it the same way her mother did.

"She was from Trilomar, and was short and had black hair. Her hair was so dark people said it looked like she had dipped her head in the centre of the universe. She was known by everyone in the galaxy and had friends on every planet, of every species, shape and age. Oh! And she had these really cool markings on her face in a pretty dark green, three triangles on her cheeks. She looked scary at first, but as soon as she smiled everyone would like her. She went on all these scary, dangerous adventures and poets would sing about

them across the galaxy; she was a hero. Even the rust water planets knew her stories." The girl's older sister started giggling when she mentioned the dark gross planets of their galaxy. Her mother sent her a look to not make fun of someone's home like that.

"Her magic was a bright-green colour that looked like jungle leaves from the forests and she had a magic stick," Aladella said.

"Scepter, darling," her mother interrupted, having to remind her every time she tried to tell the story.

"A sssepta," the girl corrected, her childish lisp butchering the word she had been trying to master.

"But as Faye became famous and important in the galaxy, another Syron got jealous. Emila wanted the power and importantness that Faye had. She wanted her name to be sung by the poets in the galaxy. She wanted people to talk about her. She wanted to be just as special," Aladella spoke, ending her sentence as if finishing her story. "You can say the rest Mama," the girl said, crawling back under her blankets to get comfy and ready to listen.

The queen helped her daughter get tucked into her blankets before picking up where her daughter left off.

"Before Faye was marked a Syron, the title of youngest Syron fell upon a platinum blonde named Emila. Emila's time in the fame and spotlight was short-lived as she soon fell under Faye's shadow. Emila's envy took over and she quickly learned to despise the Trilomarnian girl. Emila's hate became so strong she wished for a power greater than what she had already achieved, a power greater than she could handle. Emila's ambition grew and she soon formed her own plan to obtain the greatest power the galaxy had ever seen." The atmosphere in the girl's room grew a bit darker as the troubling part of the story came up. The queen had to leave out many details of Emila's horrible rise to fame in fear of terrorizing the girls with those horror stories. So, she continued, rewriting a lighter version of the history she had learnt from her own mother.

"One night, the evil Temptress Emila slid into the Syron children's quarters and stole all their Song gems. Hoping to steal the power from within. Though, a Song's power can only be harnessed by the child bonded to it, Song and child crafted by the same sun. But Emila had discovered that a little too late. She took the Songs leaving the children in everlasting sleep, since, without their Songs, they would never be able to wake up. Emila fled the Syron planet of Aladore and started building her own army. The Darion." The two girls felt shivers crawl up their spines at the mention of the evil that blanketed their galaxy, their home. They pulled their blankets over their chins, feeling safe and protected by the piece of fabric.

"Even with her silent soldiers, Emila was never an equal match to Faye. The younger Trilomarnian was much more skilled than Emila. And where Emila pulled her powers from the darkness in her heart, hate, jealousy and envy. Faye's magic was pure, coming from a fierce loyalty and bravery to protect those she loved. The Syron stood up to Emila and her new army, doing their duty to protect the galaxy. Fighting battles for the people who couldn't, and fighting for the peace they once had. But as years went on, and the Syron's already dwindling numbers became fewer. Hope seemed to fade from the galaxies that once preached peace powerfully. With few new Syron being born, there was no great Syron army to battle the steadily growing Darion."

"Emila continued her hunt of the Syron long after her army took the planet Aladore. She searched the galaxy, finding every Syron that tried to run, tried to hide, and killed them. She was a psychopath. Faye fought until she could no more, defending the galaxy to her best abilities. Waiting for the day she would face Emila, the lost Syron who was now called Temptress. And that day did come. Emila's army, the Darion, marched onto the planet Trilomar where Faye housed the wounded Syron in her small cottage home. She felt the arrival of the Darion long before she heard their footsteps outside her home. Emila called out to her rival, the girl she forever

envied and hated, challenging her to a battle. Emila asked Faye to face her, if Faye accepted Emila would let the injured Syron live. And of course, Faye agreed. She stepped out to face her enemy, her face stone cold with determination as she held her scepter tightly in her hands."

"Faye seemed to sense the child's presence before Emila even landed on the planet. The young presence was in the army swarming around her, a Syron child. Faye glanced over, following the call his presence gave off. The call faced her with a boy, no more than twenty, standing with the army, features much like that of Emila. Emila had a son, a Syron child, holding the same power and determination as his mother. The same corrupt intentions. This is where the final battle started. Syron fought Syron, in a mess of green and purple, raven and platinum, tan and pale, good and evil. Until a winner was declared." The queen looked down at her girls, the two were trying to hold on to her every word but were being lulled to sleep slowly.

"As a fierce battle ensued between Faye and Emila, neither could gain an upper hand over the other, the two seemingly being equals in power and strength. Until Faye's sceptre found Emila's greatest weakness, the dimly lit purple Song attached to her belt on her stomach. Faye's sceptre punched right through the gem, shattering it to pieces before striking the woman behind it. The army froze, the galaxy froze, everyone seemed to hold their breath at this moment in time as the corruption of the galaxy had been struck, right in her centre. Faye had destroyed the evil that had taken over the galaxy. In the long second that passed, Emila's eyes met Faye's determined glare. Then, everything was brought back to reality at the sound of a cannon. As Faye's sceptre was pulled from Emila's body, the Syron refuge was lit up in flames, the building suffocating in smoke. Faye's sceptre was held loosely in her hand as she looked down at Emila who held her abdomen trying to stop her blood from spilling out onto the ground. "I am Hope. As long as I live, Hope,

will not be obliterated from the galaxy." And Faye's words echoed across the stars with a newfound rigour, spreading a light that had almost been completely smothered," the queen said, bringing the story to a happy end, not wanting to fill the girl's dreams with fear and destruction.

The two princesses were slowly lulled to sleep, their dreams filling with their own adventures. Adventures where they could take over their own worlds and have their very own magic falling from their fingers. The two sisters curled into their blankets, their mother blowing out the candle, leaving only the soft blue glow of the moon streaming through the wide bay window.

As the queen left the room, she couldn't keep the rest of the story out of her head. Thoughts of Emila and her lasting effects on the galaxy. The constant threat of the Darion always in the back of her and her husband's minds.

Emila did not live long after that battle, since a Syron cannot live off of only one half of their Song for eternity. The pull of the other Songs she possessed being too much for her life force to handle, ripping her soul to pieces. Her last words were spoken to her son as she lay dying in his arms. "You must find the one who shares your sun, together the galaxy will fall to your feet." Her encrypted message echoing in her son's ears for years after her passing. But as she lay dying in front of him, he did not know what to think of her words. And as soon as the light finally faded from her eyes, the responsibility of the Darion fell onto his shoulders. He swore from that day forward he would make his mother proud.

Darious has ruled the galaxy for almost three hundred years now, his greed and avidity controlling his mind as he tried to harness the power of a Song just like his mother once did. No one has seen him in a few years now, his army doing his bidding, taking over planets.

He controlled the galaxy through fear and hate, stealing children to make up his ranks and searching the galaxy for Songs. Stealing them before they could reach their Syron children. Attempting to control the power of a Song like his mother once did.

The queen still believed that on the other side of the galaxy, Faye hid away on a mountain planet. A small and well-hidden academy was built by her hands. Hoping one day Faye would feel the spark of a Syron child's birth and bring them back to her new home to teach them all she knew. She stayed there hidden, watching as the Darion took over planet after planet. But knew one day hope would return and the silence would be vanquished from the galaxy.

CHAPTER SIX

The ship landed with a bit of a jerk, shaking me from my train of thought and forcing me to open my eyes. My vision blurred for a second, forcing me to blink a few times to clear the fog away before I stood up. I had fallen asleep on the transport, though I didn't remember exactly when.

I followed the flow of bright amber jumpsuits out of the ship before peeling my helmet from my head. The blinding rays of the sun scorched my skin and burned my eyes. I had to hold a hand to block the sun as I walked down the ramp, blinking to clear the little black dots from my vision.

Looking around, I couldn't immediately tell which side of Prytha we had landed on, and the more I looked at the terrain around me I started it believe we hadn't landed on Prytha at all.

Instead of the lush green forests or barren snow tundra and mountains of Prytha, the environment in front of me was dry and swampy. The trees, few that there were, were a greyish green and drooping towards the ground. The buildings around me built from grey rock, the same colour as the dusty floor. The air was so thick and humid it was easy to assume we hadn't landed on a desert planet. Beyond the tree line, there were probably marshland and swamps. It made for a dangerous environment and an even easier place to get lost.

I turned to one of the other recruits next to me, confused as to which planet we landed on. "Where did we land again?" I asked trying to make the question sound casual.

I guess it didn't work because the guy looked me down with an expression that read 'you've got to be kidding me.' "Tarkan?" he questioned, as I should have known by the grey, dusty rocks themselves. "I swear it's like they didn't say it a million times." The guy muttered to himself as he walked away. I scrunched my nose at his retreating figure, wanting to roll my eyes but ignored the urge and continued.

"Rude," I mumbled before walking down the ramp myself. I quickly split away from the group, wandering through the enclosed hangar myself.

As I walked through the base, I grabbed a few loose pieces that were lying around. The first being a black-shoulder bag, which I immediately stuffed my makeshift bag into, completing the look that let me blend in.

I slid out from the base unnoticed and took to the streets of Tarkan. From what I had heard from Gallio and my mother in the past, Tarkan was not the nicest of planets. It was filled with bounty hunters and dirty smugglers, all accumulating in one place. Gallio had told me this was where the Darion recruited their soldier snatchers.

Since the Darion's army was made up of mindwiped, hard-wired dummies, the bodies had to come from somewhere. Rust water planets like this one, would be where those smugglers would bring their picks to give to the Darion. I had to make sure I avoided them at all costs. Wiped and turned into a silent soldier was a fate worse than death.

I treaded lightly, not wanting to draw attention to myself as I slid down the streets. I knew I had made it to the main trade street of the town when the shady looking folk started popping up left and right. Small shops lining the buildings, people bundled and shrugged under the canopies for even a bit of shade.

I passed the tables, feigning interest as I slowly made my way to the other side. I moved slowly, keeping my attention on my peripherals. I just had to mind my own for the next hour or so while the Prythian ship refuelled, then I could return to the safety of its tin walls.

A glint from one of the tables caught my eye. The dealer's booth was showcasing knives. The metal seemed to melt under the heat of the sun, the nicer ones hidden in the shade of the canopy. I only had one blade on me and it was my father's, I would need another eventually. For protection. As I walked past, I slipped a long dagger up my sleeve, having learnt the trick when my sister and I were younger and stole my mother's combs and crowns. I held my breath hoping no one noticed as I continued on my way.

My luck ran out as a hand grabbed my upper bicep rather roughly and pushed me against one of the buildings. I looked up noticing the wolf-like features of the Aranese pushing his body against mine to keep me from moving. He had caged me between his sharp teeth and the stone wall.

His unnaturally sharp nails dug into my skin, making me hiss as they cut and my blood slid down my arm. He dipped his head into my neck, his snout-like nose taking a long sniff before he looked back up at me. "Hmmmmm a Prythian ... I've never had Prythian before," he growled against my ear. "Do you have a rate, Prythling, or will you be cold," he snarled.

I had never been in a situation like this before, Gallio had only taught me what he could in self defence. But as the training turned to real life, my body seemed to freeze. My heartbeat was erratic, but I forced myself to focus my mind, remembering everything Gallio had taught me as I pushed him away with a burst of energy.

Grabbing his arm, I swung myself under the limb pulling it against me and popping the joint out at the shoulder. I used the momentum to swing my fist into his jaw, the Aranese tumbling to the ground as a howl left his lips from the pain.

"You'll regret that." His words came out muffled in snarls, spit flying from his raised upper lip. He moved to stand again, cradling his popped arm, the crowd forming a type of circle around the two of us to watch the encounter. The blade slipped from my sleeve and I let it glint in the light a small smirk forming on my features. Confidence simmered around me as I fell into a comfortable stance. I could take him.

"You really think I will? Cause I don't think I do," I said with a cheeky grin. The confidence was there but I used the retort to hide my fear. I could take one Aranese, but they travelled in groups, packs. If his buddies showed up, I would most likely end up a carcass in the street.

A low growl noise fell from his lips and he jumped at me. I ducked his fist and placed my ankle behind his before rocking him back with my own closed hand. The blow made him stumble, his ankle tripping over my foot placed perfectly. He didn't stand a chance as he fell back into the dirt. The crowd started to mummer, unsettling the ring of the fight. I looked up as a shout came from the crowd and saw two Darion soldiers entering the ring, both pulling out their own blades.

"Oh, stars save me," I mumbled before turning and pushing my way through the crowd running from the two soldiers. If they discovered my identity, peace between Prytha and the Darion could be over before it even started. I raced through the thralls of people, trying to create as much distance as possible between me and the silent soldiers. My pace slowed as the crowd around me grew thicker and the people became harder and harder to push out of the way.

Suddenly a body rocked into my back. The wind was knocked from my lungs and I and my attacker were thrown to the ground. I rolled out of the Darion soldier's grasp just as a second one launched themselves at me, their blade intending to kill. I dodged quickly, swinging the stolen knife in my hand up as I rolled. I caught the soldier's side and heard the tear of fabric as the blade caught him right between his chest plate and his ribcage. No noise left the soldier's mouth as he continued his roll. No grunt of pain or flinch from the blade slicing his skin.

I bounced back to my feet as the other soldier came at me. I blocked his fist with my knife hand sending my other fist into his stomach just under the metal chest plate, causing him to double over. I pulled his arm down with my free hand, spinning him in front of me as the other soldier got up. I had seen him get up holding his side and guessed his move before it happened. Just as the injured soldier sent a kick aimed for my head, I had spun the soldier in my grip right in front of his companion's foot. The soldier's boot collided with his commander's head instead of mine and they both fell, hitting the floor. I let out a quick huff, pushing down the urge to kick dust at the two of them. I continued my sprint through the crowd before I lingered too long, knowing I needed to get out of here fast.

I sped through the crowd, dipping down a side street but heard a civilian yell out my position alerting soldiers of where I was.

I was about to run out onto another street when an arm reached out and grabbed me. I was still being pushed forward by my own momentum and the person used that to their advantage as they swung me into a doorway. I immediately found myself, once again, lodged between the solid chest of my attacker and the solid stone of the building.

I opened my mouth to tell him off and push him away from me but he brought his gloved hand up, covering my mouth and shushing me. I glared at him, feeling the urge to bite his fingers to get him to let go.

He tilted his head behind us and I watched from around his shoulder as a few Darion soldiers rounded the corner I was about to turn down. I would have run straight into them if it weren't for the masked man.

He wore a dark black helmet on his head, hiding his features, the only colour being an accent bright red stripe on the side. The colour red matched the burgundy leather jacket he wore. Though instead of a left sleeve matching his right, his left sleeve was torn off, showcasing his metal arm. It was shiny and a clean silver colour. I would have guessed it was his actual arm, if I hadn't seen the dirty white of a shirt underneath. It was armour.

I was about to speak again but he spun closer to me. The two soldiers decided to walk down the alley we were in, snooping around. The metal-armed man in front of me pushed a bit closer, dipping his head down so his helmet was against my forehead. I held in the soft gasp that wanted to leave my lips. The tension between the two of us high as he hid my body from the soldiers. The two of us barely breathing.

The cool metal of the chest plate he wore under his jacket was frighteningly cold. So cold it could be felt through the thick fabric of my flight suit. The tension and bite of the metal sent a chill down my spine. My eyes shifted upwards to the dark visor of his helmet, though I couldn't see his eyes I could tell he was staring down at me, watching every little move I made.

The close encounter between the two of us was over before I could even tell it happened. He pulled his head from mine, keeping his body against mine as he looked around, Darion soldiers gone.

I strained my neck to see over his shoulder to make sure they were actually gone, making sure I was in the clear. Not seeing a glimpse of the soldiers anywhere, I wasted no time in pushing the man off me, hearing him utter a small 'oof' from under the helmet as his head turned to look back at me.

"You didn't have to crush me against the wall," I muttered, sending him a small glare, dusting invisible dirt from my flight suit.

I could feel him smirk from underneath the helmet, cocky energy radiating off of him in waves. "And here I thought you wanted to be close to me," he muttered, not letting me catch the emotion in his voice.

I rolled my eyes at him before stepping around his body ready to head off in my own direction. "I wouldn't go that way, Princess," he said. I froze in my spot as the word princess fell from his lips. There was no way he had any idea, he couldn't know. I shook the suspicion off and turned to face him again.

"Whys that?" I asked rolling my eyes a bit annoyed that he was so vague, reminding me of a certain ghost friend I had. Who still hadn't reappeared. My arms folded across my chest as I stared him down.

He just tilted his head up, gesturing behind me. I turned around, seeing three Darion soldiers at the end of the ally pointing over at me. I froze, my eyes widening a bit.

"I can't crush you against a wall this time," he said pulling his gun from his holster and shooting over my shoulder.

I flinched and turned quickly. He hadn't indented the shot for the soldiers, instead he hit the top of a building. Brick and dust rained down on the three soldiers standing below, the rubble sending one to the ground. It didn't look like he would be getting up any time soon.

"Let's go," he said grabbing my arm and pulling me along with him. We raced down the streets of Tarkan as if he had its map sketched onto the back of his hand. He lead me quickly down streets I would have definitely gotten myself stuck in.

"We can't outrun them," I said, running next to him. We turned another corner only to find a Darion soldier waiting at the end of the street. Acting on instinct, I threw my dagger ahead of me, slicing through the soldier's visor and into his head making him fall back. As we ran past him, I pulled the knife from the body keeping it tight in my grip. Dropping it, not an option.

"Just follow me," the man next to me said. I furrowed my eyebrows wondering if I should be trusting this stranger. I reached out with my mind feeling for Aisha wondering if he was trustworthy. Thankfully she didn't ignore me this time.

"Go," was all I heard; her voice echoed around my skull. That was the only push I needed to follow the masked man through the markets of Tarkan. Though vague, it was still an answer.

The man held his arm in front of me as we slowed around a corner, the entrance to a hangar just ahead of us. I guessed we must have run across the entire city since this was not the same hangar, I had arrived in.

He held his metal arm in front of me as he peeked his head around the corner. I waited silently next to him, waiting for a signal to begin moving again. I got it when he dipped his chin subtly. We slipped into the hangar and ducked through the hallways until we reached a certain bay.

"Bay 34?" I asked wondering what was so special that we wandered all the way to this one. He only turned his head to glance back at me before he pressed in the door code and we slipped in. Sitting in the middle of the bay was a freighter ship, a bit on the smaller size. But it seemed like it would make up for its lack of bulk and size in speed.

It was a A3 fighter, usually used to transport troops, but I haven't seen one in years. Even then, the one I had seen was only a replica. A3 fighters were used in the battle of the Syron, moving

Syron troops from planet to planet. They had become famous for their speed, and the rarity of the ship post-war. I wondered how the man in front of me had gotten one, and how he expected to travel the galaxy unnoticed. But then again maybe attention was his thing. The ship was a dirty silver with bright red racing lights across the hull and around the nose, matching his own jacket and helmet.

Attention was definitely his thing.

Looking closer, I could see an imprint of a symbol just under the left wing. I would have recognized it anywhere. The crescent moon, of the Syron. A symbol of hope. It was small, if I hadn't been looking, I wouldn't have seen it. But the small moon, encircled by a ring and a proud star in the middle, stood out like a sore thumb. I would have recognized it anywhere. I made a mental note to ask him about it later. If his ship was from the Age of the Syron, it might have been a marker from its time. But if he had put it there himself, its almost an invitation to be shot out of the sky by Darion soldiers.

"You're a pilot?" I wonder aloud as he walked up the ramp, following behind him quickly, hoping not to be left behind on this shitty planet.

"And you, are not," he stated, tilting his head down to the flight suit making me realize he saw through the pathetic attempt at a disguise easily. He clicked a few buttons at the entrance before pausing. Turning his head to look me over.

"Get out," he said simply making my eyebrows shoot up a little surprised.

"Pardon me?" I asked crossing my arms across my chest.

"Nothing personal, Princess. I helped you out of a rough spot, and you helped me to my ship with no trouble. Now I have jobs to get to," he said stepping closer to me and ushering me off the ramp forcing me to step back onto the dusty floor of the bay.

"No, no, no please. I'll be killed if they find me, please." It felt terrible to stoop as low as begging, but I would be torn apart if I was left here. The worst part was I didn't know if begging would work since I couldn't read him behind that helmet. I had to figure out a way to get him to allow me safe passage. He started to turn away ignoring my plead. He had mentioned jobs, that meant only one thing could convince him to help me.

"I'll pay you, for passage," I said suddenly, making him freeze at the top of the ramp.

He turned to glance at me, contemplating my offer. He didn't have much time to think it over because a second later the door to the bay was kicked down and a squadron of Darion soldiers burst through the opening. He pulled out his gun quickly, shooting the first few at the front of the group, blocking the entrance with their fallen bodies.

"Let's go," he said ushering me inside. I quickly ran up the ramp as gunshots fired once again. His hand fell to the small of my back as he pushed me into the ship, firing at the Darion soldiers a few more times before closing the ramp and moving swiftly around me to the cockpit of the ship. I followed hesitantly and stood at the back of the cockpit. He sat in the pilot seat clicking and flipping all sorts of switches as the ship lit up. Lights flashing and coming to life.

The engines fired and lit up the bay we were once standing in, burning the Darion soldiers standing too close to a crisp. I let out a sigh of relief as we left the hangar quickly and took off into the open atmosphere, far stars shining out in front of me.

CHAPTER SEVEN

I let out a soft sigh as the ship launched into hyperspace, the stars flying past the windows in a blur. A weight lifted from my shoulders as Tarkan became nothing more than a dot of a star. Though that had been my only way home. I would figure it out, I would find a place to lie low before returning to Prytha. I had to.

My mystery saviour stood up from his seat as soon as the autopilot locked in and stepped out of the cockpit, brushing past where I stood in the doorway.

"Where are we headed? Or I mean ... where are you headed?" I asked, rephrasing my question.

He stalked into the main cargo deck of the ship, not bothering to turn and answer my question. He opened a door across the cargo bay, that I guessed led to the crew's quarters or med bay, and paused in the doorway. His stance was slightly tensed, his shoulders and back tight as if waiting for an attack. His helmeted head turned in the slightest to glance at me.

"Aladore." His voice seemed to have dropped in tone as he spat the planet's name out. I had recognized his slight accent earlier but couldn't really place where I had heard it before. It was nothing like the twang of Tarkan and was something more foreign. He might have been on Tarkan, but he had a shift in his voice that I didn't recognize from my corner of the galaxy.

The second wave of shock came mere seconds later. He was headed to Aladore. The last place in the entire galaxy I should be headed right now.

From what I knew from the stories my mother had told me as a child, Aladore was the birthplace of the Syron. The Syron were great creatures of power and magic from the galaxy's past. The Syron had been the strongest beings in existence until the Darion. They were born from the last light of a dying star and were made to be warriors of the galaxy, its protectors. Then the Darion took over the universe. The legends of the Syron were stories well known in every corner of the galaxy. Though they were told at a cost; they inspired hope, but were a taboo. If the Darion heard the word Syron slip from a person's lips, the speaker would be killed on the spot. Or dragged off and wiped. No one really knew which fate was better. To be wiped and turned into a mindless Syron soldier or to meet their end.

My mother used to tell me stories as a child about Syron's adventures and how they would save princesses like me and my sister from evil. But as I grew up, the truth of the Syron hit hard. Not all of them were sun blessed to protect us from the monsters of the galaxy. I heard the rumours that the Darion had been created by a Syron. A Syron who had gotten jealous and hungry for power. There were even rumours that the current leader, Darious, was a born Syron, that he held the same sun magic the ancient protectors did.

I turned away from the door the man had disappeared behind, almost letting out a startled scream when I found Aisha sitting behind me, lounging on one of the few crates in the cargo bay.

"What the hell! You need to stop doing that, disappearing when I need you and showing up out of nowhere!" I couldn't help the heat rising from my voice, my muscles locked up from her sudden appearance. I had to shake out my arms to loosen up my defensive stance. I glared, moving to sit on one of the crates in the corner next to her, leaning back against the cold wall. The only thing separating me from the freezing, dark, emptiness of space.

"I'm sorry, I figured speaking first would have gained the same reaction you just had," she said shrugging her shoulders from next to me. She sat with her legs folded neatly beneath her, posture painfully straight and chin tilted up a bit. It gave her a superior and powerful aura.

"Why are you showing up this time?" I asked her, pulling my stolen bag onto my lap and pulling out my few belongings, my father's knife slipping into my fingers.

"I came to make sure you were alright," she said, her gaze piercing a hole into the side of my face. She sat so still it was as if she camouflaged into the wall itself, her figure disappearing from my peripherals. The only reason I knew she was still there was the gentle white glow of her piercing gaze.

"I'm pretty sure you knew I was fine you were floating around me the whole time." I was making a guess, she seemed to always be hovering over my shoulder, so why wouldn't she have been this time. At the very least, it sure did feel like she was always creeping in the shadows.

"I wasn't this time," she said honestly. I twisted my head to look at her, my fingers freezing from fiddling with my father's dagger.

"What is that supposed to mean?" I asked, not even trying to hide my confusion. Where else could she have been if not on Tarkan? I swore I felt her comforting, slightly pressuring presence. Stars, I had even heard her voice.

"I had ... business to take care of. I wasn't watching over you," she started, sending me a glare. Her white-blue eyes piercing my own. "And of course, the one time I'm gone is the moment you need me most." I would have thought she was scolding me, though her voice wasn't condescending or mocking. It was neutral, easy.

"I didn't need you, I got out of it fine. Now look, I'm on a ship off the planet I would consider that a win," I said, my lips turning up in a half-smirk.

"You told me to run at the palace, and I think I made it even further than you thought I could have." Huffing out a laugh I couldn't have felt more lost and alone. I was so far from home.

Though, I felt almost proud of how I had gotten out of the puddle of misery that had been Tarkan. It was mostly from the help of the mystery pilot, but Aisha didn't need to know that.

"That. Is not a win," Aisha said, her voice dropping and growing raspy with anger. A tone I hadn't heard from her yet.

"You are off-planet, off the only planet where you could have found safe passage back to your home. With a man, you know nothing about and should not trust. He's a bounty hunter! Can't you see that?!" she said standing from her box and looking down at me. "And, you're headed to Aladore, out of all places ... Aladore." Her tone softened at the end of her sentence, her gaze falling down to her open palms.

"All I'm saying, is you need to start thinking through your decisions. Otherwise, without realizing it, you will be making the wrong ones. And I won't be able to help you then," she said locking her blue gaze on my gold one. In seconds she had disappeared again, and I was left feeling more exhausted and confused than I was before.

I sigh softly looking down at the blade in my hands. She was right I did need to be better. I needed to use my head, be smarter about my decisions. Though she had been the one pushing me in every one of those directions. She had told me that it would be safe to go with the pilot, then told me I could not trust him. I didn't know what to think anymore.

I huffed out an exhausted breath and pulled my hair from the messy updo it had been in since I escaped the palace. I ran my fingers through a few of the knots but gave up quickly with a frustrated huff. Then glanced down at the knife in my hands, contemplating the decision of just cutting it all off.

My thoughts were interrupted when the door the bounty hunter had disappeared through opened again. He froze for a second seeing the knife I'm my hand. I could feel his eyes travelling over my figure, looking for a threat. A threat that I wasn't posing. I put it down next to me with a small sigh, raising my hands a bit as if to say I meant no harm. The action released some tension from his shoulders, his stance becoming more relaxed as he stared at me. Or at least I assumed, he was still wearing that blasted helmet.

"Who were you talking to?" He asked leaning against the doorframe behind him. His arms were crossed in front of his chest, the silver of his metal arm shining under the artificial light. "Seems like a fight, based on what the other woman was saying." He added when I didn't speak up right away.

"It would have been a fight if I had a chance to say something back." I finally responded, a small laugh leaving my lips as I trailed my eyes across the ship, landing on him at the end.

"No, I was being lectured to apparently," I said running my hand through my hair as I glanced at the spot Aisha once stood. A small huff of laughter left the bounty hunter's lips as he moved from leaning on the doorframe and heading up past me back to the cockpit. His boots soft thudding being the only noise in the cargo bay. The dark silence of space living up to its reputation.

"Who were you arguing with?" he asked again as he passed me. I guessed he thought I had a communicator, which I actually didn't. No one had handhelds anymore. Transmitters were the only way anyone could get a message out anymore, and those spacelines were monitored heavily by Darion soldiers. I could never risk it.

"The ghosts on your ship," I answered, keeping a straight face as he looked down at me. I couldn't keep my expression neutral for very long and a teasing smile quickly took over. The man shook his head a bit, the tension in the air slowly fading and becoming a little more comfortable.

"So ... who are you anyway?" I asked following him into the cockpit and sitting in the passenger seat to his right. His hands hovered over the controls for a second and I could tell he was still hesitant about my character, unsure if I was a threat to him or not. Honestly, I felt flattered he thought I could be a threat, most people saw a girl, a princess nonetheless, and immediately thought I was weak. But no, this guy was smarter than most, or he saw me kick that guy's ass in the market.

"Bennett," he finally said before moving his hands to press a few buttons and pull a small lever.

"What's your last name?" I ask again wondering if he would give me anything else.

"That is my last name."

"Bennett?" I asked again raising my eyebrow at the masked man.

"Got a problem with that?" he asked turning his head to look at me through his blacked-out visor.

"No, I'm just realizing you're one of those strange, mysterious, galaxy guys." A silly smirk spreading across my lips.

"I'm not a strange, mysterious, galaxy guy," he said simply turning back to the controls in front of him.

"So, you say ... What's your first name then?" I asked. Before he could hesitate again, I offered a trade. "I'll tell you mine if you tell me yours." Bargaining as if we were children again. I could feel the smile he was trying to hold back as his helmet turned to me again. He seemed to observe me for a second before facing the window ahead of him again.

"Olen," he finally said. I stared at the side of his helmet for a second.

"Olen Bennett, hmm." I wondered out loud. I had to admit I had never heard a name that spoke as smooth as his.

"And yours, Princess?" He asked making my gaze turn back to the side of his shiny helmet.

"Aladella," I say, fiddling with the cloth of the jumpsuit a bit as I looked out the window.

"You got a last name?"

"Nope," I muttered softly. My family never had a last name, we were just, of Prytha.

Aladella of Prytha.

That was me. That was it.

CHAPTER EIGHT

"Here's how this is going to work," Olen started, leaning forward in his seat to flick a few more buttons. The ship seemed to whir to life and the flashing of lights and stars around the windows slowed. It felt like we had come to a dead stop once we fell from hyperspace. My stomach dropped to my feet and my head spun. I thanked the stars Olen had convinced me to use to seat belt, otherwise the drop might have sent my body tumbling to the floor.

Olen glanced over at me. "Dropping does usually make first time flyers vomit. Don't worry about it if you do." I managed to send him a vulgar gesture through my rolling head, holding it in my hands as I tried to steady the spinning world around me.

Once I got my bearings and plucked the courage to sit up, I peaked my head over the dashboard to the planet we were now looming over.

Olen had dropped us from hyperspace right over a small green and grey planet. I sat up a bit taller to get a better look. It took everything to not let my eyes grow wide in wonder. Aladore was the ancient planet from my childhood stories, the original home of the Syron. It was where magic was taught and learned, where magic was real.

I could see the rough outlines of the rivers that ran through the planet and the greyish green of the forests. Though I knew once reaching the ground, the beauty I saw from above would not be visible from the ground.

"Once we land, I'm going to need you to do everything I say. I don't trust you staying on the ship, and you're alright at fighting. From what I saw on Tarkan," he muttered, "so you could be useful."

"What exactly are you trying to get?" I had asked out of curiosity and to try and ignore the shake and rumble of the ship as we entered the atmosphere. He leaned back in his seat, pressed a button above his head, and all the lights on the ship turned off. All except for a faint red light on the floor. I was guessing he had locked down the ship, a ghost mode, to fly past the Darion ships unnoticed.

"I can't tell you that," he said, making his mission seem dangerous and mysterious. But honestly, that's the exact vibe he gave off so I wasn't too surprised. However, I was curious. Was he sent here to get someone or something? And if it was someone, were they supposed to be dead or alive?

"You can't even tell me a little bit?" I asked hoping for at least a small hint as to what he was sent to Aladore for.

"The Darion stole something from someone, and they want it back," he spoke. I pondered his words for a second wondering what the Darion could have taken. Besides complete control of the galaxy, what else would they want? Then I remembered one of the rumours I heard growing up. *Darious and the Darion travelled the stars searching for Syron children's Songs before they reached their fated child.* That's what we had to be getting now.

Gallio always said I could put things together easily; I had a good mind for that. It came to me naturally; he had always said. I didn't bother responding to his statement, believing I had figured out the problem myself.

The ship dove through the dense fog cover making it impossible for me to see anything. It made me wonder how Olen saw anything at all considering he also had a heavy dark helmet covering his head.

As we cleared the fog, the shine of metal stretched across the sky just below us. We were flying over a freighter. A huge Darion freighter. They same massive ships that invaded planets. It was hovering over the Darion camp, either waiting to be filled with soldiers, or to be emptied of bodies and wiping victims.

"Stars, you're kidding," I muttered, not believing for a second Olen had been sent on a mission like this alone. He couldn't be crazy enough to infiltrate a Darion freighter by himself. How the hell we managed to land without being seen blew my mind.

The landing pads of Olen's ship hit the roof of the freighter without so much as a shake. It had been the smoothest landing I had ever seen. There was barley a jostle of the ship as we touched down. He hesitated a second, as if waiting for alarms to go off. They didn't.

"You're like, good." The compliment tumbled from my lips as Olen stood from his seat, heading out of the cockpit and onto the main cargo deck.

"You're an actual pilot, but you're actually good. How did you do that?" I asked still confused how there weren't alarms echoing across the camp, alerting every soldier on the planet of our existence. A small laugh fell from his helmet making a smile pull up the corners of my mouth. He just shrugged a bit and placed a handgun in my hands along with a utility belt.

"Might need this, just don't shoot me, otherwise you're not getting out of here with this, *actual pilot*. This *actually good pilot*." I could hear the smirk on his features as he mocked me. My cheeks heating up, not realizing I had said it like *that*. I couldn't help but glare, trying to cover up the tint to my cheeks. I wrapped the utility belt around my waist, synching it tight. I then connected the holster around my thigh, sliding the gun into its respective place. The opposite one holding my dagger.

"Okay, look who's got jokes now," I muttered sending him another glare. I couldn't gauge his reaction, only seeing my own reflection in his helmet, making my glare falter.

The sudden urge to take his helmet off overwhelmed my thoughts for a second. I shook it off, frowning a bit, wondering where the thought had come from. Maybe my subconscious was fed up with the mystery.

I moved to stand next to him down the ramp, a shiver rolling down my spine as I sensed the familiar presence of Aisha standing behind me. I turn to look at the blue and white ghost, the words 'what' about to leave my lips.

"It is fate, trust your instincts," she said, offering a reassuring smile before vanishing with the wind.

"Thanks, Aisha, that was really, very, helpful," I muttered sarcastically at the empty air.

"Let's go, Princess." I heard from a few paces ahead of me. Turning towards Olen, he was already a few feet off the ship and knelt over a hatch to the freighter.

"Yup, let's go, Princess," I said to myself with a deep breath, trying to muster up the courage to actually go through with this.

"You got this," I whisper to myself.

I made my way over the Olen as he opened the hatch, wondering how I had gotten myself into this mess to begin with.

"So, you got a name for your ship? Or are you strange?" I asked, my voice low as I knelt down next to him, gazing down to the pitch-black hallway below us.

I heard a huff leave Olen's helmet and he tilted it up to look at me. I moved my own head, looking at my reflection in his visor. I looked like a mess. My golden-brown hair wild and loose down my back, knots in a few places but nonetheless looking decent. It was the dirt and wear that made me pause and look away. I didn't look like a princess anymore, and maybe I wasn't. With Darious's rule over my planet, titles were renounced. If I wasn't a princess, what was I?

"Yes," Olen said, his voice bringing my train of thought back to him.

"What is it?"

"You don't need to know."

"Why?"

"Because I said so, Princess."

Without another word Olen glanced at me then dropped down into the hole, disappearing into the darkness. Disappearing into the shadows beneath the hatch.

"Don't worry, I'll catch you if you're scared." His voice trailing up from the darkness. I rolled my eyes at the man hidden somewhere in the shadows.

"You better catch me, Bennett," I grumbled. I wiped my hands against the fabric of my pants, wiping away any clamminess before grabbing the edges of the hatch. Then I dropped down into the darkness of the Darion freighter.

I felt myself freefall for less than a second before hands caught my waist and lowered me to the steel ground. Even though I couldn't see him in front of me, I could hear his laboured breathing echo from under his helmet, just a bit above my head. His tight grip on my waist reassured me he was just in front of me, not letting got until I got my footing.

"See, caught you," he muttered before his hands left my waist and his body moved from against mine. I shook my head trying to get the warm butterfly feeling to leave my body. I turned on my heel and followed the rough shadowy outline of his figure. We walked around what looked like covered crates that were stacked to the roof of the room. I followed his quiet footsteps towards the distant light coming from a door at the other end of the room.

"We do this quick, in and out," he mumbled next to me from under the helmet. His voice was low enough that if there were someone else in the room, they wouldn't hear. I tried to look around to see what we had fallen into but the light from the doorway only illuminated the silver cage-like crates draped with sheets. I didn't even bother getting closer to look at what could be hidden underneath, the thought unnerving. I swear I had heard a scratching from underneath the pale sheets.

Olen nodded his head to the edge of the door and I moved to one side, taking the gun from its holster and watching the window making sure no one was coming. He ripped the panel from the side of the door and pressed wires together making the door open with a hiss. I stuck my head out looking down the hallway, confirming there weren't any Darion walking around before stepping into the grey corridor.

I followed behind Olen silently, wondering how he seemed to know his way around a Darion freighter. I figured he either had the layout put into the visor of his helmet, or he had done many missions before just like this one. I don't know which version made me feel safer.

After a few more corners we came up to another door, only, this one was guarded.

Two soldiers stood outside, blasters held against their chests, protecting whatever was behind that door. I waited by the corner looking up at Olen wondering what he was going to pull. Without a word he pulled his blaster, spinning the barrel before pointing it back at the two guards and firing. The two guards fell without a sound. The spin had been for a silencer, to make sure we didn't alert the whole camp of our presence with the sound of a single gunshot. I had to give it to him, he seemed to know what he was doing.

"Oh, okay guess that works," I mumbled from behind him as we move to the door the two Darion soldiers had been guarding. I could have sworn I heard a small breath of laughter at my comment, but I didn't have time to ask as the door to the storage unit was opened.

The room had tall, dark-grey walls and a white floor, much like the rest of the freighter. The centre of the room had a large circular table, on top sat an open case. I guessed that's what Olen had been paid to get.

It unnerved me a bit that there had only been two soldiers guarding something apparently so important, the Darion didn't offer up that much protection. Though who would have been crazy enough to land on a Darion freighter, let alone one on Aladore.

I rounded the table while Olen cleared the rest of the hallway, dragging the two bodies into the room and closing the door.

Sitting in the box sat a long, black blade with a matching onyx handle. The sword's entire blade was stained a colour so dark the light from around the room only sunk into the metal, no bounce of a reflection. I looked closer noticing down the centre of the blade, handle to tip, there seemed to be a crack, with a soft glow coming from between the metal. The room around me hummed with energy; the floor and boxes around the blade rattled. It seemed to hum from new company. The room around me felt filled with honey, I moved my arm, though it felt sluggish and heavy.

The room around me trembled when I reached out. My hand shook as I reached out for the blade. I pressed my fingers against the blackened blade, sucked into a trance by the glow coming from its centre. I couldn't keep my eyes off the abyss of the blade's colour; it was calling to me.

I pulled my hand back quickly when Olen closed the case. "Don't touch what's not yours," he stated.

I tried to shake off the trance I was pulled into and rolled my eyes at his attempt at humour. He locked up the case, the trance I was in fading as soon as the lock clicked into place. The hum and tremble of the walls all stopped in the same moment—whatever energy the sword had now locked away in its case.

I could still feel a tingle on the tips of my fingers from where I touched the sword. I half expected to look down and see the same pitch-black stain on my fingers, yet when I looked, they were completely clean. The feeling was strange enough that I had to wipe my fingers across my pants to get rid of the pins and needles.

I guess he wasn't stealing Songs, unless the weapon was something similar. Though I had never heard legends about a blade as dark as the centre of the universe.

I glanced back to Olen as he lifted the case from the table. As soon as the case was lifted, I realized why there wasn't an abundance of soldiers guarding the weapon.

A loud siren sounded throughout the building, alerting every single soldier that we were there.

"Shit." I heard the bounty hunter next to me mutter as we both rushed out the door and back down the hallway towards the cargo deck we had originally broken into.

"I'm guessing this isn't how you wanted this to go?" I asked, unable to control the amused laugh that bubbled from my lips.

I pulled out my gifted gun and shot down the soldiers as the flooded into our path. They came from everywhere. Olen didn't reply to my comment, though I knew he heard it. I wanted to think he was smiling at my sarcasm.

We ran down the final hall towards the cargo deck only to be met with ten or fifteen Darion soldiers. "Nope, not that way," Olen said, grabbing my arm and quickly turning us down another hall, pushing me slightly in front of him as the soldiers started after us.

The eery sound of humming silence echoing down the hallways. Accompanied by the sounds of their dark boots, running in perfect sync. Dark lasers started firing over our shoulders, making a small scream bubble from my lips as I ducked into another hallway to cover from the fire, Olen right behind me.

As the Darion rounded the corner behind us, their rain of dark lasers started again and I could feel the heat brush past my face and arms. I heard a grunt from next to me, making me realize Olen hadn't been as lucky. The case containing the weapon slid from his grip as his un armoured arm had been sliced by the blaster's heat. I quickly moved and picked it up as we continued down another hallway.

"Stars," I spat at the ground. "How are we supposed to get out of here?!" I cursed in Olen's direction, starting to get nervous about the ongoing escape.

"Give me a minute," he mumbled as he pressed the bottom of his helmet. It must have brought up a map right in front of his eyes. His silence made anxiety crawl in my stomach, my lungs tightening.

"I don't think we have a minute, bucket head," I said, a bit impatiently, as we round another corner.

"Oh, that was creative," he spat back sarcastically, his response getting a ghost of a smile to form on my lips.

"Ok got it. Just a bit further down then to the left, there's a hatch that leads to the roof, then we just got to make it back to the ship," he explained, ushering me forward and making me pick up my pace ahead of him. The familiar feeling of hope started to swell in my chest.

We slowed to a stop just under the hatch and Olen ran to the wall next to it, pressing a button to open the small door. It opened slowly with a screech; the slow speed of the opening hatch making me curse to the stars. As soon as the opening was wide enough, I tossed the case with the weapon up and onto the roof of the freighter.

"Alright, Princess, let's get out of here," he mumbled, grabbing my utility belt from behind me with his metal hand. I was pulled back with a single rough tug and bumped against his chest. His hand spinning me around quickly so I was then facing him. "I'll give you a boost."

He held out his metal hand, his injured arm limply held against his chest. "How will you get up? You have one good arm," I asked, putting my foot in his metal hand nonetheless. My hands rested on his shoulders, ready to jump with a boost out of the freighter.

"I'm not a damsel," he said, his voice low as if that had been answer enough. I could almost hear the smirk on his lips and smiled along with his comment. He counted down from three and I jumped, only the boost from Olen didn't come.

His yell replaced the silence of the hall as the heat of a dark laser ripped through his thigh and sent both of us tumbling to the floor. I groaned as my head smacked the ground, my vision going blurry and my teeth clashing together. I heard Olen's groan from next to me, but I struggled to sit up, my vision swaying back and forth as the soldiers approached us. I forced myself up, kneeling next to Olen only to see his metal hand gripping the side of his thigh, red blood spilling over his metal fingers.

The soldiers were advancing quickly, their blasters aimed at the floor, expecting to grab us with no problem. Unfortunately for them, that didn't mean I wasn't going to shoot. I pulled out the gun Olen had given me and took three shots; three soldiers fell before their rain of black lasers started again.

I felt energy flood my veins, adrenaline setting my body on fire. A heat rushed through my veins as I forced myself up. My vision was blurred but when I turned my gaze to the soldiers, it became focused, clearer, enhanced. My ears popped at the change coursing through my body.

It was as if I had been injected with a fiery energy, starting with my heart. A warmth spread through my body, from my chest to the tips of my fingers. I felt a warmth spread through my hands and the tickle forced my gaze from the soldiers to my clasped fingers.

From my fingertips where I had touched the blade, down my hands and wrist, my skin glowed a white sparkling light. Intricate designs spread from my finger tips to my elbows. A golden light spreading over my skin as a tattoo, glowing as if holding the light of a star itself. My body flooded with power and a sharp instinct. I didn't question the way my body reacted.

As if it was a reflex, I pushed my hand towards the soldiers approaching on the left. A glowing amber light flew from my fingertips, circling around the silent soldiers. It wrapped around one of the soldiers, the armour across his chest melting from the touch of the gentle-looking whisps. His screams were soon joined by the two others standing next to him. The gold whisps wrapped around their heads, their visors cracking and melting, their skin turning red and boiling under an invisible heat. A soft glitter had been the only residue left across their bubbling skin.

I flipped my head up, focusing on the four soldiers left. They all raised their weapons simultaneously and the blast of their shots echoed across the walls. I quickly turned, throwing my body over Olen's, expecting the blasts to rip through my body, only they didn't.

I opened my eyes slowly and looked up in front of me. Aisha stood over me, a wall of crystal light separating us from the silent soldiers.

Her name fell from my lips in relief, my shoulders relaxing a bit relief rushing through my body. She had shown up.

"You're an idiot," was all she said as she leaned down grabbing an unconscious Olen under the arms and lifting him up.

"Well ... " I tried to start, to defend myself, but she interrupted me again.

"An idiot," she said again. "Like a big ol' idiot."

I rolled my eyes at her slightly petty behaviour and watched her float up and out of the hatch, Olen hanging loosely in her grip like a child. I sighed and looked up at the hatch. I would have to jump. I groaned, bracing my feet a bit better before jumping up, my arms grabbing the edge. My fingers cut into the edge of the hatch and I groaned, using all the strength I had to pull my body up onto the roof. I rolled onto the flat ground of the roof and laid on my back, letting out a huff as I looked up at the fog cover.

Rolling over again, I grabbed the case grumbling softly as I pushed myself up and followed after my ghost friend and new, unconscious, bounty hunter friend.

My walk turned into a run as an alarm echoing in the distance. I ran up the ramp, sliding the weapon across the cargo bay as Aisha took Olen to the med bay.

I rushed to the cockpit, trying to remember the sequins of buttons Olen had pressed earlier. "I hope this works," I mumbled, taking his usual seat and pressing the same sequence of buttons, taking the controls and lifting the ship off the top of the freighter.

I knew the basics of flying having grown up on Prytha, where some of the best pilots and racers from our corner of the galaxy had been born. However, I knew the bare minimum. Shakily, the ship lifted into the fog cover. My hands moving the controls and flying us off the planet and into the atmosphere.

"Now where too?" I mumble to myself softly. I charted a course quickly before pushing us into hyperspace, leaving the ship locked on autopilot. The only planet I could think of was a long shot, but I hoped we would find friends there. Xenia.

Before getting up from my seat I glanced down at my hands in my lap, a bit frightened of the magic they seemed to admit. I made myself believe it was because I touched the weapon, whatever power flowed through my veins for that quick moment had come from touching the blackened blade. I had felt the shift of power, the blade awakened something deep inside of me.

With a sigh, I stood up and headed down to the med bay. I paused in front of the door for a second, wondering if Olen had seen what I had done or not. A shout from the other side of the door made me shake my head of the thoughts that plagued my mind, and walk inside.

As soon as the door to the room opens, I'm met with Aisha sitting on one of the beds while Olen was sprawled on the floor. Seemingly having fallen from his cot. He held is gun up with both hands, pointing it straight at Aisha's chest.

Aisha glanced over to me completely unimpressed with the bounty hunter's reaction to her presence.

"I wouldn't shoot the person who saved your life," I said from the doorway, a smile forming on my face as I tried not to chuckle at the man.

His covered head swung over to me; gun still directed towards Aisha.

"You know who this is?" He almost growled out from the floor. I stared at him tilting my head a bit. Did he think Aisha was a Darion? That she had come from the base? I guess that was the only logical reason someone could come up with as to why she was here.

"Yea, she's my ghost friend. Remember when I told you your ship was haunted?" I answered, glancing up to meet Aisha's gaze, her eyebrows raising at my statement. I just smiled at her.

"I thought you were joking!" he exclaimed, dropping his weapon to the floor before trying his best to lift himself from the ground, only to struggle since he only had two good limbs.

I moved to his side, crouching to his level and helping him back onto the med bed. As soon as he was resting and comfortably, I took a small step back. He started pulling off the armour of his metal arm, piece by piece revealing the lightly tanned skin of his muscular arm.

"Want to roll that cart over?" he mumbled, I turned around seeing the cart he was talking about, stalked up with med supplies. I roll it back to him as Aisha relaxed against the wall across the room.

Olen pulled his jacket off leaving just a black tank across his body. His uncovered arm had a black burn mark sliced across the outside of his bicep making me grimace at the sight of the injury. He kept turning his helmeted head in her direction as he took off his jacket. Probably deeming her a threat. Which honestly, he was smart to assume.

"So, who are you?" Olen asked, his question directed towards Aisha. I noticed he was struggling a bit with tying off the bandage around his arm so I moved to his side, brushing his hand away to finish wrapping the wound. Offering him a kind smile when his head tilted a bit, confused.

"I thought that was obvious," Aisha mumbled softly crossing her arms across her chest with so much attitude I had to cover my scoff with a cough.

"Hello, my name is Aisha Falleign. I am dead, a ghost now. Umm ... I was chosen to be a guide. My hobbies include floating, disappearing and giving advice," Aisha said making me giggle a bit from next to Olen. She could be difficult when she wanted to be.

"Aisha Falleign?" Olen asked, as if he recognized the name. I glanced up looking at the side of his helmet confused. How did he know her?

"Weren't you a warrior in the battle of the Syron?" Olen continued. I paused slightly and glanced up to look at Aisha, narrowing my eyes a bit at the white and blue woman. To my surprise, she just shrugged. I couldn't help but roll my eyes at her antics and turned back towards Olen. As I looked back over at the side of his helmet, I noticed a trail of dry blood rolling down his neck from the back of his helmet.

"Sorry Bucket head but identity can't stay anonymous forever, take off the helmet," I told him, tapping on the side of the helmet. He sighed, almost as if he knew I was going to point it out. He reached up with his good hand and clicked a button under his chin. The helmet opened up a bit before he pulled the black bucket from his head.

I was a bit surprised when a floppy head of brown hair fell out of the helmet, falling in loose curls across his forehead. He had a cut on his temple that had a trail of blood falling down his cheek and across his jaw. His features here sharp with a slight crook in his nose, having probably been broken a few times. I reached out and gently poked the cut on his temple making him flinch softly and grab my wrist with his good hand.

"Sorry." I mumbled looking down to meet his eyes, a deep piercing blue colour. His eyes stayed locked on mine. As I searched his face, I realized it would be hard to get any sort information from him. His features were as blank as his helmet, it was as if he still had the blasted thing on. I couldn't read a single thing from his expressions.

I broke eye contact with Olen when we both heard a loud thump coming from the side of the ship. "Stars. What next?" Olen muttered, his voice for once not muffled by the helmet.

I turned my attention over at Aisha who was staring at the side of the ship where the noise came from, slight confusion and worry across her features.

"C'mon, Princess, 'gonna find out who it is sooner or later." Olen said again and I returned my attention to him. He had just finished spraying the wound on his leg with a quick heal medication. It was strange to see his skin cells mend together so quickly. I helped him wrap it a few times before he hopping off the table.

He bounced on his leg a few times, his face contorting as the new skin probably stretched and moved. Once he knew it would hold, he grabbed his gun from the floor. I unholstered my own, following him from the med bay to see who was knocking.

CHAPTER NINE

Olen ran a hand through his hair, shaking it out as he walked through the cargo bay. He held his gun with white knuckles, weapon at his side as he skipped up into the cockpit. He peeked his head up, looking up through the window, trying to see what was going on just outside the confinements of the ship.

He was trying to see who was trying to branch onto his smaller vessel. A larger transport hovered above us; I could see the soft light of the tractor beam we had been caught in. We were being pulled to their attachment zone. About to be boarded.

"Are they Darion?" I ask Olen, a little worried as I glanced over at him. He was still looking over the ship, his expression relaxing. He looked worried, his mouth falling open slightly.

"I'm afraid it might be worse than that," he muttered, glancing down at me before exiting the cockpit. I was confused as to what he meant. From what I knew there was nothing worse than the Darion.

"What do you mean worse than that?" I asked, following after him. My chest tightening in panic. Walking passed med bay just as Aisha walked out, looking at us a bit disoriented.

"Do you have any idea what's going on right now? Because I would love to know." She just shrugged her shoulders. I narrowed my eyes at her since it was obvious, she was a really bad liar. She knew exactly what was going on.

"Really, Aisha," I muttered, silently cursing her out, I hoped she could read my thoughts. She just smiled at me before disappearing into a silvery mist. "Confusing, ghost lady," I mumbled to myself, turning to follow after the bounty hunter.

I found him kneeling over a hatch on the ground in a small room off of the cargo deck. I was guessing that was where the pirates would board the ship. I only guessed pirates by the way Olen said they were worse than the Darion. I had never encountered space pirates myself, but the flight crew from back home used to say they were brutal and ruthless, never leaving anyone left alive when they claimed ships. Only sparing those who had some sort of value to them. My chest tightened and I panicked a little more. If they had any idea who I was, I would not be safe, and neither would Olen.

A loud knock from the other side of the hatch alerted Olen they were just on the other side of the door he still crouched over. He immediately stood up and whipped his head back to me. His eyes meet mine for a second and his expression cracked, showing the slightest bit of worry before he masked it with his usual emotionless expression.

He moved across the room standing in the hallway next to me, gently pushing me around the corner. He turned his back to me, taking shielding position in front of me. He pulled his gun from its holster and pointed it towards the closed door.

"Just stay behind me and we'll get out of this fine, Princess," he said, voice thick and deadly. I nodded my head a bit just as the door opened.

The loud hiss of the airlock was the only sound echoing through the ship. Then the sound of a women's laugh replaced the silene.

"Oh, shut up Kacey, you know that's not true." The woman's voice echoing from the hatch, a soft chuckle leaving her lips. They must have thought the crew abandoned ship since they casually walked into the cargo bay. Not even looking around for a possible attack.

"Millie, I'm telling the truth. I won." A male voice echoed, following the female, Millie.

"Can I help you with something?" Olen asked from in front of me. The two pirate's voices quieted and I could hear their bodies shift to face him. I shifted my own frame in the slightest to peek around the corner wanting to see for myself what the pirates looked like.

A man and a woman stood in the middle of the cargo bay, likely in their early twenties. The man was the first one I noticed since he took a small defensive step in front of the woman next to him. His dark brown eyes were hard as he looked at Olen. His dirty blonde hair falling onto his forehead a bit but was cut much shorter on the sides of his head. He wore a shiny silver chest plate that had chipped blue paint on the sides and bottom, the metal might have once been a bright metallic blue before it had been worn down. He had matching chipped silver shoulder plates though his arms underneath were bare, showing off his sheer muscle underneath. From his bare skin I could see the dark lines of tattoo ink wrapping around his bicep, disappearing beneath his armour. His wrist guards were a shiny blue, the same colour as the chipped paint from his chest plate. Only they weren't worn down and scratched, they looked new. The two of them wore cerulean blue cloaks across their shoulders. The man's cloak was pushed to the side revealing a huge shiny axe holstered against his broad back and shoulders.

"Depends, if you have what I want," the woman answered with a fierce smirk on her lips. My eyes moved over to her frame as she took a small step ahead of the man behind her, her shockingly bright blue eyes staring at Olen. She was dressed similarly to the man next to her. Both of them sporting blue cloaks tucked into their armour, as well as shiny new blue wrist guards.

The only difference was unlike the man's old silver chest plate, she wore a stained black piece that crept over her chest and around her right shoulder, covering her neck but leaving her left shoulder bare. Like the man's exposed left bicep, her shoulder was covered in similar dark ink, I wanted to assume it was even identical. The woman's bottom half was covered in black pants, much like her counterpart only her left leg was exposed. A silver knee high boot crept up her leg, replacing the need for a pant leg. The cut-off pant leg was a decision made for mobility since the boot hugged her leg, no room underneath for fabric. It fit her leg snug just like how Olen's arm fit him.

I shifted my eyes over the pair again, taking in the aura they seemed to radiate. Power. When my eyes trailed back up, the woman's eyes had caught my own, shifting from Olen and to me quickly. So fast I didn't know if I had imagined the whole thing or not.

"Looks like you do have her," the man finally spoke up, his voice deep and plain, no emotion falling from his lips like when he was joking with his partner.

I froze in my spot behind Olen and noticed how he seemed to tense up as well. I cursed myself out under my breath, realizing I should have known this would happen.

I stepped out from the corridor confidently, glaring at the pair in front of me. "Who sent you? My mother? Or Darious?" I asked staring at the dark-haired girl in front of me. She shifted on her feet shifting the weapon she held against her shoulder, a long silver bow.

"Neither," she answered, a smile creeping onto her lips. It wasn't malicious or cocky, it seemed genuine.

"Then who?" I repeated, crossing my arms over my chest.

"I did." A voice from next to me spoke up. I glanced over at Aisha who had a sheepish smile on her face. I glared back at her, frustrated that she didn't tell me anything. My annoyance springing mostly from the fact that when she did decide to tell me something, it was riddled.

She rolled her glowing blue eyes at me before turning to the two people standing in front of me. "Della, this is Mamarie and Kasian," she introduced. I glance wearily at the two as Aisha floated over to them. They nodded their heads to me in greeting, the man, Kasian still keeping a straight face. However, Mamarie offered a small smile.

"Nice to finally meet you, Aladella," Mamarie said. I furrowed my eyebrows at the situation unfolding in front of me, but before I could voice my concerns Olen spoke for me.

"Stars, what is going on right now?" he muttered, holstering his weapon and moving to stand next to me. His hand still hovering around his belt, not letting his fingers venture far from his weapon.

"I was about to ask the same thing," I muttered. "More importantly why you needed to send for them." I added, directing the second part at Aisha. Narrowing my eyes at her.

I was utterly confused by the events that were unfolding in the cargo bay, but I knew Aisha had some kind of reason for bringing them here. I just didn't know what.

Aisha sighed softly and walked up to me, brushing the few hairs that fell in front of my face to the side. An action my mother used to do often when she was nervous. I let my eyes trail across her snow-white skin and the stark bright blue lines running its patterns down her face.

"You need their help," she finally started. She took a few steps away so she could address the entirety of the group. "I know I've been secretive and not entirely transparent with you since, well, emerging from the shadows," she said twinkling her fingers a bit. "But I do have reasons for my actions."

"Aladella, I am not a ghost, or a spirit, or whatever other strange creature you have come up with in your overactive imagination." How did she know what I thought of her? I never told her what creatures I assumed her to be. Then I remembered she could practically read my mind like an open book.

"I am ... what most call a spirit guide, but throughout my kind, we are known as Convoys. Guides or teachers," she paused, "for Syron children."

I blinked a few times, trying to process what she was saying a little faster. Of course, I knew of the tales of Convoys and their power. They were said to once have been great Syron leaders who unfortunately met death on the battlefield. Their last breaths spent surrounded by war. Only these special, courageous leaders, would come back from the dead as guides. Hoping to help the next generation of Syron to learn from their mistakes.

"So," I paused, gathering my thoughts. "So, what does that mean?" I couldn't grasp what she was trying to explain. Her words were vague and riddled.

"I was a Syron, your friend confirmed that earlier," she said, tilting her head towards Olen. I glanced to my left to see him leaning against the door frame with his arms folded across his chest. His features were twisted as he focused on what the Convoy was saying. His hair had fallen into his eyes and his brows were slightly pulled together.

I peeled my eyes from his face and back towards Aisha and the two pirates. "After I died, I found these two. I thought I would help where I could, and give them the knowledge that I was brought back to share."

"So, they are Syron as well? I thought Syron were typically women?" Olen asked from next to me, finally speaking up.

"I wouldn't say that ... " The dark-haired woman said, a smirk on her face as she sent him a teasing wink. The man's face remaining stoic.

"Syron have mostly been born women, however, men are rare, very rare." Aisha said rolling her eyes, which I assumed to be directed towards Mamarie. I bet she was hoping I didn't notice that they avoided Olen's first question. I narrowed my eyes a bit but kept the small clue to myself. I was more upset with the fact that Aisha, one of the people I had learned to trust, was obviously keeping secrets.

"Syron are typically women since they are usually the only ones with the strength and determination to complete the trials," the Convoy explained. "I taught them all I knew and all I know. But, since the war had just ended, I had to train them while constantly moving. They were raised as pirates. The only difference between them and others was the fact that they had my knowledge and my training, something usually only shared between Syron," she explained. She turned to look back at me, meeting my eyes.

"And then you were born." Her voice was soft, kind.

"Your mother called out asking for my help when the Darion first started their attack on your sister planet. I had no idea how she knew of me since my existence was," she paused, taking in a small breath, "has been, a secret to everyone. Even the Darion. But now I am not too sure I remain a secret."

As she finished her sentence, she gestured over to the two blue armoured pirates standing a little way off. "I called them because I need their help," she said. I watched as her eyes flickered to the enclosed weapon sitting on the crates just next to me and Olen. "And about that."

I kept my eyebrows from shooting up when she gestured to the weapon. I glanced up at Olen and saw the slightest lilt in his neutral expression, sharing the same flicker of emotion that I did. Curiosity.

"Why?" Olen asked, speaking up before I could.

This time Aisha wasn't the one to answer but Mamarie took a step forward from her companion. "Since you both took the weapon, and alerted the whole base of who you were and what you were taking. We figured Darious and his mindless soldiers would be searching for you. After all, you did take his—" she started but stopped. I was confused why she suddenly halted in the middle of her sentence but then noticed Kasian's hand wrapped around her wrist pulling her to meet his steely stare. It looked almost as if the two were having their own silent conversation.

"Basically, Aisha called us to help you both stay safe from the Darion. Who knows what value a princess like you could have to them?" He mused, his voice was lower than what I had first heard when he boarded the ship, and ten times more intimidating. "If you're alright with that ... ?" Kasian continued, directing the added question towards Olen. It was almost as if he was asking permission to stay on Olen's ship. It seemed the blue-clad warrior respected the pilot, even heard of his (still unnamed) ship before.

I watched Olen eye the two cautiously before nodding his head once.

* * *

The two blue armoured pirates had returned to their ship with Aisha. Sending their crew to a nearby planet to finish another job while they accompanied us on our new adventure. Once they had given their crew their orders, we had all gathered in and around the cockpit as Olen set us on a new course. There had been a bit of talk between the group, making us a little more comfortable with one another. The blue soldiers had explained that we would need to take the weapon to the opposite end of the galaxy. Further from Darious meant safety for everyone else. I didn't bother to ask which planet; all I knew was that it was even farther than home.

It turned out that Millie and Kacey had actually heard a few stories about Olen Bennett, his A3 Syron fighter attracting attention. He only basked in the attention, a smile on his face as he launched into a few stories of his exploits and adventures. In return, Mamarie and Kasian shared a few of their own adventures. Even Aisha adding a few about the war, and her lover, who she had not named.

I listened to their stories sitting on the ground of the doorway, having found a comfortable spot to listen. But just as my mother had told me stories when I was younger, my eyes slowly started to drift closed from the exhaustion that weighed over my body. I had been too caught up in what was going on and the adrenaline running through my body I had never really thought about how tired and aching my body was.

My eyes were drifting closed again for the, well what I guessed, was the fourth time in the last ten minutes. I felt a small tap on my shoulder and looked up to see Olen with a lopsided grin on his face. "Let's go, get you a place to rest," he said before helping me get to my feet.

"Thank you," I mumbled, getting up with a groan.

Looking back into the cockpit, Aisha was leaning against the wall facing Mamarie and Kasian as they whispered about something. The way their voices were lowered and their brows pulled together, I guessed something serious.

"What were they talking about?" I asked Olen, walking next to him towards the sleeping quarters. I rubbed my eyes, trying to clear the drooping pull of sleep and felt his hand snake to the small of my back, guiding me forwards. Probably there to make sure I didn't trip and fall with my tired footsteps.

"Mostly about what to do with the weapon, and what to do with you," he said with a sigh. I looked up at him the same time he looked down at me and I couldn't help the slight rush of heat that crawled up my neck to my cheeks. I shook my head a bit, clearing the rush of heat to my face, and pushed the cabin door open.

There was a single bed in the room, neatly put together, and pretty bleak and plain. There was no accent of red like his usual attire and nothing that seemed to make the place his own. There were no books or papers and pens, no clothing littering the floor or even weapons haphazardly scattered around. What I did notice was my makeshift bag had somehow managed to make it to the end of the bed, the top still tied in the bow. He must have just tossed it in here without me noticing.

"Thank you," I finally managed to spit out, stifling the yawn that followed.

He had opened one of the grey wardrobes, the airlock opening with a soft hiss. He pulled out a piece of white fabric, shooting me a corner of a smile as he tossed it in my direction. It was a white long sleeve.

"No problem, Princess," he said with a wink, slipping out of the room with the door sliding closed behind him.

CHAPTER TEN

My head was pounding.

I lifted a heavy hand and brought it to the back of my head, hissing when the brush of my fingers made my skull erupt with pain. There was a dull stinging sensation when I pulled my fingers back from my head, squeezing my eyes shut from the headache before opening them again. I slowly lifted my hand, bringing it in front of my blurry eyes

Blood.

My fingers were covered in the thick, red, fluid.

I raised my eyes back up to the room around me, shaking me head to try and clear the fuzzy feeling from my brain. It felt like someone had shoved cotton in my ears, then dunked my head in a tank of water. I felt so disoriented.

I shifted my gaze across the room when I saw a shadowy figure glide around the room in front of me. As my eyes focused, I could make out the familiarity of the room around me. I was back home, on the floor of the throne room. I was sitting across the steps just outside the doorframe. Though instead of the room I remember leaving just days before, this one was destroyed. Stone from the ceiling had fallen, crashing to the marble floors and leaving a gaping hole looking straight out to the sky. I could faintly see the stars twinkling down from above.

The rubble around the room was doused in fire. Curtains from the windows were being licked by the flames and furniture broken and burnt scattered around the room.

I focused my gaze further into the room and could faintly see two figures, battling against one another. Their moves like a dance, graceful yet dangerous. They clashed against each other, moving from one side of the room to the other.

The taller one seemed to have the upper hand as their movements clearly displayed, they had the offensive position. Their blade swung at the other shadow, aggressive and calculated. Every time their blade made contact with their opponent's, it seemed they already knew the next three the other would make.

The taller shadow's opponent, a woman most likely, her hair long and loose down her back and jewellery around her neck glistening in the light of the flames.

She blocked the attacks of the other player effortlessly and with a grace I had never seen before. She moved like a true dancer. A stark contrast compared to her attacker's moves. However, as slick and skilled as she seemed, she was quickly losing against her opponent's continuous and brutal attack.

I tried to push myself up onto my knees to help but a sharp stinging in my side caused me to stop. I grabbed my hip and immediately felt the warm blood cover my fingers. Just above my hip, under the lip of my corset, there was a deep gash carved into my skin. I hissed through my teeth and forced myself up onto my feet. A grunt of pain left my lips and I had to lean heavily against the wall in an effort to make my way towards the duel. My brain was spinning and shifting, the floor sliding back and forth making me want to roll over and vomit where I stood.

As I got closer the features of the two became clearer. The light of the fire behind them showing off the contours of their faces and helped me put names to their shadows.

My breath caught in my throat when the woman spun, her sword slashing against the man's blade, her hair tangled across her face. I couldn't help the tears that slipped down my cheeks.

"Mum?" I managed to mumble softly.

I tried even harder to get up the steps of our throne room to help her, but I only managed to get to the top stair when her sword clashed against the man's. In one swift motion, he had ripped her blade from her grasp and sent it sailing across the room.

My mother glanced over to where the sword fell, only a few metres away from me. Her eyes met mine and shock seemed to fill them before she gave me a sad smile. Her lips formed into three small words as she looked me over.

"I love you."

Not a second later I watched as the black blade of her opponent pierced through her neck from behind. Everything was still for a few seconds. My eyes locked on my mother's as I let out a blood-curdling scream. Only I couldn't hear it.

My ears were ringing from the silence as the life was drained from my mother's eyes. The silence seemed to stretch for years, but in reality, only lasted a few seconds. I watched as the blade was ripped to the side and my mothers' body and her head fell, only attached to her neck by a thread. My breath was caught deep in my chest, my throat closing as I choked on tears and sobs. My heart erratic and my lungs sucking in heaves of air.

The shadowy figure stepped forward, only his features, his identity, remained dark, hidden by shadows. It was as if my mind was blocking out who he was, to save me from the trauma. My body felt limp as I fell against the last step, my eyes locked onto my mother's cold, lifeless stare. Though I couldn't hear the scream falling from my lips, I could feel the tearing of my vocal cords and the hot salty tears that made thick trails down my cheeks.

I felt my eyes closing on their own as I stared at my mother. From my peripheral, I could see the glint of a metal arm before the faint, muffled sounds of gunfire. The fire herded the shadowed man from the room, bullets raining down on him from above.

I didn't know I had woken up until I felt arms wrap around my shoulders and I was pulled against a hard chest, my head tucked under their chin as muffled voices swirled around me.

My hearing slowly cleared up, the muffled sound lifting, the silence turning into my own shrill scream followed by thick sobs. I could barely comprehend what my body was feeling, had I really just woken up? But my dream felt so real. My screams soon softened into sobs as I gripped the person's shirt tight between my fists. I felt them rocking us back and forth, soothing me with whispers into my hairline. I tried my best to keep my emotions under control as I focused on what those soft whispers were saying.

"Della, you're okay."

"It's okay, calm down, breathe."

"It was just a dream, Princess."

I soon recognized it as Olen's soothing voice and I tilted my head up so I could meet his eyes. My sobs had calmed down and tried my best to get my breathing under control, still gasping for breath.

"My mother, m-my mother ... Olen, they killed her." I managed to get out still trying to get my outburst under control.

His eyes were locked on mine, the dark blue of his eyes seemed to lull me back into a sense of calm and I found myself drowning in their depths. I felt his thumb brush against my cheek, brushing away my tears, the cold skin of his fingers soothing the heat of my cheeks.

"It's okay, it was just a dream," he whispered softly, reassuring me nothing had happened. I couldn't help but nod, believing his simple words. I tucked my head back under his chin and felt his arms shift around me to pull me a little closer to him. I felt him hum softly above me as he rocked, the gesture calming my erratic heartbeat.

We stayed like that for a while longer; until my heartbeat slowed down and my cheeks had dried most of the tears.

I sniffed one more time making Olen tilt my chin up with his fingers. I met his eyes once more and he offered me a soft smile.

"Take a breath, then well go out to the rest of the crew, ya?" he said, nodding his head softly, his thumb brushing the last tear from my cheek. His blue eyes were a soft baby blue, the colour light and calming. I nodded my head and did as he said, taking a breath, holding it for a second, then letting it out.

Without another word I stood from Olen's hold, his hand supporting my lower back as he helped me stand. As soon as I was up, he jumped to his feet next to me and walked with me to the door and out into the cargo bay.

The rest of our group were lounging on crates in the corner of the cargo bay, their eyes turning in our direction as soon as they heard the door to the room open. Whatever conversation they were previously having was now completely forgotten.

"Are you okay?" Mamarie being the first person to break the tense silence.

"I mean it only sounded like you were being murdered. We were all ready to bust down the door to rescue you, Princess. Only Captain Olen held us back," Kasian said, a small amused smirk on his lips as if he thought the situation was entertaining.

I noticed Olen tense a little from next to me and I furrowed my eyebrows as I looked up at him quizzically. He only shook his head as if telling me he would explain later. All I knew for sure was I definitely missed something while I was sleeping.

Something that made Kasian open up a bit and caused a slightly pink colour to creep up the sides of Olen's neck. I shook my head ignoring Kasian's comment and turned back to the group in front of me.

"I had a dream, it felt real, almost as if I was actually there. I was back home; the Darion had taken over my planet and they ... they killed my mother," I said trying to cover up the slight shake of my voice by turning my attention towards Aisha. "I need to go home, at least to see her and make sure she's alright. If the dream comes true then I'm there to protect her," I said, keeping my voice hard and low as I laid out my request. I could still feel that shake of fear under my skin and one wrong move and I would lash out. Either I would burst out into tears again, or attack. Fight or Flight.

Aisha looked at me almost as if she knew something but didn't want to say it. I felt a rush of anger simmer under my skin, narrowing my eyes at her. "What are you hiding from me this time?" I almost growl at her.

"I just don't think that smart Aladella," she said with a soft sigh.

"I don't care if it's not smart! That's my mother Aisha, my mother. I can't just sit here and do nothing. What if she is in trouble and needs me?" I spat out; I could feel the anger coming off my body in waves. Who gave her the right to say my mother wasn't important?

"I'm not saying that," Aisha said narrowing her eyes at me, my eyes widened when I realized she was reading my thoughts again. The gentle scratch of her presence in my mind. "Get out of my head!" I screamed at her. I felt Olen's hand wrap around my bicep and pull me back a bit into his side.

"Stop digging through my thoughts, I can easily enough say everything I'm thinking straight to your face if you had the common courtesy to ask me!" I couldn't believe it when I could still feel the light scratching feeling of her searching my mind.

"Della! This is much bigger than you, or even your mother. You just don't know it yet! Do you have any idea of the importance of that weapon you, miraculously, managed to acquire is?! That is what is important right now! Not some silly dream you had about your home on fire and your mother's head! She means nothing right now. Nothing!" Aisha screamed back at me.

As she got angry her hair began to float around her and the light blue stripes that covered her skin became dark, a deep navy-blue colour, giving her a deep chilling look. Like a lady of the lake, floating just under the surface, making you look closer so she could pull you under. The air around her changed from light and calm to chilling in a matter of seconds. I took a hesitant step back, Olen taking it with me wearily, his hand hovering over his gun. I even noticed Mamarie and Kasian tensing up a bit as they watched the argument grow.

"That weapon is his Song Aladella, your only job now is to make sure he doesn't get it back. Without his Song, he is weak, which means there is a chance at finally ending his rule, without his Song he is only half the man he is said to be. Don't you get that?!" She snarled, her voice lowering at the end of her rant.

Her skin slowly turned back into a lighter blue colour and her hair fell limp down the length of her back, no longer suspended in the air. "If your dream was right, and the Darion are on your planet that means he knows you have his Song. It's just a trap to lure you to him so he can get his weapon," her voice low and even. "Don't do anything stupid."

With that, she disappearing into thin air. I watched as she dissolved through the wall and, with that, the constant feeling of her presence was gone and I could only feel the four of us in the cargo bay.

"That was intense," Kasian muttered said from his spot leaning against one of the crates. Mamarie rolled her eyes at him and elbowed his side making him groan softly.

"Not the time, idiot," she mumbled making him just scrunch his nose at her a blow her a kiss.

"I've never seen her get that pissed off and I've known Aisha for a long time," Mamarie said turning towards me and Olen. "But she wasn't just angry, she was trying to hide something by blowing up in anger like that," she explained, furrowing her eyebrows as she concentrated, trying to decode Aisha's burst in anger.

"Hide something like what?" I asked, still a bit shaken up after watching Aisha transform into a different version of herself. A demon version, much different from her usually angelic self.

"Couldn't you see it? It was written all over her face," Olen said, crossing his arms across his chest as he looked over the group of us.

"No sorry, I was a bit preoccupied watching her turn into some dark sea creature Syron," I said sarcastically making Kasian huff out a small laugh before covering it with a cough.

"She was scared, Princess; I just don't know what scared her," he said with a small smirk.

CHAPTER ELEVEN

"We have to go," I said as the four of us crowded into the small space of the cockpit, Olen falling into his designated seat as the pilot.

"You know, I'm just as curious to find out why Aisha seemed scared," Mamarie started, pausing when she entered the cockpit. "But I'm not sure if running straight towards Darious and his minions, is the smartest idea," she said, shrugging as she leaned against the doorframe of the cockpit. Her body language saying otherwise as I noticed her twist the few rings she had on her fingers. She was nervous.

"Well, I think it's a brilliant idea. I haven't seen any of those silent fuckers in a hot minute and I kind of want to ram their skulls into the ground," Kasian interrupted, his classic smirk still on his lips. Mamarie rolled her eyes at his behaviour but couldn't help the small smile that formed on her lips. I figured this was their dynamic. Mamarie looking out for the two of them, planning their next move, taking the brunt of the stress. While Kasian was the relief, taking that weight from her shoulders and making her relax with his off-handed comments.

"We don't even know if they're actually there. It was just a dream," I reasoned. As I spoke, I tried to get myself to believe it was just a dream. An effort to push down the feeling of dread that sunk into my stomach. What I dreamt of was nothing but a really, really, really bad dream. But as I rehearsed the words in my head, the less I believed them.

"What say you, Bennett?" Mamarie asked him. Our attention turned towards the pilot. He paused in his button-pushing for a second and glanced over his shoulder at the two blue-clad warriors.

His eyes then drifted over to me. "I say if we have a shot at Darious, then we take it." A cheeky smirk on his lips, his eyes lingering on me for a few seconds. The look he gave seemed to calm the sinking feeling in my stomach, returning a small smile of my own.

He turned after a few moments and rested his hand over a button flashing a warm red light. "I'd take a seat." The order was given to the three of us. I slid into the seat next to him, Mamarie and Kasian sliding down to the floor. A second later we were launched into hyperspace.

Taking off into hyperspace was not nearly as bad as dropping from it.

"Aisha would murder us for being such idiots right now," Mamarie mumbled a bit.

"Good thing she's not here then," I replied with a small smile.

Kasian moved over to Mamarie and pulled her into his arms, hugging her back against his chest. When he moved his head into the crook of her neck, whispering sweet nothings. That was when I averted my gaze. A small smile formed on my face at the two and I turned my attention back towards the window, my mind wandering to all the things I would face when I arrived back home.

The conversation became natural in the small cockpit on our journey to Prytha. Mostly Olen and Kasian trying to come up with a more impressive story. Kasian seemed to have enough adventures for three hundred years. Olen's ranging more from childhood pickpocketing to getting caught by a Mug monster on Brennia. The more they told stories, the more comfortable we got with one another. Mamarie and I even sharing a few of our own. I had to admit mine were much bleaker than the three smugglers around me, but they listened to the stories anyway. Mamarie tried to tell a few of her and Kasian's adventures, but the man got too excited and started recounting them for her.

I already found the two blue-clad warriors very impressive, immediately from the way they held themselves, but even more as they explained their companionship. It was as if they had been through everything together. I could tell by the way they both subconsciously reached out for one another, to make sure the other was always close by. Also, the fact that they moved around one another so gracefully it was as if the other was just an extension of their own bodies.

They seemed so in sync with each other I figured they must have been stuck by each other's side for a very long time, longer than the twenty-one years they've apparently been alive.

"So, you and Olen. How long have you been partners?" Mamarie asked me, ignoring the boy's conversation just ahead of us. I had swapped seats with Kasian once he and Olen had started comparing armour, Olen's metal arm to Kasian's own protective metal. Mamarie and I had taken up space in the doorway, appreciating each other's company as we laughed at the two children who occupied the cockpit.

I moved my attention away from the two men and over to the warrior who sat next to me. "I'm not sure I know what you mean," I answered with a small laugh, "almost three days, maybe four? I'm not too sure how long has passed since I left home if I'm being honest."

If I thought about it, I must have been away from home for at least a week, maybe two. Most of that time spent awake and running around. Trying to stay alive and not be murdered by the Darion ... and others.

Mamarie only gave me a small smile and looked up from the piece of fruit she was peeling with a small dagger. "It just seems like you two have been together a while, years even," she said, voicing her thoughts.

"When Kasian and I became partners, we were so uncoordinated it was almost pathetic. We could never figure out where the other was, it took years to get it right. A lot of mistakes," she continued, cringing a bit as memories resurfaced. "But that flow, connection, whatever you want to call it. You and him have what took me and Kasian years to perfect."

I couldn't help but turn my attention from her to the pilot just a few feet ahead of us. His side profile shadowed by the darkness of space, the soft red light the only thing illuminating his features.

"I guess I've never thought about a connection, it's just easy," I answered with a small shrug, twisting my fingers in my lap a bit. When we were running through the Darion freighter I had known where he had been standing the whole time, never running into his body as we spun around each other. I wonder if he felt it too.

"That's the point," Mamarie's voice pulled my attention from the two in front of us and back to her. "It's supposed to feel easy. When you fight together, you'll see, you'll fight as if you are a single being. You will be totally and completely aware of where the other person is even with your back turned to them. It's pretty cool if I'm being honest." Glancing back at Olen I wondered if we would ever reach the same level of trust that Mamarie and Kasian obviously had. We had come a long way from him almost kicking me off his ship.

I guess what she was saying made sense, it was easy. I didn't know exactly what she was talking about but there was a buzz of friction in the air whenever we were close. I wonder if he felt it too. I only really began to notice it when Mamarie brought it up, but now that she had, I couldn't help but think back to the last few days and how the pieces seemed to fall together seamlessly.

"We're coming up on Prytha now," Olen announced from the cockpit making me break from my train of thought. I took a small breath and felt a hand grip my shoulder, giving it a small squeeze. I look up and see Mamarie already standing and giving me a tight smile.

"Let's go," she said, as if knowing if she asked if I was ready, I would have said no.

Helping me up to my feet, I gave a subtle nod of my head and took a shaky breath. I didn't even want to look out the window and see the possible destruction of my home planet.

I was surprised when I finally did look out the wide windows. Everything seemed normal, perfect even. There were no Darion ships in the atmosphere, no fires raging across the forests and towns, no war, no bloodshed. Nothing that I had seen in my dream. I felt my brows knit together as I looked down at my home planet.

Confusion washed over me along with embarrassment. I felt a little stupid for believing in my dream in the first place. Though, when I had left the planet with the flight crew, Darion freighters had been hovering in our atmosphere. I remembered it clear as day. So where had they all gone?

"I'll drop us down on the outskirts of the city, close enough to get where we need to," Olen said as we entered the atmosphere, the ship shaking a bit as the planet's gravity sucked it down.

"And far enough so we aren't noticed," Kasian added with a grin, "I like the way you think." I shook my head at the two and their bonding, glancing at Mamarie and seeing her huff a laugh, the same thought probably flying through her mind.

"Alright. It won't take me long to go in and out. We should be quick. Since the Darion aren't here, we won't have to fight our way in and out. That means we can get off the planet and get his Song far away from here by nightfall," Mamarie explained, taking lead on our small mission into the palace.

"I just need to see her, that's it. Just to make sure she's alright, then we can go," I said. Mamarie giving me a nod before she and Kasian left the cockpit, heading to the cargo bay to grab their weapons and what ever else they deemed essential in our infiltration mission.

I watched Olen gently land the aircraft in a small opening of trees. The branches of nearby trees scraping the hull as the ship lowered, the screeching echoing through the room. The sound made the pilot wince, earning a small chuckle from me. He turned his head at the sound of my laugh and sent me a glare. I couldn't help but move back into the cargo bay with a small shake of my head. This ship was his baby, he would never let anything happen to it.

The door to the cargo bay opened as we hit the ground, falling down into a ramp onto the soil of my home world. The familiar clean smell of Prytha filled the musty cargo bay and I took a long breath. The smell of recent rain and the chill of a breeze sweeping through the ship.

I took a step down from the ramp but my pace faltered as I looked out into the trees. Memories of Gallio plaguing my mind. I never got a proper chance to mourn his death, being immersed in action since the day I left Prytha. Yet, as I looked out into the forest, I couldn't help but wonder if they ever found his body. Did my mum think he had gotten off the planet with me? Did she even know he had been shot down by Darious's soldiers?

I closed my eyes to rid any tears that were about to fall and took in a shaky breath, letting it fall from my lips slowly. There would be time to remember those who have passed. Eventually.

I felt a heavy arm drape across my shoulders and quickly wiped the under of my eyes to make sure I hadn't let any tears slip. I was met with the comforting side smile of Kasian. I offered him my own smile—though it probably looked like a wince—to thank him for the small moment of comfort.

His hand squeezed my shoulder, the gesture saying 'we're all here with you, don't worry'. He removed his arm from my shoulders when Mamarie called us over to where she and Olen were standing. Turning around, I noticed Kasian had been holding his massive axe against his shoulder with his other hand, and I swear that thing was as big as I was. Yet he carried it effortlessly.

Mamarie had her longbow across her back, the string across her chest holding it to her body while her quiver was attached to her hip. They both looked ready for a fight. Though I guess they always did.

"Here's what we're going to do. Della and I are going to the castle, while you two are going to take the town. See if you can find anything odd or any trace of the Darion. We know they were here because that's why Della had to leave in the first place. So, if they left, we need to find out why. Della and I will see what we can find in the palace while we check in on her mother. If you see anything, anything at all, tell Kasian or tell me," Mamarie said, addressing the last part to Olen then to me.

"How would that warn the other group of a threat?" Olen voicing the question before I could. His arms were crossed against his chest and he loosely held his helmet in his fingers. Brows furrowed a bit as he thought about Mamarie's plan.

"Kasian and I have a link, we'll know," she said simply. I glanced between the two. A link? Did she mean they were telepathic? They could read each other minds? I glanced at Olen who made eye contact with me but just shrugged. I guess nothing fazed him anymore.

"I know how to get in without being seen, it's kind of a hike though," I told them, ignoring Mamarie's link comment and focusing back on the task at hand.

"Alright, lead the way, Princess," Olen said, earning an eyeroll from me at the nickname.

I heard Kasian mumble something about nicknames to Mamarie, only to receive a slap to his arm. "The only nickname you will ever call me is Millie," she responded, her tone fierce and dripping with a threat.

"What about the baby? Pumpkin? Sweetheart ... c'mon that's a good one," Kasian continued. I heard an 'Oof' from behind me than the sound of the tall man hitting the ground. I rolled my eyes with a small smile and turned to see Olen grinning next to me. I was starting the love this small group of friends surrounding me.

CHAPTER TWELVE

Mamarie and I had split up with Olen and Kasian halfway into our walk: Mamarie and I splitting towards the tunnel system that ran under the palace, and Kasian and Olen moving towards the city.

There were a few gated entrances into the palace just outside the wall that surrounded the city of Prytha. I had directed Kasian and Olen towards the tunnel that would take them to the city centre, hoping they would figure their way through the tunnels and not get lost.

My mother always told me they were built for an easy escape into the forest and mountains. She told me if there ever was a need for us to evacuate the city, Prythians would escape using the tunnels that ran under the city and up into the mountains where a bunker had been built for our protection.

I never thought I'd be entering my home through those same tunnels.

We had been walking through the forest for maybe ten more minutes before we finally arrived at the wall. The barrier wasn't that large, but was built into the side of a cliff. The walls carved from dark-grey stone, a few holes here and there. But only one way in.

I lead Mamarie up to the stone wall, pushing around vines and other overgrown brush until I found what I was looking for. I tore some of the leaves down, revealing the gate that closed off the tunnels.

"At this rate, we will be in and out before Kasian and Olen even get into the city," Mamarie said with a smirk. I laughed, nodding my head as I reached for the door and pulled, but the metal didn't even budge. This exit had never been used as long as I've been alive, so it made sense it had rusted shut. It was only extremely inconvenient.

"Locked?" Mamarie asked from just over my shoulder.

I shook my head and wrapped my hands around the bars, giving it another pull. Feeling a bit of give that time. "No, just rusted," I explained. I took a small step back, hoping my idea would work, and kicked the handle of the door with as much force I could muster. The gate shook and made a god-awful screeching sound against the stone as it swung a few inches.

"Once more?" Mamarie asked with a small chuckle at the end of her sentence.

"I wonder how people were expected to get out of here if the gate doesn't even bloody budge," I muttered before sending another powerful kick into the gate. This time the gate slid out a bit farther, still scraping the concrete, not wanting to swing open all the way.

"Perfect," Mamarie said as she pulled her bow from around her body so she could slip between the gap I had broken open. "No wonder this was a job for us ladies, Kasian's fat ass wouldn't fit through here," the girl muttered as she slipped through the gap.

The only sound that echoed around us as we walked through the tunnels was the faint drip of water and distant scurries of an animal.

I remembered running down these tunnels as a child and hearing the distant laughing and chatting of the workers.

A feeling of uneasiness fell over me at the echo of silence through the halls.

"Somethings not right," I muttered to Mamarie, who had come up next to me as I rounded another corner that would lead to the kitchens.

"What do you mean?" she asked, glancing over her shoulder as she did, making sure no one was following or trying to sneak up on us.

"It's too quiet. It's never been this quiet in these tunnels. People's voices used to echo all the way through them, even from the farthest parts of the palace," I explained glancing over at her. Her brows furrowed and we slowed to a stop in the tunnels.

"They must have heard the gate," she said. By 'they' I hoped she didn't mean the Darion. But for some reason, I felt like she didn't even know who 'they' were.

I nodded my head, understanding what she meant before leading her further down the tunnels. I made an effort to keep my footsteps as silent as I could as we continued. I rounded a few more corners before we finally made it out and into the kitchens.

I was surprised to see no one there whatsoever. I turned back to Mamarie a bit worried as to what the lack of staff could mean. She met my eyes, the same confused look on her face.

As we continued our way through the palace towards the throne room, the silence of the palace made the hairs on my arms stand up and a chill run down my spine. I froze when I heard the click of heels echo through the hallway, other footsteps getting louder as we approached the hall. I quickly moved out and grab Mamarie's arm pulling her back around a corner before the footsteps turned down our hallway.

"- I don't care what they said, I want a search party sent out again. If Gallio is not off of this planet with my daughter, then I want him brought in." My mother's voice bounced off the walls of the palace and I felt a breath I was holding in easing from my lungs. A weight being lifted from my shoulders realizing she was alive.

But she didn't know about Gallio. Though how could she, I left with no way of communicating with my mother, no way of knowing what was happening on my home planet. I figured if I stayed away long enough, I would eventually return home to find the Darion gone. I guess that's exactly what had happened. I left, only returned to find the Darion gone.

I glanced around the corner catching a glimpse of my mother as she walked from the throne room. She looked okay; she didn't seem to be hurt in any way. The one thing I did notice was how tired she looked. As if she hadn't gotten a wink of sleep since I had to run from the planet. Though she probably hadn't, the look on her face told me everything. The stress of the Darion was heavy on her shoulders and with me gone and Gallio missing, her two right hands positions were empty. She had no one to confide in.

I turned back to Mamarie with a sad smile. I probably looked just as tired and stressed as my mother these past few days, I wanted nothing more than to run up to my room and sleep for the next month. However, I knew it still wasn't safe for me to stay here. I wouldn't be returning home for a while. The thought itself was too much to think about.

The responsibility and stress of the dark blade had extended my stay away from home. My priority now was to get it as far away from Darious as I could.

I shook my head a bit, to rid myself of the sad feeling of hopelessness and followed Mamarie out of the palace, the same way we had come in.

The walk back was completely silent, I was too engrossed in my thoughts and I think Mamrie knew that, not wanting to interrupt.

If my mother was still worried about the presence of the Darion, then where were the soldiers? Where was their army? If she thought Gallio was with me, then was his body never retrieved from the woods? It had to have been, we weren't far from the river and the main trail wasn't much further. I knew plenty of children and mothers who picked the berries in that area. His body would have been easily discovered.

If it wasn't found, did that mean the Darion soldiers had taken it? Had hidden his body? Or was he still alive? If he was alive, why hadn't he returned to my mother?

Why would the Darion not tell my mother what happened with Gallio to begin with? It was almost as if they wanted my mother to believe he and I had gotten away so she wouldn't try to find me. If she knew I was alone she would have found a way to contact me. If she still believed I was with Gallio, however, there was no worry or need for pressing contact. She believed I was safe.

Darious must have known I would run, that's why those two soldiers were on us right away. He must have expected the princess to flee so she wasn't used as leverage. The Darion soldiers had completed what they had set out to do, kill my guide. Darious must have believed it would be easier to catch me if I was alone, then he could bring me back and use me as a piece in his game for my planet.

But his plan didn't work. He was expecting a princess, he was not expecting me.

He thought I would be an easy catch for his soldiers, he never would have believed I could gather my own small battalion. Aisha, Mamarie, Kasian and Olen had helped me more than they originally thought. Darious would have never expected us to steal his weapon, meaning his plan was falling apart in his hands, and he had no control. Not until he got his weapon.

Mamarie suddenly nudged my shoulder, pulling me from my train of thought.

"Okay, I couldn't take it any longer. What?" she asked. She had probably seen the thoughts flying through my head just from the concentrated expression I wore. I couldn't even feel where my brows had pulled together, making me rub the area a bit to loosen the tension.

As we walked from the tunnels and into the forest, I told her everything. Since leaving my home, sneaking into a flight crew, meeting Olen, stealing the weapon, and her appearance on his ship.

Then I told her what I was thinking, the pieces were starting to coming together.

Only as they came together, I started to wonder what we were doing here.

* * *

Mamarie and I were sitting just outside the ship when Olen and Kasian finally returned to our makeshift camp.

I had been telling Mamarie more about what I had been thinking about on our walk back and she agreed with me on more than one occasion. Agreeing with my thoughts about how Darious knew I would run and that it would have been easier to catch me if I was alone. She had joked about how she was my guardian angel and saved me from the clutches of Darious and his silent soldiers. I had only laughed and brushed off her comment.

"What'd you find then?" Mamarie asked as Kasian took a seat on the ground next to her, Olen walking up into the ship silently. I furrowed my eyebrows at his odd, mysterious, behaviour before glancing at Kasian. The man only shrugged his shoulders at me as he wrapped his arm over Mamarie's shoulders and pulled her into his chest.

"Well, I thought it was going alright. Quiet little town, few people walking around in the market, doing normal people things. No trace of a Darion soldier anywhere, just people minding their own. Olen had a weird feeling the whole time, was tense about it as we walked around. Said it was just a chill up his spine. I felt nothing though," Kasian explained glancing around the trees behind me. I figured it was a subconscious thing, to survey the area for threats before actually settling.

My brows pulled together again at his description of town. Much like the palace his description was empty, hallow, quiet.

"I think Olen might have been right," I said finally.

"In the palace, it was too quiet, and empty. I thought maybe everyone would be in town or out in the fields but if the town was quiet too then something is wrong." It was quiet, empty, so where was everyone? Had the Darion killed them when I was running or had they been taken?

I looked up at Mamarie as the pieces finally click together.

"The Darion, what are they also called? They're known across the galaxy but what name is used more than 'Darion'?" I asked her standing up from where I was sitting as I started pacing. Nerves getting the best of me.

"The Silent Soldiers," Olen answered. He had moved onto the ramp leaning against the side of the ship with his arms crossed in front of him. I nod my head along with his answer, seeing the wheels turning behind his eyes and his mind running a million miles a minute in sync with my own.

"My people are gone somewhere; their fear must have driven them to the mountains. The ones still here must be stuck. There must be Darion somewhere," I said wringing my hands in front of me a bit. But where? Where had my people gone if not the mountains? And why hadn't my mother gone with them?

"That's not possible, I didn't hear that annoying ringing that seems to be hardwired into their mainframes," Kasian said, scratching the back of his head a bit as his expression turned to one of confusion.

"You didn't hear it because it's not strong enough. This is my home, it's never quiet, it has never been quiet. Walking through the palace was unfamiliar, like walking through an abandoned version of what it once was. I knew where I was going but it wasn't the same. It's their presence here. It's just not as potent as on other planets," I explained looking at them. Mamarie was staring at me as she started nodding her head, believing every word that fell from my lips.

"Where are they?" Olen mumbled from his place on the ramp. I glanced up at him and our eyes locked for a second. I couldn't focus on the look he was giving me because of the thoughts running through my head.

But before I could even get my thoughts in order, an echoing bang split through the atmosphere, the sound was powerful enough to make me drop. The sound wave sent me to my knees, my hands flying up to cover my ears.

I glanced up through blurry eyes and saw a ship entering the atmosphere. It had broken the sound barrier, sending a ringing bang loud enough to break windows and pop eardrums. The ship had dropped from hyperspace inside the planet's atmosphere.

Once the ringing in my ears calmed down, it was as if the bang had messed my hearing completely. The world around me was silent, the buzz of life that rumbled through the forest stopped all at once, it got so quiet I could hear my own heartbeat.

I was brought back to reality when I felt Olen's hands on my arms helping me up. I glanced up and even though his mouth was moving I could barely hear what he was saying. I couldn't hear what he was saying at all.

He got me to my feet, pushing the hair from my face and tilted my head to the side. Confused I brought my hand up to my ears. I felt it before I even brought my hand in front of my face. Blood.

I looked back at Olen who was staring at the blood trailing from my ears, his thumb brushing the hair from my forehead. Looked over his own features, I noticed a small cut on his cheek. His ears weren't bleeding, meaning he had been protected from the blast by the spot he had taken just inside the ship. The rest of us, however, were suffering from it.

His lips moved but I couldn't tell what he was saying, trying to read his lips, but he was talking too fast for me to understand. He brushed the hair from my face once more before glancing at Mamarie and Kasian, who both had matching trails of blood down the sides of their heads and necks.

Olen moved in their direction next, trying to tell them whatever it was he told me. I glanced back at the sky, looking up at the giant ship hovering in the sky.

"The Darion," I mumbled softly. My voice was only a whisper and I wasn't sure if I had even said the two words out loud. I noticed Olen tilt his head to me for a second then turning back to the couple in front of him.

"He knew I would come; he knew I would eventually come back to her." This time I knew the words fell from my lips. Again, my eyes travelled over the dark ship looming in silence, just outside of the atmosphere.

"Mum." I gasped softly. He was here for her; he would use me to get to her. I had to get there first. Without so much as a backwards glance at my friends, I got up and started sprinting towards the gate, to the tunnels. I wouldn't have listened to their yells for me to stop even if I had my hearing.

I couldn't if they were following after me. Not looking back once I started moving. I couldn't even hear my feet hitting the ground, or the breath leaving my lips.

All I could hear was the ring of silence echoing around me.

CHAPTER THIRTEEN

The farther I ran into the palace, the less my ears rang. My hearing was slowly returning, with every step, the world around me grew clearer. The first thing I managed to make out beside the echoing ring was the pounding of my boots under me. Gone were the silent steps I had taken before.

I was moving with urgency, not caring if the things listening could tell exactly where I was. My mind was too caught up with the thoughts of my mother. Images of her severed head and the blood clouding my mind. That was the only thing that mattered right now. Getting to her, and getting her out.

My sprint slowed as I reached the kitchens. With my hearing returning I could just faintly make out the sound of synced footsteps. Coincidently, heading in my direction. I silently cursed myself for not taking the precautions to keep still and silent. Getting caught by Darion soldiers was not an option.

I slipped the short blade from its sheath against my thigh, sliding the cool metal up my palm and wrist. Spinning it to get a tight grip on the handle. Surveying the empty kitchen around me I looked for a place to hide, for now.

There was a large counter in the middle of the room, an island top for the workers to have more space to move. The centre of it hollow to allow boxes to be placed for easy reach. The island was on wheels for easy moving, not a good place to hide.

The room was lined with shelves and pantries, the wall to my right being the odd one out having short counters where the sink, stove, and hearth took up space. The kitchen also looked like it had been ransacked, much different than I had left it only hours before. The pantry doors flung open, bags and baskets on the floor around the kitchen. All empty. The staff must have cleaned it out when they escaped to the mountains. Though that would have meant they had been here only hours earlier.

The footsteps were getting louder. Though I didn't know if that had to do with my hearing returning, or the soldiers were simply getting closer.

Not wasting another second, I slid myself behind one of the taller pantry doors. It was wide enough to hide my entire body, save for the bottoms of my shoes. The gap between the bottom of the door and the floor would give my position away if the soldiers noticed.

The footfall finally silenced just outside the door to the kitchen. There was a breath of silence before a bang echoed across the kitchen, followed by the loud splinter of wood and the broken door swinging inward with a creak. As the door opened, the buzz of silence took over the entirety of the room. Wrapping around any other noise and muffling it.

Darion soldiers.

I put my hand over my mouth to muffle my breathing. Light streamed in from the hallway they had entered from, casting their shadows onto the wall in front of me. I kept my stare on the shadows, counting three heads.

I took a deep breath and counted to three in my head, mustering up the courage to put all the skills I had learned from Gallio, and on my own, to use. There was a reason I had trained for hours on end. I had to be prepared for moments like this, when an evil infested my home, I had to be able to defend it. I was a Prythian princess. I had to stand for every Prythian under my mother's rule. I had to prove myself to the Darion, that they couldn't just take what they wanted. I had to stand as a symbol of hope for my people, maybe even the galaxy if it came to that.

I hardened my features as I heard the soldier's footfall right next to the cabinet, I was next to. With a quick breath I swung the door I had hidden behind into the soldier knocking him a few paces back. I grabbed onto the wood of the door and swung myself at the silent soldier in front of me, my feet colliding with his chest and sending him back into the soldier behind him.

I landed with one knee on the concrete and my hand with my blade brushing across the floor keeping my balance. I flipped my head up to see the two soldiers I had knocked over were still struggling to get up. The third had rushed the island in the centre of the kitchen, flipping himself on top of it so he had a higher position over me.

He made his movements obvious as he took a step before leaping at me. I immediately grabbed the edge of the table and swung myself under the shelves back to the other side of the counter. I stood up quickly, turning to see him look a bit confused before turning back to me. The other two had straightened themselves out and had moved to join their counterpart on the other side of the island. All staring me down utterly silent. The trio, as if in sync, all pulled out their blades in the same moment. As a unit, lifted them above their heads, holding their weapons in a reverse grip, as if they were spears.

I glanced down quickly and kicked the side of the table, sending the moving island into their unprotected stomachs, rolling on the wheels I had cursed out earlier. The three doubled over as the air was knocked out of them and I ran to the door they had left open, grabbing one of their discarded blades as I moved. I had gotten out of the kitchen just as they kicked the island across the room. The wood splintering as it crashed against the wall just next to me. Without looking back, I slammed the door behind me and pushed a few of the vegetable crates that were in the hallway in front of it so it wouldn't move.

I backed away as the door shook from their efforts to get it open. I waited for a second to make sure it held before continuing down the hallway.

Brushing the loose hairs stuck to my cheeks out of my face, I skipped into a jog down the hallways of my deserted home.

I needed to find my mother before something happened. If the Darion soldiers had found me in the kitchen, there must have been more wandering around the palace. I needed to find her before they did. My dream flashed across the back of my mind, making me cringe and move a little faster, hoping to see her and get her off the planet safely.

My feet carried towards the thrown room, slowing down as I reached the entrance. I ducked behind the corner of the doorframe, moving quickly enough through the shadows.

From my place behind the door, I could hear voices whispering in the room, meaning it was someone other than Darion soldiers. I didn't think it was even possible for the silent soldiers to open their mouths.

I poked my head around the corner to see the long dining table, which still looked set from the day I had fled my planet. Placing for my family and the Marques's.

Sitting in my seat was my mother, her hair a mess around her face, her posture straight as a board and her expression as blank as a sheet of paper. Her brows were furrowed together, letting me know the conversation she was involved in wasn't going well for her.

My eyes drifted to the other two figures in the room. Standing behind my mother was an older woman, an Aranese. Her arms were crossed in front of her chest and her eyes were trained on the back of my mother's head. The sharp angles of her facial features made her look dangerous. She watched my mother like a predator stalking her prey. The glimmer of sharp teeth pressing against her bottom lip making her look even hungrier, I wouldn't be surprised if the Aranese started drooling.

The last person my eyes shifted to was sitting at the head of the table with their back to me. I couldn't make out who they were but I could see their dark hair and tan skin from where I stood. The man's hushed conversation paused and his head tilted a bit in my direction. I sucked in a breath and quickly moved back behind the door before he could turn his head to look through the doorway. The room was silent for a second before I heard the man mumble something and the scraping of a chair followed.

Another chair was pulled out and I heard the faint clack of my mother's heels as she left the throne room. She was headed across the hall, the opposite direction from where I was hiding. Complicating my mission to grab her and go.

I let my lips mouth a few curses as I figured a route around the throne room that would lead in her direction. Then I could cut her and the Aranese off. It wouldn't be taking out the single wolf woman, but would be easier with my mother's help.

"You can come in now, little dove."

My entire body froze at his words, my muscles tensing and my posture straightening instantly. He knew I was here. The man sitting with his back to me had known I was hiding behind the door, that's why he had sent my mother away.

Hardening my features, I prepared myself to face whatever general sat in my throne room. With a quick breath, I took a step from where I was hidden into the doorway, then another into the throne room.

My eyes met his instantly, not wanting to show him I was afraid. I met his dark green eyes with a fire of my own, showing him, he didn't scare me. I cursed myself when I did hesitate my step for a second when I finally saw him.

He had dark hair, almost a raven colour but with warmer tones. Cut short on the sides leaving the top messy and spiked, falling across his forehead a bit. His features reminded me of a panther as he looked me over. He was leaning his hips back against the table and had a small blade between his hands, spinning it as he watched me, a small smirk on his features. His actions silky and mediated. He knew how to instill fear into his enemies. I had never seen someone with his features before, though I had seen the spark of chaos that trickled across his eyes. I had seen it in the slick Prythian panthers. Dark creatures covered in scales as dark as night, their eyes glowing yellow.

I had run into one when I was a child. Running into the forest with my sister seemed like a good idea until the smoky creature had started circling us. The panthers were one of the reasons the townspeople didn't venture into the mountains unless necessary. The creatures slipped down into the town occasionally, always leaving a trail of destruction behind them, slaughtering anything that happened to cross their path.

My sister and I had been lucky that day. Saved by a herd of Rawa's as they trampled the creature about to steal our lives. Raya had been one of them. The panther's pelt hung in my father's study after the incident. A reminder of the beauty and destructive nature of Prytha.

"Now isn't that better?" His grin was sweet, though the look in his eye shifted it to something else. Something chaotic.

When I didn't respond right away, he let out an audible sigh and rolled his neck back before pushing himself from where he was leaning.

He was dressed in all black, his dark pants scrunched around his ankles where his boots were laced up. He had a black shirt, buttoned up, save for the few at the top of his chest. The exposed skin had dark wisps of a tattoo peeking around his neck and shoulders. Over, he wore a long black leather coat, I compared it to the scaly skin of the Prythian Panther. It was rolled up to his elbows, showing off his forearms and fell to just around the backs of his knees.

Attached to his hip was a long dark blade. My gaze stuck to it as shock rippled through my entire body. My heart trembled at the sight of the weapon. The dark blade rested against his hip. The one that was supposed to be safe on Olen's ship, far away from him.

"You recognize it don't you?" he continued, brushing his coat behind the blade to show it off. "I must thank you for bringing it back to me." He said, the cocky smirk not leaving his lips. He trailed his fingers down the exposed blade and I watched as the ink seeped into his skin where he touched the metal, crawling up his arms in intricate patterns.

When I had touched the metal of the sword, I had felt as though the black pigment had been staining my fingers, only it didn't. But it stained him, showing its true power, where its loyalty lay. With its wielder. The dark stain of the blade covered his fingers before trailing over his exposed forearms, the dark raven colour creating intricate designs over his tanned skin.

My mind wandered quickly to my friends. The friends I had left at the ship, were they okay? Or had this man killed them to get his weapon?

"Well, I do think introductions are in order, don't you? My name is Darious, and you are little dove?" he asked, though there was something trailing just behind his eyes, his expression remained lilted in a slight smirk.

His stained fingers rubbed the sides of his neck as he looked me over. As his fingers touched the exposed skin, the tattoos around the back of his neck seemed to creep around the curve, a slight shimmer of power growing beneath them. It was as if the tattoos were affected by the stain of the blade.

My heart stopped in my chest.

This was Darious, leader of the Darion. *He* stood in the middle of my home, acting as if he owned the place. And he was getting away with it.

I glared at him harder and started towards where my mother had gone. As soon as I started moving, he had unsheathed his blade and held it out in front of him. Cutting me from my path, the tip of the blade against my hip. I half expected for those same dark tattoos to cover my own body where the blade cut the fabric of my pants and grazed my skin.

He tutted, shaking his head at me as if I were a child who had done something wrong. "I don't think so, Aladella," he said, my name falling from his lips in an almost sickly-sweet way.

I turned my head to glare at him, "I guess there were no introductions needed, Darious," I growled back, spitting out his name. His brows shot up a bit and he let out a low whistle at my words before the cocky grin spread across his face once more.

"Now, now, is that how you treat your sunmate?" he asked with a dark chuckle. Keeping his blade on my hip he moved to circle me, picking up a piece of my golden-brown hair once he faced me again. The edge of his blade pressed into the fabric of my flight suit as he circled, though not cutting the fabric any further.

My brows furrowed in confusion at his words, not understanding a single word from his sentence. I searched his face for an explanation for what he meant by sunmate but was only met with his eyebrows raising for a second time. This time genuine surprise it seemed.

"You have no idea, do you?" he muttered before his face fell into one of deep thought. "They haven't told you anything," he continued, humming a bit as he ran his hand through his hair. Leaning back against the side of the table, his sword at my hip. The tip of the blade catching just under my corset.

"I wonder why?" he mused, his lips pursing a bit as he glanced me over.

He tutted again and straightened his back, his free arm across his chest letting his stained finger tap his chin. "Well, now who can you trust? I can tell you everything," he offered, a wicked smile returning to his features. "Anything you want to know. I could tell you it all, right now."

"But where's the fun in that." He said with a cocky smirk.

My eyes searched his face, for anything, an answer of any kind. But all I was met with was his dark chaos-filled stare and casual smirk. There was no reading him, his features, though relaxed, gave away nothing.

What did he mean? What haven't they told me? And stars, how did Darious know? Out of everyone, he was the one with the answers. I tried to put the pieces together but before I could get a word in to drop the obnoxious smirk from his face, the sound barrier was broken again, an explosion sent the ceiling caving.

I let out a cry when I felt Darious's black blade slice across my hip, drawing blood. The cut made me stumble backwards, towards the steps I had come up.

The cement was raining down from the ceiling and crashing down to the floor. I didn't have time to cry out as a big part of the ceiling came crashing down above me. I lifted my arms to block my head but it did nothing against the stone. The piece hit me hard, bouncing off my arms and straight into the side of my skull.

My vision was blurry and my ears ringing. I didn't register I had tripped down the stairs until I hit the ground and my elbows and forearms were screaming, taking the brunt of the impact. I groaned sitting up and reached up to my head, gasping as my fingers hit a small spot on my head, bringing my hand to my face I noticed the bright red of my blood smeared across my fingertips.

I forced my lagging vision up back into the throne room to see two shadowed figures. They were blurry at first, but I blinked a few times to clear my vision. Darious had his blade out and was bringing it down on his opponent, his movements calculated and brutal. His opponent, however, was graceful as they moved. A stark contrast to his brutal striking motion.

I stumbled up a bit to get back up the stairs but gasped as I felt a sharp pain from my hip. I looked down, noticing how big the gash was that Darious had inflicted. The longer I looked at the wound, the more familiar the situation I had stumbled into became.

I glanced up in a panic at the two figures. Darious's opponent shifted their face, the flames from the explosion lighting up her face.

Mum

My whole body went into a panic as I realized what was about to happen. Still disoriented from the ceiling falling in, I managed to stumble up the steps as Darious disarmed her weapon, sending it sailing across the room.

"Mum!" The words came out in a scream, and her eyes shifted to meet mine. Her sword just a few feet in front of me. Her eyes mirrored my concern, though hers were clouded with shock when she realized I was actually there. Crumpled on the steps and bleeding, but I was there.

"I love you," she mouthed to me, the action finalized my dream and I could only watch as Darious's sword ran through her neck, swiping to the side and cutting it almost completely off. I let out a scream as her body toppled to the ground but couldn't get myself any farther up the steps.

Darious glanced over at me, his expression void of any of the playful banter and cocky behaviour he was showing before. Instead, he looked completely serious, angry even. A soft purple dancing behind his dark green eyes. Though that angry expression seemed to melt as he stared at me from across the hall. His green eyes glanced around, as if taking in the scene, before focusing on me once more.

"I had no choice; I hope you see that eventually," he said to me. His voice seemed to whisper across the battlefield. But somehow every word found me as crystal clear.

I only let out another cry of pain, a searing burning coming from the wound on my hip. I heard another explosion and saw the gleam of a metal arm, followed by a flicker of blue fabric before the firing of bullets began. The clang of metal on metal echoing soon after.

Disoriented from the stream of blood coming from my head. My vision blurry, from the head trauma mixed with the salty tears streaming down my face. I stumbled over to my mother's body. Grabbing her hand.

The next few moments were a blur as I pressed my head into her stomach and cried, my hand squeezing hers not wanting to ever let go. At some point, Mamarie had moved to my side, grabbing my shoulders to guide me away.

I started screaming and fighting to get out of her grip and back to my mother, not wanting to leave her like this. But Mamarie's grip around my waist was strong. As she pulled me from my mother's body, my gaze shifted across the room.

Kasian's axe was held loosely in his hand, slain soldiers discarded around him. Olen stood next to him, his gun in his right hand and his metal arm a bit bloodied.

Glancing across the room I caught the green eyes of my mother's murderer. Darious was running away, glancing over his shoulder and his eyes meeting my own. He was nursing his shoulder, where I assume, he got shot. Or sliced by Kasian's axe.

The part that haunted me was the look in his eyes, as if he was sorry. It was the way the corners of his eyes had almost tilted down, an apology.

He doesn't get to feel sorry for me, not after what he did.

CHAPTER FOURTEEN

We landed on Mamarie and Kasian's safe world three days ago, a moon off of the water planet Neptune. They had so cleverly named it Nep's Lune. The planet was quite beautiful. It was mostly water, like the planet it orbited, but was covered in forested islands. We had landed on one of the bigger ones before taking a hover to a smaller island where the cyan soldiers had a safe house. A bunker they had only used a few times before. I had to admit, it was a nice place to brood.

When Mamarie had dragged me back onto the ship it took me a few hours to calm down from my hysterics. She had been there the entire time, sitting next to me and holding me close. The only reason I didn't run back onto my war-torn planet was because of her. She had left me when I had calmed down a bit, to help Kasian chart the course to Nep's Lune. As soon as she had left, Olen had taken her place. Sitting with me on the floor of the cargo bay.

Not a word had been exchanged between the two of us. He had just sat down next to me, his back against the wall, tossing his arm over my shoulders and pulling me close. I had rested my head on his chest and his hand had run through my hair, pulling out the knots gently. It had calmed me down enough to fall asleep there on the floor, wrapped up in his arms.

When I woke up, I was once again in Olen's bed, alone. I had met the rest of the group in the cockpit, mostly to ask where we were going. I didn't mention a single word of the conversation between Darious and me. I had already put pieces together at that point but didn't voice my thoughts.

When I asked what they knew, Mamarie had suggested waiting for Aisha to show up and explain it all. That was three days ago, or maybe four. There had been no trace of the spirit guide. I hadn't felt her presence anywhere. And I haven't spoken a word to the three others on the island.

The first day Mamarie had tried, then Olen, I had a feeling Kasian knew that I needed my space and he pulled the two away leaving me to sulk by myself.

Since then, I've spent time either in my room or on the beach. Today I chose the beach.

I had plenty of time to think about everything that was crashing around my mind. Darious, Aisha, Mamarie and Kasian, Olen and my mother. Wondering how they all seem to fit together in this problem so perfectly.

I had figured out what Darious meant by sunmates yesterday. I was Syron, I was a Syron child. That was the first thing I had figured out.

It explained why Aisha had been with me since I was a child. It explained why Gallio had gotten me out of the palace and away from the Darion. It explained why I had pulled magic from thin air to save Olen. The magic had been my own. It explained why I had been so drawn to Darious's weapon. Why it called to me.

I had only heard my mother talk about sunmates twice in my childhood. She would often tell my sister and I stories about the Syron before we went to sleep, and only once had she told us the legend of sunmates.

She had said that occasionally, when two suns had lived their long lives together, sharing each others' power and warmth over millions of years, they would become bonded. Sharing the light and power they both radiated as they illuminated their solar system.

She had said sunmates were incredibly rare, but would be born when two suns, bonded suns, from the same solar systems created Syron children of their own. Just like the twin suns, the Syron children would be bonded for life. Created as equals, just as the suns had been.

I had been born from the sister star of Darious's power. He and I were equals; I would be the one to take him out when it came down to it. I don't know why it took me so long to figure out, but I had. I think I had a feeling when Aisha was explaining how she was Syron. When she said she trained Mamarie and Kasian before my mother called to her. It only made sense I had been born a Syron and Aisha had reached out, becoming my guardian soon after. I just didn't know why they had hidden it like a secret.

Maybe keeping it a secret from me, kept it a secret from the world. If we never spoke about it, Darious would never know. But somehow, someway, he did.

I also figured out Mamarie and Kasian are Syron as well, Aisha was their mentor after the war, she raised them here on the island. Then when they could protect themselves, she was called to my side. That's when I saw her during my training with Gallio, she helped me tap into that dormant Syron side of me. Aisha had slipped up there too, saying she started training the two after the war, that was three hundred years ago.

Kasian and Mamarie weren't human, they were immortal Syron. I knew they had stories beyond twenty-one years of life. Olen would rip into Kasian when he found out.

The one piece that didn't seem to fit was Aisha. Why had she hidden the information, why not tell me? I would have hidden better had I known. At least I thought I would. I probably would have mastered my power and tried to take Darious when I saw him in my mother's throne room. That's probably why Aisha hadn't told me, I could be reckless.

Now I was just waiting for her to show her face. So, I could scream at her for all I had lost, just because she kept a secret. Though I knew deep down she had done it to protect me.

I glared out at the water in front of me, the pebbled beach digging into my ass. With too many thoughts running through my head, I gave up on my thinking for the day and stood up.

I stripped down to my underwear and tank before wadding into the water. I ducked under to cool waves, letting the feeling of the water wash away my frustrations. I swam out a bit before surfacing. Taking a breath as I moved my hair from my face. The chill of the water helped soothe the fire that licked just under my skin.

"Della!"

I turned my head at the shout of my name echoing out across the water. Olen stood on the beach, a crooked smile on his lips. Since arriving on the island, he had left his armour and signature red leather jacket on the ship. Opting for the comfort of a grey long sleeve and black combat pants. He looked more relaxed like this, not burdened by wars or battles. No protection needed.

He waved me in from where he stood before dropping a towel. Something I had definitely forgotten to grab from the house before coming down.

With a slightly embarrassed blush on my cheeks for forgetting. I sent him a small wave of thanks. He shook his head with a cheeky grin, probably laughing to himself over my forgetfulness. He sent the small wave back over his head before running his fingers through his curly brown hair and retreating back to the house. Offering a final throw of his arms as he left.

I took a breath before diving back under the water.

I couldn't ignore them forever.

* * *

I changed into a white long sleeve and black combat pants, tying my boots back up around the bottoms of the pants.

All given to me by Mamarie.

I headed out to the sand pits at the back of the house where I knew my friends would be sparring. The closer I got, the more I could see Mamarie's dark hair whip around as she threw a shirtless Olen straight into the sand making him groan. From the sidelines, Kasian's laugh tore through the air. Doubling over from where he sat in the grass, leaning back on his hands. Mamarie only jumped up dusting off the sand from her hands and navy tank before reaching a hand down for Olen.

"You're good. I'm just better," she teased before helping the curly haired boy to his feet. He winced a bit, a blow to his pride. A grimace of a smile pulled at the corner of his lips sending Kasian into another fit of laughter. A real smile pulled at his features and he ran a hand through his hair shaking the sand out. Right over Kasian's head. The blonde warrior spat the sand from his mouth and glared at the pilot.

I couldn't help it as my eyes trailed down his chest, there was no denying the bounty hunter was attractive. There was a thin layer of sweat covering his body making his skin glisten. Also causing sand to stick to his damp skin. He made no move to brush it off as he moved to sit in the grass.

Before someone caught me starring and I embarrassed myself, I turned my gaze back to Mamarie and Kasian who had collapsed next to each other on the grass.

And with a small grin pulling at the corners of my lips, I made my way across the field to where they had been sparring.

"Well then, who's up for a real challenge?" I asked with a cheeky smile across my face. My voice hadn't come out as strong as I hoped, but the effort was still there. The group turned to face me and Kasian immediately laughed a little, his reaction made me smile. I had hoped that they hadn't taken my ignoring personally. I didn't want there to be an uncomfortable awkwardness between us because I was coping. Though, I didn't think they would let that happen anyway.

"I don't know, Princess, you sure you got what it takes to go up against me?" Kasian asked raising an eyebrow.

Mamarie laughed a little from next to him and nudged his shoulder. "I wouldn't be talking, I bet she could kick your ass easy," she said making us all smile, Kasian grunting a little as if a challenge. Which it was.

I trailed my gaze over at Olen, who was grinning down at the couple, his arms folded across his chest. He must have felt my eyes on him because his attention turned to me, his smile not faltering.

"You've healed then?" he asked, his arms tightening over his chest and his eyebrow raising a bit in question. He shifted his weight as he assessed me, looking for the answer himself.

My head still ached sometimes, more so at night before I slept, and sometimes I got dizzy when I stood up, but it wasn't nearly as bad as it was three days ago. Three days ago, even getting up too fast, forced me into a fit of dry heaving, the spinning being too much for my aching body.

As for my hip, Olen had stitched it up when I was unconscious after breaking down on the ship. I didn't remember the interaction, but Mamarie had told me when I had tried to shower and noticed the stitched skin.

I lifted the edge of my shirt, pulling the waistband of my pants down a bit to show off the stitches on my hip. The skin was almost completely healed, I guess I had to thank my Syron power for that one. Though I knew the skin was still tender and if I fought my hardest, I could split it open.

"Healed enough to move, just go easy on me," I said with a pointed look.

Olen only sighed a bit, rolling his eyes, "It's not like I can stop you," he said raising his hands a bit. I smiled and turned to the other two on the grass.

"No more hand to hand, you've got to have some kind of armoury around here. Training swords?" I asked looking around.

Mamarie thought for a second before glancing over her shoulder, towards the tree line a few metres away from us. "I don't know about training swords but there is something, be back in a second!" She said with a smile. She got up from Kasian's arms and went to go get whatever she was talking about.

I dropped myself down to the grass next to Kasian. He had pulled his arms behind his head and was looking up at the sky, ankles linked and eyes squinting under the bright sun. The sky was a bright blue, reflecting from the water planet below. Few clouds in the sky with the sun shining down, almost perfect.

"How are you feeling?" he asked. I had guessed Kasian would be the first to ask, he was blunt like that, getting straight to the point.

"Better than two days ago," I muttered with a soft sigh. I tilted my head to look back at Olen who was still standing with his arms across his chest.

"I know what you want to ask me," I said with a pull at my lips. I could tell by the way he was looking at me he wanted to know what had happened between Darious and I when we were in the throne room. And to be honest I didn't even know what to think, I didn't know what to think about what he said, or specifically what my friends haven't said.

He sent me a small look, almost like a playful glare before moving to sit next to me, lying down on his back. "I wasn't going to ask, not if you didn't want to talk about it. But I can't help being a little curious," he admitted.

His confession made Kasian bark out a laugh from next to me. “A little curious?” he said looking over at Olen, I raised my eyebrow a bit confused before turning my head back to Olen.

He rolled his eyes a bit at Kasian but the small smile stayed on his lips. “He hasn't stopped wondering what happened since we landed, you're welcome for not letting him attack you with questions,” Kasian muttered with a small laugh, nudging me with his elbow.

“I don't know why I tell you things,” Olen mumbled moving his arm so it was covering his eyes, I smiled a bit over at him, noticing the slight pink tinge to his cheeks.

Kasian only let out a laugh before moving to stand up. “One day you'll realize I'm actually, very helpful,” Kasian said, sending Olen a wink before ruffing my hair and walking off to where Mamarie had disappeared.

“I think you mean useless!” Olen retorted making Kasian laugh as he walked away. I let out a few chuckles from my spot on the ground before glancing over at the man lying next to me. I rolled onto my stomach next to him and looked over at his still covered face. He let out a breath before moving his arm from over his eyes and under his head again, only glancing at me a bit with a smile on his face.

“It took me three days to actually figure out what anything he said meant,” I said to him, pulling at the grass between my fingers. I felt him shift a bit to watch my face as I spoke. He seemed a bit surprised I was even talking about it, but I trusted him, I trusted them all. Keeping it to myself would only make me worry and more confused about the whole situation. I would over think until I had thrown myself into a panicked frenzy. That wouldn't have helped anyone.

I pulled a few more pieces of grass out and let them blow out of my finger tips in the soft breeze. “He knew I was just outside the room, hiding behind the door. He had waited for everyone to leave before confronting me. I don't know why he didn't just drag me from where I was and execute me right there. But he didn't. He thanked me for bringing his weapon back. When he said that I realized how dumb I actually was to even return home, he must have known I would come back eventually," I explained a bit, ripping more grass out, a clump of it this time.

"Then he called me his sunmate. At first, I didn't understand, and I guess he could see the confusion on my face. He told me he could tell me everything I wanted to know, the things my friends wouldn't tell me," I said with a soft sigh. "I figured out what he meant when we got here. What Aisha had said earlier, I'm the Syron who shares suns with Darious. I was so confused at first, and angry at you all for not telling me. But then I guessed you had no idea, and Kacey and Millie had to have kept it a secret for a reason. Maybe the longer I didn't know, the longer I would have been hidden."

I didn't look up at him for a second, still ripping at the grass absentmindedly. I only realized I was creating a hole in the ground when his hand came over and covered mine, pulling them away from the grass. His hand was warm and enveloped both of my hands in his larger one. I glanced up to look at him to see he was turned on his side, eyes already on my face, his brows furrowed a bit as he thought over my words. I let my eyes trail over his features for a second as he gazed over mine.

"When did you figure it out?" I asked as I tore my eyes from him, a soft blush on my cheeks.

"I think I always knew you were a little special," he said with a wink. I had glanced up to catch the gesture and I huffed out a laugh pushing his shoulder so he fell onto his back again. He laughed a bit with me and tilted his head to look over at me.

He reached up softly and tucked a loose hair behind my ear making me blush a bit harder, I tugged my bottom lip between my teeth trying not to let him see my nervous smile. His eyes lowered from mine to where I was biting my lower lip softly, his eyes turning a shade deeper.

I watched the colour change curiously, wondering if that was something that happened to all of his people, if it was, I wanted to see his planet, where their emotions were shown so prominently in their eyes. Though when I had met him, he had kept his eyes a cool light blue. He must be able to control it, like his own magic power.

His lips tilted up into a sly smile and his hand moved down to the side of my neck, his thumb brushing across the skin of my throat then landing just under my chin, the warmth of the palm of his hand enveloping the soft skin of my neck.

His fingers pushed into my skin a bit as if to pull me towards him. His eyes moved from where his hand was, to my lips that had slightly parted from surprise and back to my eyes. His eyes darkened again, from their light blue colour to a deep admiral blue.

The sound of Kasian laughing and Mamarie swearing pulled me out of my trance, Olen's eyes lightened again and the warmth of his hand left the side of my neck as he sat up.

I looked over at the treeline seeing the couple walk out holding sparring staffs, grins on both of their faces as they tried to trip each other as they walked. I grinned at the two, figuring that's why Kasian had been laughing, he had tripped the brunette as they walked back. I glanced back at Olen who was watching the pair with a grin. He glanced back down at me and I noticed his jaw clench a bit before he offered me a cheeky smile. I rolled my eyes a bit playfully, not ignoring what had just happened, but pushing it to the back of my mind for now.

I had turned my attention back over at Kasian and Mamarie just in time to see her sweep Kasian's feet from under him and sending the man toppling to the ground. I stifled a laugh as I stood up raising an eyebrow at Mamarie, she just shrugged at me with a smile before tossing me a staff.

"Let's see what you got, Princess," Mamarie said, teasing me with the nickname the group seemed to have taken a liking to. Thanks to Olen, of course. I sent her a playful glare before spinning the staff in my hand, moving across from her in the grass. I saw Olen move to help Kasian up in the corner of my eye. Olen laughing at Kasian, the blonde glaring at the blue-eyed boy only to accept his help anyway.

Turning back to Mamarie I held up the staff across my body, straightening my stance. "I promise to go easy," I said with a teasing wink making her only smile at the challenge.

Without a second of hesitation, she brought the wooden staff down at me. My reflexes instantly kicked as I raised my own staff in defence. The sound of wood hitting wood mingling with the sounds of life across the island as we sparred.

CHAPTER FIFTEEN

We had stayed out in the fields until dark, training and joking around. It had helped me forget about the pit I had been stuck in the past few days.

I had caught myself staring off into the treeline a few times, my mind wandering to darker thoughts, but one of the three always pulled me out of it. Being surrounded by friends helped lift the darkness around my heart.

I should have realized it sooner but the few days alone had been crucial to figuring myself out first. The longer I was alone the more I fell into myself. The first day had been the worst. I had stayed in my room, just my thoughts floating around the dark room. I could vividly see that day in the throne room. It replayed as if projected onto the walls around me.

The second day I had ventured to the beach, sitting on the stones for hours. Moving outside had helped me clear the stuffy thoughts. The friends I had somehow surrounded myself with made it easier. The longer I was around them, the easier it was to smile, the less my heart ached.

I was pulled from my thoughts as I felt a heavy arm swing over my shoulders, I tilted my head up to see Olen grinning down at me. "So, tomorrow, Kacey and Millie want to show you something new. They didn't really elaborate on what it was going to be, but I'm guessing its only something for special people," he said, sending me a teasing wink.

I couldn't help rolling my eyes as I jabbed my elbow into his side. He let out a small grunt and grabbed his side with his other hand, his eyebrows pulling together in a small frown.

"What was that for?" he mumbled taking a few longer steps to catch up to me, matching my stride.

"Just felt like it," I answered sending him a wink, mocking the one he had just shot me.

He scoffed, a smile still on his lips. The movement dragged my eyes down to his smile, noticing it turn up into a small smirk. I had to get out of there.

I spun on my heel, my eyes a little wide from the flicker of embarrassment for being caught, and continued towards the homestead. When I swung the front door open, Mamarie and Kasian were already lounging inside.

They swung their heads in my direction when I entered the kitchen, all smiles as they snacked on packages of food I couldn't identify.

I hopped up on the counter next to Kasian, Mamarie leaning on the counter across from us. Olen found a place in the doorway, leaning his shoulder against it, his arms folded across his chest. I stole the bag from Kasian's hands making him huff and send me a glare. I just sent him a cheeky smile before digging into the bag. Crackers.

"We thought Aisha would be here by now and she could explain things to you. But she's not, so me and Kacey were debating explaining. And we will, if you want to listen," Mamarie finally burst out, breaking the brief silence as we settled in the kitchen. My hand paused on its journey to my mouth with the snack I had stolen from Kasian.

"Sorry what?" I spoke. I figured they would explain the whole Syron thing, thinking I didn't have a clue of what I had figured about them and myself.

"Kasian and I are Syron. The reason we don't have the powers or sparkly skin ... " Mamarie started before Kasian cut her off.

" ... or get to brag about the title," he said adding a wink. Mamarie just rolled her eyes at him before continuing.

"Aisha took us in, gave us training and a place to live. Learning what it was to be a Syron, the responsibility that came with that kind of power. We also trained under Faye," Mamarie said. I raised my eyebrows at the new piece of information.

I had my suspicions that they were somehow Syron related, but to be actual Syron who trained under Faye? *The* actual Faye, the symbol of hope through the galaxy? That shocked me, might have shocked Olen even more since his eyebrows shot up at the mention of the infamous Syron.

"And we were Syron! Full on badass Syron! For a full three months, then Darious showed up to where we were hiding, ransacked the place and stole our Songs," Kasian continued, his voice bitter as he stole the snack bag back from me.

Mamarie nodded along with him. "We still have our magic, our power. But its not as saturated as it would be with our Songs, we also don't get the sparkly skin," she added.

"Or the immortality, don't forget about that, it sucks ass, being mortal. I don't know how you do it," Kasian added, cutting in again, the last part directed towards Olen. The pilot only smiled back at Kasian shrugging his shoulders a bit.

"You're telling me you're just a little old man trapped in his younger body?" Olen asked, raising his eyebrow as he joked with Kasian.

"Three hundred and twelve and still look better than you, Bennett," Kasian growled. Olen tried to hide the smile with a shake of his head, a soft huff of a laugh falling from his lips.

"That's why Aisha called you both," I realized out loud. "She said you were protection, which I'm guessing you still are, technically. Because of what I am. But also, because his weapon gave you leverage, to get your own Songs back."

The realization sunk in slowly. I had lost their only chance at getting back the power they once held. I had ruined their one shot at regaining their Syron magic.

"I'm so sorry," I said. I could feel the back of my eyes sting as the shame and embarrassment made my cheeks heat up.

I had been so caught up with my own problems I didn't even stop to think I could have been messing it up for everyone else. Stars, I was acting selfish, like a child. My mind had only been focused on one thing, my mother, and how important she was to me. I didn't realize maybe the others had something equally important they had to protect. And look where my self-absorption got us. My mother was still dead, her eyes haunting me at night. Olen was out the bounty he would have gotten from the Song, paying for his ship. Fixing the weird rattling sound, you can only hear from his room when it was dead silent. I had also managed to drag him into this whole Syron vs. Darion mess. Kasian and Mamarie now powerless and slowly gaining all their years back at once, their bodies growing weaker the longer they were away from their Songs.

I was brought back from my thoughts when I felt an arm around wrap around my shoulders. I blinked quickly, clearing my eyes, a few tears slipping down my cheeks as I leaned into Mamarie's embrace. My arms wrapped around her torso and I hugged her back tightly. I felt a warm tear fall onto my shoulder, letting me know she was crying just like I was.

"Its okay," she mumbled into my shoulder, "if it was my family, I would have done the same." Her head shifted a bit in the crook of my neck and I could tell she was looking over at Kasian.

It didn't take him more than a second for him reach over and wrap his arms around the two of us, his forehead pressing against Mamarie's for a second before he rested his cheek against the top of her head.

Their acceptance of my somewhat pathetic apology made me feel a little better about the situation. The mention of my mother stabbed at the healing wound in my heart. A few more tears slipping down my cheeks. I squeezed my eyes closed to cut off the flow.

I let out a soft laugh and pulled away from Mamarie a bit. Kasian's arm fell over my shoulder, pulling me into his side a bit like a brother would, I sent him a small smile of thanks to which he sent me back a teasing wink.

I looked back at Mamarie as she held my arms, just above my elbows, bringing my attention back to her. "You're a part of that family now, Aladella. We're stuck together, through the good and the bad." Her lips tilted up into a small smile at the end of her sentence. I couldn't help the smile that grew across my face. This was my family, all of them, even Aisha. Who is like that distant aunt, that nobody really knew what she did, but for some reason has a ton of money and always has the advice you need in that moment?

I glanced over at Olen who still stood in the doorway, a soft smile on his face. "C'mon," I said, patting the counter next to me to he could come join our little family hug.

"Yea c'mon, little brother," Kasian teased with a little laugh. Mamarie only rolled her eyes, Olen ignoring his comment completely, most likely used to it by now. I couldn't keep a straight face at Kasian's comment and huffed a small laugh, earning a grin from the blue-clad warrior.

I only smiled at Olen before pulling him into our group hug, feeling a sense of safety with my friends—the people I knew I could count on and would be with me no matter what, for the rest of our lives.

Surrounded by the people I loved, my family.

* * *

Later that night I felt more relaxed, lighter. The heaviness on my heart being lifted by the comfort of the rest of my group.

I dropped my towel at my feet, feeling fresh and clean from my shower, and started pulling on undergarments and a t-shirt I had stolen from Olen to sleep in. Considering all I really had from home was a corset, a ball gown—that seemed like it was from a different lifetime—and a flight suit.

I ran my fingers through my long hair, letting it air dry and tugging out the few tangles I came across. I had a small giddy feeling in my stomach as I pulled at the hem of Olen's shirt. I don't know if he knew I had it, I had announced I was taking some of his things, but that was when I was ignoring the group and mumbling my sentences.

I pulled back the covers of my bed, the training today and our emotional moment had draining me, mentally and physically. I knew as soon as my head hit the pillow, I'd have an easier time getting to sleep than most nights.

I paused when I heard a knock on my door. My door had been left a crack open in case Mamarie had anything else she wanted to say before going to sleep, which she usually did.

I sat down on the side of my bed and started pulling my hair back into a braid. "Yea?" I asked turning my head to greet Mamarie, only instead of the taller brunette girl, Olen Bennett stood in my doorway.

"Can I...?" he started, trailing off a bit as he stood in the doorway. I smiled at him, rolling my eyes a bit at the question, unable to keep the grin from my cheeks. "Of course, door's always open," I said with a smile, turning a bit in my spot to face him, my hands still up and working on braiding down the back of my head.

I only had light from the small side table lamp next to me, the light barely reaching the dark corners of the room. Because of the lack of light, Olen was cast in shadows where he stood in the doorway. When he took a step forward, the side of his face light up under the warm light. He moved into my room slowly, looking around as he closed the door behind him.

He looked almost nervous to be in the room, but I knew he wasn't, he was cocky, just trying to fool me into thinking he had never been in my room before. I knew he had gone through the room looking for his gun yesterday, he was stupid enough to misplace it and thought I was pulling a prank on him. Kasian had taken it.

"Stop, with that whole ... thing." I said, taking my hand away from my hair to gesture to his whole body. Immediately a cocky smile pulled at his lips.

"You just gestured to all of me," he said with a lazy smirk.

"Mhmm, then you must know what I mean," I said back with a small smile.

"Sorry," he added with a smile before his eyes looked up to where I was braiding my hair, my fingers fumbling with a few of the wet, tangled strands.

"You want me to?" he asked, lifting his hand a bit to gesture to my hair.

I raised my eyebrows a bit surprised, "You can braid hair?" I asked, my eyes following him as he moved across my room. I had turned so my back was facing the edge of the bed while he moved to stand next to the side table behind me.

He didn't answer until he was standing behind me, his fingers brushing against mine as he took the strands into his own hands. "There was a little girl in the group that raised me. One of the pilot's daughters, she made me learn so I could do her hair," he said, I could hear the fond smile in his voice, the sound contagious as a smile pulled at my lips as well.

"So, did you need something?" I asked after a moment of silence, closing my eyes as he raked his fingers across my scalp pulling hair into the braid.

"Mhmm," he hummed out, "I wanted to see what you were doing."

I let out an amused huff at his reasoning. "That's it?" I asked, an involuntary shiver rolled through my body when his fingers brushed across the back of my neck. His fingers paused for a second, hesitating before he continued.

"Maybe that's not all of it," he mused tying off the bottom of my braid. My eyes stayed closed from when his hands were running through my hair, trying to remember the soothing feeling.

As his fingers left the tie at the bottom of the braid, they moved up to the back of my neck again. Pulling at the neckline of my shirt. "That was until I saw you in this," he said, his breath fanning across the back of my ear. A shiver rolled down my skin again and I held my breath, biting my lip to hold back the grin trying to pull through.

"I didn't think you'd mind," I said before pulling away from his hands. I turned around, sitting up on my knees so I was almost the same height as him.

"Do you?" I asked, running my hand up his chest, pulling on the fabric of his shirt. "Mind? Do you mind?" I continued, glancing up to meet his eyes. The deep blue colour had returned and it took everything to not smirk at the effect I had on the man in front of me.

I couldn't hold it a second longer, my lips pulling up a bit. He closed his eyes tight when he noticed my tone change from worried, to sarcastic. I fell back onto my heels with a little laugh.

"Alright, bucket head," I said with a small smile and pulling myself under my covers, tugging them up to my chin. I shouldn't have done that. Toying with Olen was fun, the way his eyes changed into that deep blue colour was alluring and I was afraid if I kept teasing him, I would become addicted to the colour. Maybe that's why I had pulled away, scared I would fall in too deep.

"What can I help you with?" I asked with a small grin.

He opened his eyes again, returning to the light blue as he looked down at me with a small smile. "Well, Princess, I know how hard it is for you to sleep at night ... since ... " he said trailing off again. The smile on my lips faded and I averted my eyes from his and to the ceiling.

"I figured maybe some company would help," he said. "I grabbed a cot from the ship. I can put it down; be right here in case you need someone."

I glanced back over at him, my eyes stinging a bit at how much he was willing to do to make sure I slept at night. He looked down at me almost expectantly, waiting for me to say it was okay. I let out a small sigh before pulling the covers open next to me.

"Turn off the light," I said with a small smile before turning so my back was facing him. Cuddling into my pillow a bit trying to hide the smile on my lips.

I heard him pull of his boots, with a bit more shuffling before the light was turned off and the bed dipped behind me. The lamp next to the bed flicked off, blanketing the room in darkness. I felt his arm brush across my back as he got comfy, his hand moved just above my body to fix the blankets, pulling them to his chest. I waited a few seconds, closing my eyes and listening to his breathing. I got a bit nervous, contemplating if he could, not only hear my heartbeat, but feel the intensity and speed of how hard it was hitting my ribcage.

"Olen?" I whispered out finally. I felt him shift a bit, moving the arm closest to me up, probably to put behind his head.

"Yes, Princess?" he asked, the grin evident in his voice, which had somehow dropped deeper than it had been when he entered my room.

"Are you comfy?" I asked softly, my eyes trained on the wall in front of me, my vision adjusting to the dark room.

"Yes Della, I'm comfy," he mumbled softly. "Are you comfy?" he asked back after a few seconds. I stayed quiet for a second, not entirely sure how to tell him I wanted him closer without sounding weird or clingy.

He let out a huff of a laugh before the bed shifted again and his chest pressed against my back, his arm sneaking over my waist.

He pulled me close, my back pressed tight against his chest. "Better?" he mumbled against the back of my ear, his breath on the back of my neck making me shiver. I reached down and threaded my fingers through his, holding his hand against my chest and shifting into him a bit.

"Yes," I said softly, closing my eyes and feeling sleep start to pull at me immediately.

"Hey Olen?" I said again softly as I felt sleep come easily, not like how it had been impossible to find the last few nights.

"Yea Della?" he mumbled, his voice sounding just as tired as mine.

"Thank you."

As sleep tugged at my mind, I faintly felt lips press against the back of my neck while Olen whispered out a soft, "You're welcome, Princess."

It didn't take me long to fall asleep after that. My dreams peaceful, with no nightmares about my mother. Only the good memories I had with her.

CHAPTER SIXTEEN

"Milly, I swear to god, you said I would learn how to use my magic." I groaned from my spot on the grass. Where I had landed after she had thrown me with a single hit to the chest. I should have expected the strength she had and not have been so overconfident.

Besides the two extra inches of height, she had on me, she also had the training of someone just over three hundred years old. More than enough time to build the strength to knock anyone on their ass with one hit.

"Yea well, I'm trying Della. If I knew what your power was this would be ten times easier," she said, kicking my foot lightly with her own as she stood above me.

"Now get off your ass and let's try again," she ordered.

I groaned loudly before getting to my feet again. "I told you, all I remember was a sparkly little yellow wave coming from my fingers and then the soldiers were melting," I responded.

"How is a little gold wave supposed to tell you what my magic is?" the last part came out in a grumbled question. I had expected a sassy retort from the older woman, but when I looked up the brunette's gaze was glaring a hole into the dirt.

"Well, what I can tell you, is that you are very different from Kasian and I. That's for sure," she said, her head tilting to meet my eyes again, meeting my very confused expression. She saw the look and sighed, staring at me as if I should already have internalized the entire history of the Syron. I hadn't. I would most likely never know the entire history like she did.

"Kasian and I are Mind Syron, Syron of the Soul, whatever you want to call it. I am really good at manipulation of the mind, compelling people to do things, telepathy that kind of thing. With my Song I can even manipulate objects. Kasian is the real Telekinetic though. I can only manipulate my arrows, guide them to their target. Kasian can move anything, he sucks at the telepathy part though, that's why our connection is mostly from my mind to his," she explained, a nostalgic look on her face as she thought about when she and Kasian had their powers. I had to keep reminding myself that she was over three hundred years old, and that she had three lifetimes of memories involving her full power.

"You, however, are something completely different. You have visions and can melt people with physical magic," she started. I flinched a bit at her reference to my dream, the pain still fresh in my mind. "Its almost like you have this power of destruction, but the ability to avoid disaster," she said.

"So, Della is a chaos fairy, eh?!" Kasian said. I tilted my head over my shoulder to see the two boys approaching where Mamarie and I were in the field.

They had gone back to the ship to see if they could figure out what was happening in the galaxy after Prytha was burnt to the ground. By the looks on their faces, they had promising news.

"Ha ha ha, very funny," I muttered sarcastically, sending the boy a small glare.

"I actually remember a bit of that, it was gold, and shimmery. It left residue on the ground," Olen added as the two men joined our small circle.

"You remembered that and didn't say anything about it?" I questioned aloud. Wondering why he would keep quiet about something like that. I would have definitely said something immediately if he had yellow waves of wispy shimmer coming from his finger tips.

"Well, Princess, there are a few things I've seen in the galaxy that are weirder than a Prythian with glowing eyes," he said pointedly, wearing a feigned annoyed expression before a small smirk took over his features.

"Her eyes were glowing?" Mamarie asked, I turned to look at her as she paced a few steps, looking more confused than anything.

"Yeah, can't you all do that?" Olen asked, a bit hesitant to ask why that piece of information seemed important.

Kasian's eyes were wide when he let out a mocking laugh. "Well, yeah. But that only happens at peak power, usually linked with a powerful emotion. And is basically only possible with a Song," Kasian explained, his eyebrows furrowed together. His expression reminded me of our first meeting, his expression void of any charming charisma. Instead, stoic and expressionless, deep in concentration.

"But I didn't have a Song, or really any emotion, if anything I was scared out of my mind," I said. "That could have triggered my magic, but I don't think it was anything like what you are saying." I remember the way it felt, I felt powerful. But I haven't felt the same shiver of magic since. The four of us fell into a confused silence. I could see gears turning behind Mamarie and Kasian's eyes, trying to put pieces together that we didn't have.

"To add to the confusion, we got a message on the ship, it might be something useful?" Olen said, his tone lilting at the end to make his sentence end in a question.

I looked up seeing him already looking me over, trying to decipher how I was feeling about the situation unfolding. If I was being honest, I had no idea. I still was heartsick over my mother, I wasn't getting anywhere with my Syron magic training, and Darious was still out there, getting away with murder.

"Who was it from?" Mamarie asked.

Olen and Kasian glanced at each other, a smile growing on Kasian's face while a familiar smirk settled on Olen's. "Well, we know what Aisha was looking for now," Kasian said. He trailed his sentence, leaving a breath of air making my toes curl in anticipation.

"Oh, shut up and tell me, I hate this suspense thing," Mamarie interrupted.

"Oh, should I shut up or should I tell you?" Kasian asked, bickering with his partner. Mamarie sent him a look that should have sent him six feet under. She even took a step forward as if she was about to put him there herself. Thankfully or not, Olen interrupted their small dispute.

"Aisha found Faye, the Syron that beat the Temptress," he said, a look of wonder and pride pouring off of him.

"Faye, as in killed Emila, Darious's mother, Faye?" I asked, completely taken aback by what he was saying. They had really gotten a message from Aisha, saying she was with Faye? *The* Faye.

I had thought her long gone. But I guess my mother was right, she still was here.

* * *

I stood in the cockpit with Olen, Aisha's message playing in front of me for the third time. "I found her. I found Faye. We'll be coming to you soon, as soon as we can get off the planet, we'll be heading your way. It might take a week or two since getting her on a transport might get difficult as we go through major star systems," Aisha's voice said, echoing through the speaker system.

I put my head in my hands, rubbing my temples a bit. We couldn't see Faye in the video, but Aisha's voice was low and the mic had picked up distant gun shots and explosions. Wherever they were, it wasn't safe.

"Della?" Olen's voice rung through the room and I tilted my head in my hands to the entrance of the cockpit. He stood leaning against the doorframe, arms crossed, like always. His hair fell in front of his eyes a bit as he looked down at me.

He raised an eyebrow at me and moved forward, dropping himself in the seat next to me. He proceeded to kick his feet up onto the dash, his hands moving to the back of his head.

"What's goin' on?" he asked, his tongue flicking out to wet his bottom lip, distracting me from his question. I felt my cheeks heat up a bit and I turned my head back into my hands. Groaning as I sat back in my chair, bringing my knees up and hugging them to my chest.

"Aisha finding Faye means I have to try five times harder now. I have to do everything I can to help her kick Darious', and all of his little silent soldiers' asses. Enough to break their reign," I answered, admitting to the thoughts I've been having all day. Olen looked at me a bit quizzically and I sighed, I would have to explain everything to him. Everything.

"Darious and I are sunmates, he called me his sunmate. We were born from twin suns, Olen. You've heard the stories about twin suns, twin Syron, we are meant to be on the same side. But we're not, meaning I have to be the one to kill Darious. No one else would even come close to the power he has," I said with a sigh. I tilted my head back against the chair and closed my eyes, squeezing them shut tight for a second.

"Only problem is, he's got at least 300 years on me," I muttered with a sad huff of a laugh.

I felt his hand reach over and wrap around my own, tangling our fingers together. I opened my eyes, tilting my head to look over at him.

"Maybe, maybe he's got the years, the experience. But you have something he doesn't," Olen said, his thumb brushing across the back of my hand.

"You've got us, you've got a family. A family who will be there to help you, no matter what. We'll figure this out, help you find control of your powers, hell, I'd fly to the other side of the universe to get you your Song if I knew where it was," he said with a soft smile. I grinned back up at him, his words melting my heart a bit. But that's when it hit me.

"That's it!" I said suddenly. I got up from my seat quickly, my hand still in Olen's as I rushed out of the ship, dragging him along with me. "My Song, Olen, we need to find my Song," I said, excitement in my eyes, buzzing with new found hope.

I was going to take down Darious.

* * *

For the third time that day I was standing in the training field with Mamarie. The sun was starting to set and we were still trying to get my non-existent powers to work, trying to find a tether, to bring them back.

"Darion pulls his magic from dark thoughts, dark memories. So maybe we shouldn't be trying to pull memories from your family," Mamarie thought out loud.

Olen and Kasian had went off to the ship again, sending a message back to Aisha and Faye to see if they could get a location on the two, and made excuses about fixing something. Probably so they wouldn't have to wait around, bored, like I was.

Mamarie had been trying to get me to pull memories with strong emotions for the past hour, trying to get some kind of magical reaction. But whenever I thought about them, I just felt sad, and it was like a dark cloud hung over any happy memory I had from my childhood. The only magic I was able to form with that were sad, dark sparkles from my fingers, kind of like a hickory colour. Nothing like the gold sparkles I had seen before.

"Oh really?" I said sarcastically. I glanced up from my place in the grass, I was lying down watching the sky change from blue to a pinkish orange colour.

"Well, do you have any really happy memories then?" she asked.

I hesitated for a second. I had grown up with my mother, father and sister always around me, but now their absence only made my heart ache. I knew in time I would be able to use them as good memories, but the wound in my heart was still fresh. Being reopened and cut even deeper from the recent death of my mother. Whenever I thought of them, I only thought of how they were no longer here. I could no longer see them, smile or laugh with them. That void would take a while to heal, a century even.

The only other people to have ever been around me were Gallio, and Erick. One now dead and the other? ... I had no idea what happened to the Marques after the Darion infiltrated my planet.

"No," I finally said. I felt my shoulders slump a bit in defeat, Darious had ruined everything, every part of my life. He had taken away my happiness. If it hadn't been for the friends now around me, I think I would have lost myself a long time ago. I closed my eyes softly, thinking of the people around me as I slipped into a small trance.

Memories flew passed my eyelids, Kasian being a sarcastic idiot with a heart of gold. Mamarie an absolute badass but at the same time a friend worth fighting for. And Olen, more of the silent type, but definitely the most loyal and caring person I had ever met. Moments from the few days that I ignored, started to rush through my head.

I pulled the comforter of the bed I stayed in closer around my body, trying to keep my tears at bay. My head pounding from the amount of time I had spent crying and probably dehydration.

I didn't know what time it was, only that I had been in this position for more than a few hours already. My entire body was numb, and I could feel my heartbeat in my fingers and toes. I kept hearing footsteps pause outside my door before they would eventually go away.

Then they would come back.

This time though, they didn't stop and walk away, this time they stopped and a small knock echoed from my door. I didn't move, just kept my eyes glued to the plain grey wall in front of me.

"Della?" Mamarie's voice was quiet, almost a whisper as the door creaked open. I stayed where I was, a small breath leaving my lips. I knew one of them would show up eventually, but I had hoped for at least a day alone.

I heard her feet tap against the floor before the bed dipped at my back.

A small sigh left her lips and I felt her turn a bit, I could feel her eyes on the side of my face for a second before she looked away again. This time instead her hand landed gently on my shoulder, rubbing it softly. "We're always going to be here for you. I know you don't want to talk about it right now, but when you do, we are all ears," she said softly. Her words brought tears to my eyes again, this time for a completely different reason.

"We all want you to know were not giving up on you, no matter how much you are going to think it's annoying. You can't get rid of us that easy. We'll with you until the last star in the universe finally goes out," she said softly. She patted my arm one more time before getting up.

"I left water next to you, drink it," she said. I could hear the teasing smile in her tone. And I felt a small one pulls up on my own lips. Her words helped stitch up the deep cuts in my heart. I knew I would eventually be okay.

My vision got a little blurry before I was pulled into another memory.

I was sitting on the beach of the island, tossing stones at the water, watching as they plunged into the small waves, sinking beneath the dark surface, leaving ripples of their own. I had my knees pulled up to my chest and my chin resting on them. I hadn't let any tears spill today, not yet at least.

"Aladella!" I heard someone shout from behind me. I let out a soft, slightly annoyed sigh, closing my eyes as I heard Kasian's voice shout my name again. "There you are, jeez, could have answered the first time. I know you heard me," he said as he stepped down the path and onto the pebbled beach where I was sitting.

I didn't say anything as he came and sat next to me. I glanced over at him, watching how me copied my position and brought his knees up to his chest. His ankles crossed and arms lazily wrapped around his knees. I ignored him and just tossed another stone into the water, this time it only skipping once before sinking.

"Well, you know, as incredibly fun as this is," he started, stressing his sarcasm as he said incredibly I felt my lips want to pull up in a small smile as he said that, but I pushed the feeling away, continuing to ignore him.

"I made food," he finished, looking at the side of my face, almost expecting me to get up right away and follow him. If I was being honest, I had lost my appetite completely. I didn't want to do anything.

"Oh, come on. I know you're hungry," he continued, his voice a bit softer as he nudged me with his shoulder. I glanced over at him for a second. A small smile on his face, not the usual cheeky grin, this one friendly and supportive.

"You know that's how I found you," he suddenly added. I looked at him with a raised eyebrow, completely confused as to what he was talking about.

"What do you mean?" I finally asked, my voice soft as I turned back to look at the water.

"Your stomach was growling. So loud actually, that I thought there was a predator on the island. I had to come save you so it wouldn't eat you," he teased.

A small smile managed to make its way on to my face this time.

"There she is!" Kasian said, nudging me with his shoulder a bit. "I'm not forcing you to come back and hangout with an awesome group of people, I'm just saying, could be fun. Plus, there's good food."

I stuck my face in my arms that were crossed around my knees, hiding the small smile he had brought to my face. I heard him get up a second later and his footsteps retreat back to the homestead. I looked back up at the water, watching how it rippled gently.

With a small huff I got off my ass and started making my way back the way Kasian had left.

My vision faded again and for a third time I was pulled into another memory.

I was about to run out onto another street when an arm reached out grabbing me and pulling me into a corner, pressing my back against a wall and my chest against theirs, my body stuck between the person and the wall.

"Shhh," the man in front of me said when he noticed my mouth open to speak. I watched from around his shoulder as a few Darion soldiers rounded the corner I had been seconds from turning down. I would have run straight into them if it weren't for the masked man.

He wore a dark onyx helmet on his head, hiding his features, a bright-red stripe on the side of the helmet. The colour red matched the burgundy leather jacket he wore. Though instead of a left sleeve matching his right, his arm was covered by silver armour, a metal arm. I would have guessed it was his actual arm if I hadn't seen the dirty white of a shirt underneath.

I was about to speak again but he spun closer to me as the two soldiers decided to turn down the alley, we were in. The metal-armed man in front of me pushed closer and dipped his head down so his helmet was against my forehead. I held in the soft gasp that wanted to leave my lips.

The cool metal of the chest plate he wore across his chest could be felt through the thick fabric of the flight suit I still wore, causing a shiver to crawl up my spine. My eyes shifted upwards to the dark visor of his helmet, though I couldn't see his eyes I could tell he was staring deep into my own.

The close encounter between the two of us was over before I could even tell it happened.

He pulled his head from mine, keeping his body against mine as he looked around, Darion soldiers gone. Once I realized they had disappeared, I pushed the man off me, hearing him utter a small 'oof' from under the helmet as his head turned to look back at me.

"You didn't have to crush me against the wall." I muttered, sending him a small glare.

I could feel the smirk from underneath his helmet, an arrogant energy radiating off of him. "And here I thought you wanted to be close to me, sweetheart," he muttered, not letting me catch the emotion in his voice. I rolled my eyes at him before stepping around his body ready to head off in my own direction.

"I wouldn't go that way, Princess."

My vision faded quick into another memory.

I broke eye contact with Olen when we both heard a loud thump coming from the side of the ship. "Stars," Olen muttered, his voice for once not muffled by the helmet. I glance over at Aisha who was staring at the side of the ship were the noise came from, slight confusion and worry across her features.

"C'mon, Princess, 'gonna find out who it is sooner or later," Olen said, making me return my gaze to the blue-eyed man.

There was a swirl of colour as I was thrown into a new memory.

"It was just a dream, Princess."

I soon recognized it as Olen's soothing voice and I tilted my head up so I could meet his eyes. My sobs had calmed down and tried my best to get my breathing under control, still gasping for breath.

"My mother, m-my mother ... Olen, they killed her," I managed to get out still trying to get my outburst under control. His eyes were locked on mine, the dark blue of his eyes seemed to lull me back into a sense of calm and I found myself drowning in their depths. I felt his thumb brush against my cheek, brushing away my tears, the cold skin of his fingers soothing the heat of my cheeks.

"Its okay, it was just a dream," he whispered softly.

Soon they were all muddling together ....

"And yours, Princess?" he asked making my gaze turn back to the side of his shiny helmet.

"Aladella," I said, fiddling with the cloth of the jumpsuit as I looked out the window.

Another quick shift ...

"Thank you," I said. It didn't take long after that to fall asleep but I faintly felt lips press against the back of my neck while Olen whispered out a soft, "You're welcome, Princess."

'Hey, Princess,' kept echoing through my memories as Olen seemed to take over, my heart beating wildly against my ribcage. Memories of the four of us together, Olen, Mamarie, Kasian and I. Together, as a family.

I slowly opened my eyes, looking up at the sky when I heard Mamarie gasp from next to me. She was staring down at me, her blue eyes wide as they raked over my body.

I sat up looking down at my hands, a bit surprised when it wasn't just my hands covered in the bright sparkly gold magic, but my entire body. It was as if I was on fire with the strange gold glitter.

"Oh, my stars," I breathed out, excitement coming off of me in waves.

"Damn princess," I heard from behind me. I quickly turned around standing up. Standing a few feet away were Olen and Kasian, a proud smirk on Olen's face as he stood with his arms across his chest. Kasian next to him looked awestruck.

"No fucking way," Kasian mumbled, looking over the gold magic making my body appear on fire.

"Ahhh! yes!" I yelled, my heart beating fast as I looked at my friends around me, completely ecstatic about the new achievement. This was way more than what we were expecting. This was a good sign. The universe was telling me I could do it.

I met Olen's eyes and he smiled at me; the grin unable to fall from his face. I could tell my excitement made his heart flutter, because I could feel it happen to my own.

"Okay, Della!" Mamarie said laughing along with me, a big grin on her face. "Try to control it, centre it to your hands. Imagine all that power, all the heat, just in your hands, let it flow through you, don't force it."

As she instructed, I closed my eyes and let her words guide me. I felt the warm thrum of magic tingle across my arms and legs in the direction of my hands. It left a warm trail as it all gathered in my hands. And when I opened my eyes again, I held two gold flames in my hands, the glitter of them rising up into the sky before disappearing. I watched them for a second before closing my hands, the light disappearing completely.

I looked back up at my friends, doing a little happy dance before running into Olen and Kasian. I pulled Mamarie with me, wrapping my arms around their waists, my female friend squeezing in between the two, pulling ourselves into a small group hug.

No matter what would come at us, no matter what we would go through, I just knew we would make it out together. I looked up from my head on Kasian's shoulder in a smile, meeting Olen's eyes. He was already looking down at me, an emotion in his eyes that I couldn't quite decipher, but whatever it was it made me feel warm and my heart flutter a little faster.

CHAPTER SEVENTEEN

I felt a shake on my shoulder, stirring me from my sleep. The gesture pulled me from the warmth of my dreams and forced a small groan from my lips. I rubbed my eyes, turning over a bit before I opened them.

Olen was looking down at me with a small smile on his face. His hair was still a mess on top of his head letting me know he had just woken up; however, he was already changed and any trace of sleep had been washed away from his features.

"Rise and shine, Princess, got a full day of new powers to train," he said with a small smirk on his face. I groaned and rolled back over in my bed, pulling the covers over my head.

"Ten more minutes," I mumbled softly making the pilot chuckle.

"If I come back in ten minutes and you aren't up and ready, I'm tossing you in the lake."

I groaned a bit more, knowing he wasn't bluffing. I stretched out my body, still a bit fuzzy and stiff from sleep. I stretched my legs and arms out in a starfish, one foot poking out from under the blankets. A cold shiver rolled over my foot—exposed as it was, outside of my cocoon of warmth.

Olen only chuckled a bit before I heard the door close as he left.

He had stayed again last night. The group had lingered out by the fire pretty late, celebrating our small victory. It made me smile remembering the soft shimmer of magic that fell from my fingers. When we all headed in, Olen had walked me to my room, he had hesitated walking in, not sure if I needed him there with me.

To be honest I don't know if I *needed* him there, but I did know, I definitely *wanted* him there. I had just nodded my head and that was all he needed as conformation. He had returned to his own room to change from his smoke-scented clothes, saying he didn't want to smell like a cig hole on Tarkan. I only laughed at his comment and showered as well, knowing I would regret waking up with musty sheets.

I had crawled into bed, half asleep, with the lights already off when he had opened the door coming in. I had muttered a soft hello to which he just chuckled and crawled in behind me, his arm wrapping around my waist and pulling me against his chest. I fell asleep seconds later, mumbling a soft goodnight.

I pulled myself out of bed, the thought of his arms wrapped around me making me stay in bed a few seconds longer, savouring the warmth. I couldn't help but silently curse the pilot when I rolled from my covers and felt the freezing cold floor under my bare feet.

It didn't take me long to pull on my combat pants and a one shouldered black top. I tied up my hair in one long braid down the centre of my head, braiding the sides of my head in smaller ones. It took a little longer than I though but I needed it out of my face and I had been graced with thick hair.

When I stepped out of the homestead, I started cursing Olen out again.

It was dawn; the sun was just starting to rise. I would have run to find him and give him a piece of my mind, if I didn't find the slightly cold air and wet smell of morning calm and refreshing.

Olen was sitting by the sand pits with Mamarie by his side, the dark-haired girl wrapping her hands, wearing a blue long sleeve and grey combat pants.

Kasian was walking towards me from the other direction, coming from the beach. His hair was wet and he carried his shirt in his hand. He had gone swimming before the sun had even come up. I didn't know if he was just strange, or insane.

"There is something seriously wrong with you, seriously wrong," I told him as I fell into step next to him. He only laughed at my comment, shaking out his hair over me letting the cold drops fall on my skin. A slightly annoyed groan fell from my lips as I ran a few steps ahead, getting to the other two a few seconds before him.

I plopped down on the wooden bench Olen and Mamarie were sitting on, putting myself between the two, closer to Olen since Mamarie had a bag resting next to her.

"Someone please explain to me why Kasian thinks himself sane when he jumps into an ice lake at dawn, for fun," I grumbled, feeling Olen's arm wrap behind my back, resting on the back of the bench. I found myself leaning into him a little as he laughed at my comment.

"Because he's definitely not sane," Olen answered for me.

Kasian moved to stand in front of the three of us, putting his hand over his heart as if we had actually hurt him. He had pulled his shirt back over his head, the neckline damp from the water still falling from his hair.

"And I thought we were Brothers!" Kasian exclaimed, sending Olen a glare.

I just rolled my eyes at the two and turned to Mamarie. "What are we trying today boss?" I asked her, grabbing the wrap as she finished and started on my own hands.

"Well, we need to refine the boundaries of your magic. I have no way of going through Syron archives to figure out what you are, so we're going to have to do this the old-fashioned way. Try everything," she said, turning on the bench so she could go through the bag between us.

"We know that you aren't a Mind Syron, so that takes that off the table. But your fire could be anything, Element Syron, Chaos Syron. However, your colour is gold, yellow, I don't remember that being brought up anywhere. The visions too, that's a whole other complex section I didn't even know existed," she explained.

"We'll figure it out," I said as I finished wrapping my hands, passing the tape to Olen.

"If Della turns up being a Chaos Syron I called it," Kasian said, referencing yesterday when he called me a chaos fairy.

"What do you mean by sections?" I asked Mamarie, ignoring Kasian's comment. I had never heard of there being specific types of Syron before.

"I thought it was just 'the Syron' not different breeds," Olen added, Mamarie only huffed at the comment with a small smile.

"Well, there are only really two kinds, physical and emotional, elemental or mental. Kasian and I are emotional, mental Syron. We deal with people, what they think, what they feel, only some of us have the mental strength for telepathy, like Kasian," she explained, sending a teasing smile the man standing next to her.

He looked like he was about to boast about himself when Olen interrupted before he could. "Hurry, continue, we don't have time for Kasian to talk about himself for the next ten minutes." Kasian just glared at the other man.

"I was just going to say that it seemed one of us was more important than the other. Special even," Kasian said right back to the man sitting next to me.

"Oh, you're *special* all right," Olen said, making Kasian's face contort into one of disbelief. Mamarie and I only shook our heads at their banter before she continued to explain.

"The others are elemental Syron, their power is physical. Just like how you create fire from your fingertips. That's something an elemental Syron would be able to do, only their magic would be the actual element, fire, water, earth, air. Not gold magic like what you have," she explained, I nodded my head along with her before thinking about Aisha, her magic was different, not like either of those.

"What about Aisha?" I asked, voicing my train of thought to the group.

"Aisha is a spirit guide now, she was an elemental Syron in her prime, but after death her powers were enhanced. The only thing is she doesn't have the same capacity she used to." Mamarie's words confused me a bit, not knowing what she meant by capacity, what I had seen from Aisha had shown the amount of power she had. And she seemed very powerful.

"Think of it like this. While alive, your heart is pumping, constantly running through your body, magic running through your blood. The way our magic works is like a giant fuel tank, but our hearts are constantly circulating that magic, refilling the tank. Aisha has a fuel tank that isn't constantly refilling. She has a limited amount of magic before she passes on, this time for good," Mamarie explained, having seen the confused look on my face.

"What if its different for Della because she has a sunmate, Darious. Maybe she doesn't just have her own powers but is also influenced by Darious's," Olen said, speaking up. I raised my eyebrows, a bit surprised by his suggestion.

"That would make sense. It would also explain why my eyes were glowing when I used my magic when we were on the Darion ship," I added, pieces clicking together the more I thought about it.

"Milly, you said my eyes would only glow like that with heavy emotion, more than that, I had to have my Song. Well, my Song wasn't there, but Darious's was," I explained, my eyes growing a little wider. I knew Darious and I had this strange connection from being sunmates, Syron created from sister suns, but I didn't think that would affect me as much as it did.

"That would make sense, the whole 'stronger together' thing would mean double the power because you would be pulling from each other's magic. Not only more powerful because you are fighting together, but you are literally more powerful, feeding off each other's Songs," Mamarie explained, her face contorting into one of complete surprise as she pulled things together.

"But what happens when they are on opposing sides, like Della and Darious are?" Kasian wondered, asking the question everyone was thinking but didn't want to say out loud.

"I don't know," Mamarie answered. A slight tension formed across the group as nervousness bubbled in all of us. I knew the strength I would have with Darious on my side, but he was what we were trying to escape. What we were fighting against.

"We'll figure that out another time, I think you all woke me up to train, am I right?" I said, easing the tension a bit.

I gave the group a small smile before turning to Kasian, "You think you can manage me now that I've got melty hands?" I asked, wiggling my fingers at him a bit. He only huffed out a laugh, kicking his shoes off next to the sand pit.

"You're not the only one with magic Della," he answered.

Mamarie let out a small snort from where she sat on the bench making Kasian glare at her a bit. "Sorry Kacey, but you don't have a chance," she teased. I smiled, raising an eyebrow as I looked at Kasian.

"C'mon Kacey," I said, taunting him a bit as I kicked off my shoes and took a few steps into the sand. He huffed before joining me in the sand pit, Olen and Mamarie smirking at him.

"No powers for the warm up," Kasian said, shaking his arms out as he lowered his centre of gravity, getting into a fighting stance. I nodded my head, knowing I had to beat him without my magic. Even if it was only to hold my victory over his head.

I tightened my fists and watched as he did the same.

The one thing about Kasian was that he never made the first move, he would dance around the circle for hours waiting for you to make the first move. He said it was because it gave him an advantage.

So, without waiting another second, I took offence. I jumped towards him with a step, swinging my fist, aiming for his throat. He brough his arm up, blocking and pushing my hand to the side, while he did that my other fist came up, this time going for his stomach, taking steps forward the entire time. I backed him up to one corner of the sandpit, keeping him in a defensive position.

Knowing I couldn't give him the upper hand, I faked a left swing and ducked under his left arm, jabbing him in the side with my right hand. He let out a huff as I made my way behind him, backing up a bit so we could restart the sequence.

"Dead if I had a knife, Kacey," I taunted, tilting my head a bit with a grin as I brought my fists up again. "Yea? Well, you don't have one, Della," he said, taking a step forward and waiting for me to make the first move.

Again, I met him in the middle, punching my arm out. He grabbed it this time, pulling it up, the movement bringing me closer to him. I grabbed his wrist while he pulled me and twisted my body so my arm wasn't in an awkward angle. With his arm in my grasp, I pulled him forewords, grabbing his forearm quickly and dropping my body weight, kicking the back of his knee and making him drop to the ground. He dropped and rolled with me, only spinning us so I landed on my back with his forearm across my throat.

"Dead," he said with a cheeky grin. I grumbled rolling my eyes a bit and let him help me back up to my feet.

"I almost had you though," I said, "if you weren't so bloody huge." I mumbled under my breath.

He feigned a hurt look, his hand clutching his shirt right over his heart. "Are you calling me fat?" he exclaimed, pulling his face into an astounded expression. I only pushed his shoulder a bit and stood up again, rolling my shoulders back.

I glanced at the bench seeing Olen and Mamarie chatting with each other, he must have felt my gaze shift to him because he looked up, a crooked smile on his face. I felt my cheeks heat up a bit at being caught. I shook it off and stepped around the circle a bit before looking up at Kasian.

"Can I use my magic now?" I asked, on cue lighting my hands, the gold flames licking at my fingertips.

"Only if you promise it won't actually burn me," he said, eyeing my hands wearily.

"Of course," I said with a giddy smile.

We had ended up training for most of the morning, only taking a small break to eat in the middle of the day before spending a few hours on our skills. Mamarie's archery skills were something I was never going to mess with, I understood why she kept that silver bow on her all the time, she was a perfect shot.

Whereas Mamarie's skill was elegant, and sophisticated, Kasian's was brutal. He carried around a massive axe on his back, not necessarily for throwing, but he had gotten cocky and tossed the thing at Mamarie's target. Almost cutting the tree completely in half.

Olen however, was more resourceful, he had an understanding of every single weapon Mamarie brought from the shed she had been to earlier. It was kind of scary how he knew how to use each one. I had grown up fighting hand to hand mostly, and I was good on Prytha. However, against the group in front of me, I still had a lot to learn.

Looking at the options Mamarie had brought out, I immediately gravitated towards a long blade. I was very much a beginner, but I was picking it up pretty easy.

The sun was a few hours from going down and the group was pretty gross after rolling through the sandpit fighting throughout the day. I ran to catch up to Mamarie, helping her put the weapons back in her makeshift armoury.

"Swim after?" I asked her as I put my pile down on the table in the shed. She let out a sigh before a big smile took over her face.

"I think I forget we live on an island," she said with a small laugh, "that is exactly what I need right now."

I grinned back at her, helping to put everything back in their respectful places before heading back out towards the field. We had left the boys lying out in the grass, Kasian complaining about how he had a burn mark across his side. Pouting about how it hurt, while Olen only laughed at him.

"Time for a swim?" Mamarie asked the two sprawled out on the ground. I laughed a bit at them, a genuine smile on my face. Where Kasian was on his stomach with his head in his arms, Olen was stretched out on his back, arm crossed over his eyes to block out the lowering sun.

Kasian's head immediately lifted at her words, nodding his head like a puppy as he bounced up quick. He took a large step to Mamarie and grabbed her hand in his, walking off towards the beach, swinging their hands between each other.

I glanced back down at Olen as they started running towards the path to the water laughing. "You coming?" I asked, kicking his foot with my own. My arms were crossed against my chest as I stood, leaning on one hip a bit. A smile spread across his features as he heard me waiting for him. He didn't move from his spot, only lifted up the arm over his eyes—just enough for me to get a peek at his deep blue eyes.

"Help me up," he mumbled, flexing his fingers in a grabbing motion with the arm not covering his face. I rolled my eyes at him as he acted like a child before wrapping my smaller hand around his large one.

Before I could even move to pull him up, he tugged on my arm and sent me toppling onto him.

I landed with my hand still in his on his chest, while the other hit the ground just next to his chest. I let out a small groan from the impact against his body.

"Come on, Princess, you were supposed to help me up. What are you doin' down here?" he asked, a cocky smile on his lips as he moved his arm that was covering his eyes to look at me.

"That was rude," I said with a small laugh. I shifted a bit, my loose hairs falling in front of my face as I moved a leg over his so I could get up.

I felt his free hand brush the hair from in front of my face, making me freeze against him and look up. I shifted my gaze to meet his eyes, but he was watching his own hand as it ran down the side of my face. The arm he had been covering his eyes with now resting behind his head.

My skin sparked as I felt his fingers brush down the side of my neck, moving the loose hair over my shoulder. His hand didn't stop at my shoulder like I thought it was going to. It traced over my shoulder and down the side of my back until it rested on my waist. It felt like there was a trail of fire down my back where his hand had been, making me shiver from the light touch.

His hand wrapped around my hip, holding it and pushing his thumb into my skin a bit. He pushed us closer together a bit and

I felt myself relax on his chest. Only after he had gripped my hip tightly did he move his eyes back to mine, his eyes a deep shade of blue, so dark I couldn't seem to look away.

I felt something spark in my stomach, heating up every part of my body before I felt my eyes shift, burning as they sparked with the familiar gold flame.

"That's a nice colour on you," he mumbled, his hand moving from my waist to brush his thumb under my eye. I looked at him a little confused making him smile, the cockiness replaced with something else.

"Gold," he said, answering my silent question.

"I could say the same about you," I said softly. I gently moved my free hand up and traced under his eye to his temple with the pads of my thumb. His eyes closed for a second at my touch before opening them again, being an even deeper shade of blue.

"Almost Prussian," I said softly. My comment making him grin a bit.

"You noticed how the colour changed," he said, not asking but stating that I knew. I sheepishly smiled at this nodding my head.

"Of course," I said, feeling the fiery gold from my eyes fade back to their hazel brown colour.

He only hummed softly and trailed his fingers down my back again, as his fingers trailed across my spine, I couldn't help the shiver his touch sent through my body. His grin turned up into a smirk, realizing I was reacting to his touch.

"Oh, shut up," I grumbled, rolling my body off of his and standing again. Trying to hide the way my face was flaming.

"I didn't do anything!" he exclaimed, the stupid grin on his face not dropping.

I couldn't help the smile that pulled on my lips and just shook my head at him. My hands moving to my cheeks to hide the pink colour.

"I'm not helping you up either, bucket head, you can do that yourself," I added before spinning on my heel, dropping my hands to my side and heading off in the direction of the beach.

I heard Olen roll over and get up, jogging a few paces until he was walking next to me. His hand brushed across mine softly as we walked, the action making me glance up at him. I don't know if he didn't notice the small contact, or just ignored it. He kept his gaze forward and we continued walking in comfortable silence down to the beach.

Mamarie and Kasian were both already in the water, Mamarie sending a huge wave of a splash at the larger man making him dive though it and grab her waist, lifting her over his head before tossing her further into the lake. Both of them laughing their asses off.

When she surfaced again, she looked over to me and Olen who were just coming up onto the pebbled beach. "Della! Hurry up I need your help drowning Kasian's ass," she yelled, her body stripped down to her underwear much like Kasian, the slight burn I had left on him visible on his side, a bright red mark in the shape of my hand. Oops.

With a giddy grin, I started pulling my combat pants off, my feet still bare from training. Once down to my underwear I glanced over my shoulder at Olen. His eyes were raking down my legs making me smirk. His eyes moved back up my body meeting my own, I only raised an eyebrow at him.

"Take your clothes off, bucket head," I said, teasing him where he would have called me princess. He only rolled his eyes at me before pulling his shirt over his head.

Of course, I let my eyes trail over him like he had done to me, not even two seconds before. I could feel the slight tint of a blush take over my cheeks but I ignored it as he ran his hand through his loose curls.

"I don't know why you have to keep calling me bucket head, Princess," he said with a grin, taking a few steps towards me.

"The same reason you call me princess," I said with a cheeky shrug, my smile still stuck to my face as I took a step back towards the water.

"I call you that because you are a princess, Princess," he answered, taking another step towards me, making me take a small one back.

"And you are a bucket head, aren't you, bucket head?" I teased, he brought his bottom lip between his teeth and tilted his head to the side quickly, a hum coming from between his lips.

Then he reached out, moving so fast I barely registered he had grabbed me. His hands encircled my waist and tossed my body over his shoulder. I let out a surprised squeal and grabbed his hips to keep myself upright.

Before I knew what was happening, he was tossing me into the lake next to Mamarie.

CHAPTER EIGHTEEN

"Little Dove ... " a sing-song voice said, echoing across the dark room around me. Moving like a soft wisp of smoke, a whisper in my ear.

"Look at me, little dove," he said again, coaxing me to open my eyes. His voice made my heart beat skip a bit, fear coursing through my veins, slow and thick. His deep voices rattled through my brain as I was pulled from the warm depths of sleep. I slowly peeled my eyes open, blinking a few times to adjust to the blinding light around me.

As soon as I opened my eyes that fear slipped away. I was still dreaming. It was proof enough when my eyes adjusted and I was in a room I had never seen before. I hadn't woken up in Olen's arms, therefore I was still dreaming.

The room was dark, the walls around me were a deep shade of green, so dark almost black. Each wall decorated with elegant moulding. There was a bed to the left of where I stood, covered in black and green bedding with white pillows. The only bright thing in the room.

Straight ahead of me were two huge doors, probably double my height, the dark wood matching that of the floors. The only light came from the open windows behind me, lighting up the couch and desk to my right, both placed in front of a fire place.

I was standing in the middle of the room alone.

A little curious as to where I was, I turned to open the windows more, wanting to let in more light. The curtains were a black velvet that was soft under my fingers, as I moved them behind the claws at the edge of the windows, my breath caught in my throat at the view.

I was expecting the room to gaze out onto a city, or field, I was half expecting it to be Prytha, I was dreaming after all. But it wasn't.

There was a vast valley of bright yellow and green grass, white flowers dotting out in every direction. As the wind moved, the grass waved and rippled like the ocean, the grass dancing as it moved along the currents. There was a small stream through the middle of the valley, its water clear enough to see the red rock beneath, the orange and rusty rocks matching the warm tones of the valley.

Though, what startled me was the fact that I seemed to be looking out onto the edge of a planet. Just passed the vibrant valley, the planet dropped off to nothing, the darkness of space lingering just beyond. Unlike Prytha, or any other round planet, where the atmosphere mimicked the colour of the planet, this world had no air protection. It was like standing in the middle of space, stars shining brightly in every direction and the outline of a galaxy spread across what would have been a sky line.

I had never seen anything like it.

I moved my hand to the glass of the window, trailing my finger down the freezing glass until I reached the latch, about to open it to the strange world outside.

"I wouldn't do that, little dove," a voice spoke from behind me, I recognized it right away from the pet name he had given me. I turned quickly, almost bumping right into Darious's chest.

He stood so close I could faintly smell a hint of cologne, and the fresh smell of rain. It took me a second to realize what was happening before I took a step back, away from him, my back pressing against the window. My veins grew thick with an undertone of fear and I guarded my emotions as I looked up at him. I watched him wearily, however, he only moved to stand next to me, his arms clasped behind his back.

"Beautiful isn't it," he said, his voice low and slightly rough. I turned a bit and glanced through the window. I was on edge, confused about what exactly was going on. I couldn't be dreaming about Darious. Maybe this was another vision.

"Calm down, your anxiety is muddying my mind," he mumbled from next to me.

I turned, looking straight up at him. Was it that obvious I was confused and on the verge of a panic attack from this nightmare? My surprised look changed quickly to a glare when I looked at him longer. The emotions rushing through me as I remembered how he murdered my mother and destroyed my sister and father on Diarna. I took another step back, further into the room.

"What is this, some sick game?" I spat at him, my hands clenching at my sides. I could feel the crackle of energy forming in my fists, the spark of fire about to light.

My anger faltered slightly when he let out a sigh, turning from the window to look at me. His hands dropping from behind his back and one moving to run through his dark hair, almost as if he was stressed.

"That's not any better," he grumbled, leaning his hips back against the window pane. He stared at me for a second before a small smirk pulled at his lips.

"Hmmm, I can feel the heat from here," he said with a small gesture to my body. For a second, I thought he was talking about the growing energy in my hands, but the way he was looking at me I could tell it was something else.

"What do you want?" I spat out with a glare; my tone harsh. This man didn't deserve my time, he didn't deserve to be alive. He only smirked back at me, a small hum leaving his lips as he pushed himself from where he was leaning against the window.

"As much as I adore chatting with you, love, I need to ask a favour," he said, the pet name dripping from his lips with enough sarcasm for Olen and Kasian combined.

I let out a small huff, unbelievable.

"You think I would, ever, help you?" I growled, the word leaving my lips in a snarl. "I should be gutting you right where you stand," I spat.

He only raised a small eyebrow at me, as if expecting I would agree with him immediately. "Then why don't you, little dove?" he said, opening his arms wide in a confident gesture. Leaving his body exposed, acting as if I couldn't even touch him.

A low growl sound left my throat and in a second my hands were ablaze, I could even feel my eyes light up, a bright golden colour. Darious's expression changed immediately, from cocky it changed to genuine surprise.

He raised his eyebrows at me before a smile spread across his face. "Now this, this is something else," he said, as if genuinely interested in my magic. His reaction only made my anger burn more and I brought my hands together, creating a web of magic between them before sending it at Darious.

I saw a flash of concern glow in his eyes before my magic wrapped itself around his entire body, his clothing smoking a bit when it touched the sparkling gold mist around him. If he was ever intrigued, he hid it quickly, only looking right back at me, his eyes glowing a dark green colour as our gazes connected.

In that moment I felt him dig himself into my brain. Whereas Aisha only prodded at my mind, searching through it carefully. Darious forced himself into it, a searing pain erupting in my head. I let out a screech of pain as my vision blurred and I fell to the ground, my fire fading from my hands as I reached up and grabbed my head.

"Get out!" I managed to scream at him, the pain in my skull burning.

I heard him tut from above me, walking over, kneeling down in front of me. "You are still young Aladella, I have over three hundred years on you. This is not a battle you can win," he said softly, a hand reaching down and brushing the loose hair from my face.

I felt his presence in my mind retreat and I was left visibly shaking on the ground. Feeling violated and vulnerable. My cheeks were dry of tears, but I could feel them welling in my eyes, close to falling.

"Now, help me," he said, asking once again for my help. I moved my gaze from my hands up to him, meeting his eyes once again, his green meeting my gold.

"No," I said, I felt the anger return quickly. My eyes shining before I spread my magic across the ground, the entire room going up in gold flames. Darious let out a painful yell as the flames engulfed his body. I slowly stood up, the gold sparkle of the flames licking across my body, keeping me safe. My gaze followed him as he dropped to the floor, his clothes burning and his skin turning black and glittery where ever my magic brushed against him.

"I am much stronger than you think, Darious. You may have a silent army; you may have worlds falling at your feet, but you are nothing to me, and never will be. You have taken everything from me, and I will take everything from you." I could feel the tears leaking down my cheeks as I screamed at him, watching as a pained expression tore across his face.

"I haven't taken anything from you, little dove," he said, emphasizing on the I. Before I could retort, the world was spinning and I was tossed into a new environment.

I felt the searing ache of Darious in my head, knowing he was the cause of this. He had thrown me into my memories, only I didn't recognize my surroundings at all.

"Darious," a sing-song voice rang out through the trees. I was a bit hesitant before I started following the voice. The forest was nothing like the vibrant green of Prytha, it was very much a dark green and grey colour, as if death had been caught in its leaves. I broke through a line of trees to a small clearing, ahead of me I could see two figures.

I recognized one immediately as Darious, only he was much younger, maybe fifteen. Next to him was a beautiful young girl, her platinum blonde hair pulled up and out of her face in a half up bun. The hairstyle messy, but she didn't seem to care. Darious had a strange expression on his face, a genuine smile. Something I thought impossible for the man. He tucked a piece of hair behind the blonde girl's ear, his hand moving down her arm to hold her hand.

I was too far to hear what they were saying, but the girl's excited giggles were everything I needed to understand. They were in love.

Darious had leaned forwards to press a loving kiss to the girl's cheek, making her blush a bright pink and turn her face to hide it. Moving to hide her embarrassment, flustered by his display of affection.

Suddenly a new figure barged into the clearing. A platinum blonde woman, her hair long and flowing down her back, a deep-purple gown adorned on her body and a harsh silver crown across her forehead.

Fear spread across Darious's features.

"Mother," he said, immediately standing up and offering his mother a small bow. He was genuinely terrified of the woman. His mother was Emila, the Syron who turned and started the war. Created the Darion.

"What do you think you are doing?!" She spoke harshly to the boy, the girl staying on the ground and keeping her head down, almost as if trying to stay as small as possible to hide from the woman in front of her.

"If you think it is acceptable to be frolicking around with a useless girl like this one ... Darious I have told you the consequences for socializing with this pathetic thing," Emila spat out. She glared down at the young girl, as if imagining putting her six feet under right then and there.

Darious's young expression changed to one of pure terror. "No, mother, please," he said suddenly, pleading her to not do something. I was guessing it was the punishment she had mentioned about being around the young girl next to him.

I don't know what I was expecting to happen, but what occurred next was far from what I could have imagined.

Darious suddenly fell to the ground screaming, holding his head in pain, much like I had been seconds ago when he had infiltrated my mind. I could only guess that's what was happening to him now. Emila was digging into his mind, her son's mind. I cringed back a bit at the sound of the boy's screams, wishing to do something to help, but knowing this was a memory from his past.

Slowly the screaming died down, and Darious's small body was left panting on the ground. Completely defeated, he was exhausted and I could only watch as his eyes closed slowly. Not even seconds later they snapped open again, this time glowing a vibrant purple, Emila's eyes glowing the same eerie shade. The boy slowly got up from the ground, turning towards the young girl slowly.

Without hesitation Darious's body lunged for the girl, his hands wrapped around the blonde's neck, gripping her tightly as he positioned himself on top of her. A sickening grin spread across Emila's face as she watched her son cut off the young girl's airways. Startling enough, the same smile was mirrored on Darious's features.

I watched as Darious gripped the girl's neck and shook, her body making choking sounds as she scratched at his hands and forearms, trying to get his hands off of her. Then, girl's struggling stopped, the life drained from her grey eyes and she fell limp under his body.

His hands stayed around her neck, shaking it for a few more seconds after she was obviously dead, the action causing me to look away from the scene. A tear fell from my eye and trailed down my cheek, mixing with the others that had fallen while I had to watch the scene play out in front of me. What brought me back to the trio was Darious's heartbreaking scream that shook the trees around us, animals scurrying away and birds flying up into a frenzy in the sky, circling and almost blocking out the sun completely.

"Distractions, Darious. That is all they are," Emila, Darious's mother said before turning and walking back to where she came from.

Darious held the girl's body close to him, rocking back and forth slowly as he stared down at her bruised neck. Her eyes open wide in eternal fear.

I watched the scene, my heart breaking with theirs. I looked down at the girl, her eyes staring up at the sky. I felt another tear slip out my eye as I looked at Darious, sobs raking his body. When I looked back at the girl, her dead grey eyes were staring right at me.

I shot up screaming, the room around me dark and unfamiliar for a few seconds.

I thrashed a bit in the covers, trying to get them off my body as they suffocated me. Arms quickly wrapped themselves around me and I was pulled against someone's chest. I fought against them, scared from the girl's gaze, I could see her in the dark corners of the room. Blank grey eyes watching me.

My senses slowly started coming back to me and I could hear Olen whispering against the side of my head softly. The door suddenly opened, light flooding into the room. The dead girl disappearing from the dark corner as light entered the room.

Mamarie was immediately by my side, brushing hair from my face and grabbing my face turning it to meet her gaze. Olen's arms were still wrapped around me, one around my waist, and the other around my shoulders, holding my wrists with his hands. Keeping me from hurting him, or myself.

"Della, hey, Della you're okay," Mamarie said to me softly. I focused on her face, feeling the panic slowly seep from my skin, my heart rate slowing down only a fraction as her face became clearer in my vision.

"It was just a dream," she continued gently, running her hand through my hair, pushing it from my face again.

I tried to calm my erratic breathing as I looked up at her, a bit worried. "I don't think it was," I said softly, my voice cracking in the middle, a bit rough from screaming. I felt Olen's arms wrap around me just a bit tighter, the comfort making me relax into his chest a bit more. I wanted to ask why Darious had shown me that exact memory. But a small itch in the back of my brain made me think that maybe I already knew.

CHAPTER NINETEEN

I was sitting on one of the kitchen chairs, a warm mug of tea between my hands, thanks to Olen. He had pushed it into my hands as soon as I had sat down, his only explanation being a small smile.

My vision, or dream, with Darious still rattled around my head. It had been a few hours since I woke up screaming, Olen had taken most of that time trying to calm me down and reassure me that I was safe, I was home, as he said.

I was spooked from my thoughts when I felt something heavy fall over my shoulders. I jumped a bit and whipped my head around.

"Calm down, Princess, just me," Olen said, wrapping the blanket farther around my shoulder. I gave him a soft smile as a thank you before turning back to my half empty cup.

"You want to talk about it?" He asked, pulling one of the other chairs next to me out and leaning into it. I glanced up at him from the edge of my cup as I brought it to my lips again.

He was slouched down in his seat, leaning his head against the back of the chair, arms folded across his chest. His eyes were closed but I could tell he was paying attention to every move I made. His hair was a mess which meant he had been running his hands through it, stressed or nervous, that's the only time he ever did it.

"She's has to talk about it," Mamarie said as she entered the room. I tilted my head to see her walking into the kitchen, her own blanket wrapped around her shoulders. She hopped up on the table next to me, taking the head of the table, a small smile on her face. Kasian moving to lean his hip against the table, across from me, hands rubbing his eyes before crossing them across his chest.

"We should talk about this in the morning, you guys should get your sleep," I said, scratching my hair, pulling at the few hairs that were tugging uncomfortably.

"If you think Ill be able to sleep after the straight possession you went through, nope, that's haunting my dreams for the next few days," Kasian said, muttering the last bit with wide eyes.

I rolled my eyes at his over-dramatic behaviour and glanced at Mamarie, who was looking down at her hands, fiddling with her fingers. Confused, I glanced to Olen, who was still sitting with his head back and eyes closed. The only reason I could tell he was also being weird was the fact that he sighed, running his hand through his hair as he opened his eyes, glancing over at me.

"Wait, what? No way, you guys must be kidding. Possessed? Really?" I said, trying to laugh it off a bit, when the group just looked at me a bit awkwardly, shuffling around. That's when it dawned on me, something had happened before I woke up.

"What happened?" I asked again, sitting up a bit straighter, putting my mug on the table in front of me.

"Your eyes were glowing Della," Mamarie finally answered.

My brows furrowed a bit at that, I had been using magic in my dream, is that was she was talking about? That seemed normal if anything, I did have strong emotions running through me.

"Oh, well that's not too bad, is that not something that's normal? That can happen, right?" I said, brushing it off as I tried to convince myself I was fine.

"It's not just that Della," Kasian said, glancing over at me, an almost pained expression on his face.

"What? What do you mean?" I said, a little annoyed they were taking so long to tell me what had happened.

"Your eyes were green, Princess, dark green," Olen said, speaking up for the other two Syron in the room. I spun my head to look at him, furrowing my eyebrows a bit. He sighed again running his hand through his hair, sitting up a bit straighter in his chair. He met my gaze as he leaned forward, resting his forearms against the table.

"You said something too," he mumbled, running his hand through his hair before meeting my eyes again. "You said 'keep calm in Eden, little dove. Hell is coming, and it burns hot. Sleep well, for tomorrow we fight' then you started screaming," Olen said softly.

I froze a bit at his words, my gaze dropping back down to my hands, not even realizing they had started shaking a bit. "It's a message from Darious," I said softly. The room seemed to be sucked into a thick tension, covered in silence.

"He ... He appeared in my dream. I thought it was a vision, like the one I had of my mother. But I'm not so sure anymore," I said, wrapping the blanket farther around my shoulders. I felt frigid suddenly, my body shivering at Darious's words, the words that he forced from my mouth. My heartbeat became erratic as I thought over the dream, over and over again.

"He said he needed my help, but I said no. He dug himself into my mind ... it hurt," I said, trying to keep myself together as I told them what happened.

I felt Olen shift closer, pulling one of my hands between his, squeezing softly.

"Aisha has been through my thoughts before, I could feel her in my mind but that was more like an annoying itch. This was something else, something vile. He made me angry, wanted to see what kind of magic I had. The power I had. So, I set him on fire," I said, then stopped, hesitating when the flash of the memory he put in my head resurfaced.

For a reason I could not explain, I kept that to myself, not sharing it with the group around me.

"He was trying to figure out how strong you were becoming, seeing if you found your Song," Mamarie said, linking ideas and coming up with possible conclusions. "He wanted to scare you, show you what it would mean to go against him." She ran her hand through her loose, dark hair briefly. She hopped from the table and started pacing, something she did when trying to put pieces together in her head. Something I used to do as well.

"He asked for my help, why would he do that?" I asked the group, moving the blanket from my shoulders, warming from the conversation, letting it drop. Olen rubbed his eyes, Mamarie and I'd words hanging in the silence, only interrupted as a soft sigh left his lips.

"He wanted to know if he could beat you, being sunmates, he said those things to help lower your guard. He really only wanted help figuring what you were capable of, probably wanted to know if you had found your Song," Olen said, thinking off the top of his head. He put his chin in his hands, his brows furrowed a bit as he glared down at the table. Wheels turning behind his eyes.

"He might have thought I found it," I realized, following their train of thought.

"When I got angry my eyes started glowing, I showed him the power I had. He looked genuinely surprised for a second, but then he murdered my mind," I said with a soft sigh. He was much stronger than I thought.

"No, that's perfect Della. Darious is an idiot, he believes you found your Song. That's why he attacked your mind, he wanted you to remember you were inferior. But you aren't," Kasian added, a big grin forming on his lips as he stood up.

"Darious believes he beat her, meaning he can beat her again," Mamarie said softly, the pieces finally clicking together. It was like all four of our brains were working in perfect synchronization.

"But he didn't beat me, he beat a weak songless version of me," I said with a small smirk on my face. The group let out a sigh of relief, weight falling from our shoulders. We were one step ahead of him.

Olen let out a soft laugh from next to me. I turned to face him, watching as he stood up, shaking out his hair before looking down at me. "I guess that's our next mission then," he said with a grin. I only smiled back at him; the smile genuine as the feeling of butterflies filled my stomach from the look he gave me. Pride.

"What about the whole creepy possession to deliver a message," Kasian asked, looking across the group. "As much fun as it was figuring this out, I don't want to wake up in the morning to find an infestation of goggled soldiers."

I nodded along with him, thinking over his words. "I don't think Darious literally meant tomorrow. I think he only said that to be dramatic. He wants us to come to him, just like Prytha," I said softly, wringing my hands out a bit, the mention of my home no longer stinging my heart but making it itch uncomfortably.

"In a few days, Aisha and Faye arrive. We'll talk about it more then," Mamarie said, giving the group a small nod with a smile before grabbing Kasian's hand and pulling him back down the corridor to their room.

"Are you going to try and sleep again?" Olen asked, leaning his hip against the table, looking down at me with his arms folded across his chest. I thought over my answer, hesitating for a second. I wondered if Darious would control my dreams again, scared of what I might relive, the pain I would feel again.

"Come on," he said softly, reaching his hand out. My lips tilted up in a half smile and I laced my fingers through his. I let him pull me up to stand next to him, his hand moving from mine to pull the blanket tighter around my shoulders. Wrapping me in a warm cocoon.

"Let's go," he said softly, pressing a kiss to the top of my forehead before spinning me around. His hands staying on my shoulders as he guided me down the hallway. A small laugh bubbling from my lips making him smile.

* * *

"Della! Della they're here!" I looked up from where I was tying my boots back up from my place in the grass, hearing Kasian's voice echo across the field.

I knew right away who he was talking about, Aisha and Faye were here.

It had been two days since Darious broke into my mind in a dream. I had been hesitant to sleep since then, but Olen always seemed to coax me into bed and I would find myself waking the next morning well rested.

Since then, I had been trying to figure out how to find my Song. Mamarie explained to me that a Syron's Song finds them, it's never been the other way around, and it always comes exactly when you needed it. So where was mine?

I hopped up quickly from the grass, pushing my loose hair out of my face as I took off across the field to the beach, where the rest of my small family was waiting.

I skidded to a halt on the pebble beach, Mamarie next to me on one side, Kasian and Olen on the other.

Across the lake we could see a small boat like the one we had taken, speeding across the water.

I froze when I couldn't see Aisha's bright white and blue skin, everyone on the boat wore black.

"That's not, Aisha," I said, my voice barley over a whisper. Before I could even take a step to grab my friends and run back up the beach, black lasers started pelting the beach.

"Get down!" Kasian yelled. I immediately grabbed Mamarie and tossed us both to the ground, her body shielded by my own. I looked up, trying to see through the dust explosions around us. A few feet away was the tree line, not safety but cover. "Go, go the tree line," I told her, glancing back at the approaching boat.

The rain of lasers eased up a bit as they recharged, and in that moment, I pushed off Mamarie, grabbing her arm and pulling her with me to the tree line.

I glanced across the beach seeing Olen and Kasian hidden behind the boat we had taken to get here. Much better cover than what Mamarie and I were hidden behind.

"I don't have anything. I-I don't have a weapon," I stuttered as I looked over at Mamarie, both of us dropped to our stomachs on the grass. I could hear Olen's own gun firing from across the beach, the ricochet of his bullets against the metal of the boat.

"Aladella, you do not need a weapon. You have these," Mamarie said, grabbing my hands with her own. "Now use them," she said, a determined look on her face as she squeezed my hands. My heartbeat slowed down as I registered her words; I had my own built-in protection.

My features hardened as I looked back at the Darion soldiers, their boat only a few hundred metres from shore now. The boat was only big enough to hold around thirty soldiers. Only. But it was better than facing off against one hundred.

I stood up slowly. Feeling my body start to tingle as I pulled the energy from around me, my hands set ablaze with gold flames.

The Darion soldiers sent their rain of explosions towards me. Without thinking really, I sent my magic out in front of me. The gold glitter started sticking together, creating a translucent web. A shield wall. It was practically invisible, though when the sun hit it, you could see a flowing current of sparkly magic.

The blaster fire that hit the wall dissolved immediately. I could feel the hot energy recharging my energy as the wall absorbed the blasts feeding into my power.

The boat got closer and closer to the wall, and in a second it was slamming against it. The ground seemed to shake as a few of the soldiers flew out of the boat. I focused on the energy I could feel leaking off of the Darion's weapons, the whisps of black energy feeding into my own. I imagined myself draining power from their batteries, pulling every drop of power from the weapons. Sure enough, the soldiers across the lake started tossing their guns off the sides of the boat, their weapons being rendered useless. With their guns useless I pulled my magic defence back and in seconds their boat hit the edge of the rock beach.

Immediately, I felt Mamarie take my right side, Olen and Kasian on my left. I felt a tiny smirk pull at my lips as we looked at the small army taking up the shoreline of the island.

The five soldiers that fell from the boat trudged up from the water, their blasters still intact since they didn't go through my magic. The soldiers pulled their silver swords from their sheaths in sync, preparing for battle. I got a little nervous looking at the twenty-nine soldiers in front of me.

"Need some help?" I suddenly heard from my right. I turned immediately, recognizing Aisha's voice.

And there she stood, eyes glowing white, dressed in gold and pearl, floating an inch from the ground, her hair breezing around her as if underwater.

Next to Aisha stood a shorter woman, dark raven hair cut short at her chin and dark eyes, with green facial markings around her eyes and on her cheeks. She was dressed in a green, one-shouldered top, one long black pant while the other leg was cut short, the rest of her leg was covered by a shiny black boot. And in her hand, a long gold sceptre, adorned with a green gem.

It was Faye.

A smile pulled across my lips at the sight of the two, Faye moving to stand next to Mamarie, Aisha floating above us. I turned to look at my friends, laughing a little when I saw Kasian's mouth drop so far it was almost hit the floor. Olen had a determined smile while Mamarie looked excited to fight next to the legendary Faye.

"Come on Della, this is where you say some cheesy-ass line and we run off into battle like badass Syron. Something about Aisha and Faye heard your call and came to help you save the day," Kasian said, almost giddy from next to me.

I smiled and looked back at the approaching soldiers, trying not to laugh at Kasian's comment. "What, like the Call of the Syron?" I asked him. He only grinned back at me looking back at the soldiers.

"So, you want to start a war," I said softly, my hands lighting up a bit as I cursed out Darious and his silent army.

Kasian only whistled lowly next to me. "He really did ask for it didn't he. I hope he hears this call: the Call of the Syron," Kasian said, winking at me before running forwards to the army. A loud yell leaving his lips, a battle cry, sounding a bit too excited for the bloodbath about to occur.

I only rolled my eyes and ran after him, Faye and Mamarie next to me.

Olen and Aisha staying up the bank, acting as snippers.

The flames grew in my hands and I sent them towards the soldiers, some of them turning and running back to the water. I used my magic to melt through their armour, burning their skin or destroying their visors.

Kasian and Mamrie moved to fight back-to-back, their hand-to-hand tactics taking out soldier after soldier. To my right, Faye eliminated soldiers left and right, not even bothering to use her magic, at least from what I could tell. From above Aisha rained down white spheres of energy, blowing soldiers apart. Olen remained up on the bank, shooting down any soldier that got too close to one of us.

Was it wrong to say fighting with them felt natural, or that it felt like it was what I was meant for?

I had always been a bit rebellious, but this was further than that, this was starting a rebellion, a resistance against the dark silence that had covered the galaxy for far to long.

CHAPTER TWENTY

It took awhile to get the blood from my hair. Too long honestly. I didn't feel good about it either. The guilt was settling in the bottom of my stomach. I hadn't had to with that much death before. Olen had to keep reminding me the soldiers had slaughtered innocents like livestock. That helped a bit. I knew it was healthy to feel a little guilty about taking a life, I didn't think it was something I would ever get used too.

I hoped it was something I never got used to.

I didn't realize I had been staring at myself in the bathroom mirror until a knock on the door broke me from my thoughts. "Hey, Della? You almost done? Faye has an idea about how to find your Song. Get dressed and meet us in the kitchen," Mamarie's voice said from the other side of the door.

I took a shaky breath, wiping the tears that had been close to falling, hanging on the edges of my eyes. Ruffling my drying hair, I left the bathroom pulling on the first thing I saw, my amber jumpsuit.

I was only in my socked feet when I shuffled down the hall to the kitchen. Faye was sitting at the table with Mamarie and Kasian while Aisha hovered in the corner. Olen's back was to me where he stood in the doorway. I couldn't help but smile when I noticed his tense stance, arms crossed over his chest and one foot kicked out a bit.

I lifted my hand, brushing it down his arm as I moved next to him in the doorway. He shifted a bit to the side, his head tilting down to look at me. I could tell from the way he was looking at me he had heard me pad down the hallway. He had been listening behind him instead of to the conversation happening at the table.

His hair was wet and brushed back over his head, a small cut just above his eyebrow. The red of his jacket surprised me a bit, seeing as he was dressed the same as the first day, I met him. Only difference was his arm and helmet were still on the ship.

I reached up and brushed my thumb against his cut, wondering how I had let him get hurt. Even if it was a tiny cut.

"I'm fine, Princess," he said softly, his voice just above a whisper. His hand moved up slowly and encircled my wrist, pulling it down from his head. His hand was warm over my skin as he guided my hand to his mouth, pressing a kiss to the palm of my hand. I felt my cheeks turn a soft pink. A grin pulled at the corners of his mouth when he saw my cheeks heat up and he sent me a wink. I scrunched my nose at him, pulling my hand from his.

"So, you had an idea about how to find my Song?" I asked the group as I entered the kitchen, moving to standing at the head of the table, leaning my hip against its edge. Olen moved from his place in the doorway, following after me to join the conversation.

Faye smiled up at me as she crossed her hands together in her lap. "Yes, its rare for a Syron's Song to keep itself hidden, especially when it is so obviously needed. That must mean Darious has some kind of control over it. At least that's one of the only things we could come up with." Faye explained, a huff of a laugh falling from her lips.

"But when Darious appeared in my head, I made him believe I already had it," I said, not sure what she meant by Darious had control over it.

"It is possible, that to hide you from getting your Song he hid it, not physically, but veiled it. He is a Mind Syron, which means he could be able create entire worlds around whoever he wants, changing our physical environments to one from his imagination. Much like what he did in your dream," the Syron explained.

"He could have used that same technique, only instead of presenting a fake reality to you, he hid your Song. Keeping it out of your reach," Faye explained, tapping her fingers together a bit as she looked over the group.

"Is it possible for me to remove the veil?" Mamarie asked. Being a Mind Syron herself she had the same kind of magic as Darious.

"You might have been able to if Darious hadn't taken your Song, unfortunately the only person who can find it now, is Aladella," Aisha answered, all eyes turning to me again.

"What do I have to do?" I asked. She glanced down at her hands, shifting a bit, even Aisha shifted her weight left to right.

"You'd have to go deep into your subconscious. Only there, will your mind be able to decode Darious's magic. Your Song would appear as if it's always been there. You would be reliving your memories without Darious's magic veiling it. Then you can follow your steps up until the last place it was in contact with you. We'd go from there," Aisha explained, stepping forwards a bit.

I glanced over her and Faye's expression, noticing the uneasiness and uncertainty immediately. "If it's that easy, why do you both look nervous?" I asked, shifting my weight to my back leg as I crossed my arms over my chest.

"Aisha would have to dig through your mind," Faye said. The sentence itself made me flinch, thinking back to the pain I was in when Darious dug through my mind.

"That's not all. We'd have to lower your core temperature so you couldn't use your magic, if your temperature is warm enough you could subconsciously burn us to crisps for tampering with your mind," Mamarie added, figuring out where Faye and Aisha were going with this.

I sucked in a small breath, looking around the nervous gazes of the group. "How low?" Olen asked.

I glanced over at Faye, whose brows furrowed a bit in concern. "Basically dead," she said softly.

My breath caught in my throat for a second as I looked at her, startled by the comment.

"Absolutely not," Olen said, speaking up before I could. His jaw was tight and his brows furrowed a bit. His arms crossed tightly in front of him. I wanted nothing more than to agree with him. To have to lower my body temperature to almost dead was a huge risk. But it seemed to be our only option.

"This might be the only way, Olen," I said softly, turning my body a bit to look at him. He didn't meet my eyes, only glared at the wall on the other side of the room.

"No, not happening. Are you kidding, basically dead? Do you know what that will do to you?" he asked, his voice low but I could hear the concern and anger in his tone.

"Bennett, without her Song we're all lost to Darious. He's too powerful," Kasian said, trying to take the heat off of Faye and Aisha. He knew how important this was, even if it meant risking my own life.

Olen only glanced down at me, eyes hard for a second before he turned and walked out of the room. I could see the conflict behind his eyes, but it was only there for a split second before his walls came up and he shut me out. His expression returning to the vague look he had when I first met him.

As soon as he walked out, I sighed softly, knowing I'd have to talk him into this idea. "You guys figure out a way to make this happen," I said with a sigh, "and how to not kill me in the process."

Mamarie only shook her head at me with a small smile, entertaining my attempt at a joke. Without another word I turned and walked straight out of the homestead. Heading towards the beach, where I knew Olen would be.

I could make out his figure immediately as I walked down the small path to the pebbled beach. He was sitting on the stones, knees tucked to his chest as he tossed stones into the water.

The beach looked the same as it did before the attack. Faye and Aisha had cleaned up the bodies and mess. Sending them back on their boat to another island. I don't think I could have taken a seat next to Olen if there were still bodies floating around.

I slowly sat myself next to him. Letting our arms brush against each other as I pulled my knees to my chest, folding my arms around them and resting my chin on my elbows. I waited, watched the stones as he threw them, sitting next to him in silence as I let him calm down. After a minute or two I could feel the hot anger seep from his body as he relaxed a bit.

"I can't let you do that Della," he said softly, cutting through the silence with his broken tone.

I tilted my head on my arm so I was propped up a bit using my hand. I gave him a soft smile before looking down at the stones between us, rolling them between my fingers as I started the conversation.

"I have to, Olen. This is bigger than just me; you have to see that right?" I reasoned softly, waiting for him to turn his head and look at me. But he didn't, instead looked down at the rocks between his legs and picked up a few more.

"I'm allowed to be selfish. I'm allowed to want to keep you safe," he said, as if trying to say something else entirely. His tone was hard, yet, his expression staying soft and neutral. I reached into his lap and pulled his hand into mine, lacing my fingers together with his.

"You can't protect me from everything," I said, trying to ease the pressure he seemed to hold on his shoulders when regarding me. I wondered when that had happened. We had been stuck on this journey together for a while, but I guess we had come a long way from him debating leaving me on Tarkan. He, for some reason, now felt responsible for my safety.

"I can try," he said, his voice low and scratchy, his eyes focused on our hands. His thumb brushed over the back of my hand gently, running over my knuckles. His confession stirred something deep in my stomach. There was something there, something that meant more than just trying to keep me safe. Just like how I felt about him every time he got a bit too close. The warm fluttery feeling that swam in my stomach.

"I'm going to be selfish, Della. I want you. And I wouldn't be able to live with myself if I let you get hurt," he said, finally looking up to meet my eyes. My breath got caught in my throat for a second as I watching his eyes swirl with light and dark blues, his emotions fighting behind his eyes.

"I won't get hurt, I promise," I said softly, giving him a small smile.

His lips tilted for a second in a half smile before his eyes went back to our intertwined fingers. His side profile was still a bit tense, his brow furrowed and jaw clenched, though his grasp on my hand was gentle. As I observed him, I knew I had to say something about the shooting stars of emotions I'd been feeling the past few weeks with him.

"I wouldn't be able to live with myself knowing I died without..." I started, trailing off a bit as I got a bit embarrassed. My breath got caught in my throat. He noticed and tilted his head back to look at me, dark-blue eyes searching my own.

"Without what?" he asked softly, his other hand reaching to push my hair behind my ear gently.

I looked up catching his eyes again, my heart was racing a million miles a minute and I felt like I could feel the heat of the stars in my chest. I let my eyes trail over his features slowly, his soft, slightly crooked nose, deep-blue eyes, sharp jawline. The small cut above his eyebrow, the curls forming as his hair dried. The way his lips were slightly parted as he waited for me to answer.

"Stars, save me," I mumbled. Without thinking about it, because if I thought about it, I would have winked out. I leaned forward.

I let my hands cup his face softly as I pulling myself closer to him, my lips pressing against his.

My movement was quick and caught him off guard. I felt him stabilize himself with his arm behind him as the other quickly responded and tangled his fingers through the hair at the back of my neck.

His lips brushed across mine, kissing me back immediately. The warmth of him being so close made my body tingle, it felt like I was being kissed by stardust. He took over almost immediately, his hand that supported him moving to my hip. He slid his palm down my thigh slowly before gripping the back of it and pulling me over into his lap. I kept one hand on the side of his neck, my fingers brushing his jaw while the other gripped his red jacket to keep him close to me.

Before I lost control to the tingly feeling going through my body, I pulled away slowly. I kept my eyes closed for a second longer before opening them, meeting the deep-blue of Olen's irises.

"Without doing that," I said, answering his question. A small breathy laugh left my lips as I watched a wide smile take over his lips. He laughed a bit lightly before it turned into a teasing groan and he pressed his forehead against my collarbone.

"How do you expect me to let you go now, Princess?" he groaned against my throat. Pressing slow wet kisses on the sensitive parts of my skin as he made his way back to my lips.

Before he could get there, I grabbed his jaw lightly, pulling him a bit away from me. His cheeks squished between my fingers. "You don't get to let me go anymore, bucket head. You're stuck with me," I said with a teasing wink. He only groaned before pushing forwards. His lips connecting with mine once again.

His fingers dug into the waist of my jumpsuit, as I slid my hand down from his jaw to the base of his throat, digging my nails into the soft skin. He groaned against my lips, his hand holding tight to the back of my neck as he brought me closer to him. His tongue brushing across my bottom lip teasingly before he deepened the kiss.

My body felt on fire as he kissed me, all the small daydreams I had about him fading away when I realized a kiss alone, was ten times better than I expected. With my hand still around the base of his neck I pushed him away softly. "As much as I would love to do this all day," I started softly, leaning forwards to peck his lips once more. "We should probably get back; I'm trusting you to make sure they don't screw anything up."

He reluctantly nodded his head before loosening his grip on me. I stood from his lap and helped him up as well before we headed back towards the homestead.

"Sleeping next to you is going to be ten times more interesting, Princess. You don't have to keep your hands to yourself, you know," Olen said, sending me a cheeky wink. I rolled my eyes at him nudging his shoulder as we walked back.

* * *

I looked down at the tub of ice water sitting in front of me, wringing my hands together a bit nervously. I knew what the plan was, but that didn't stop the nerves from bundling in my lungs, making it a bit harder to breathe.

I was only in my sports top and shorts, Mamarie hooking me up with some of the med bay equipment from Olen's ship. Stickers were placed on my chest, temples and ribs. To send them my heart rate and brain waves, to keep track of what was going on with my body while Aisha was in my head.

"And that's the last one," Mamarie said, pressing the sticker to my sternum, making sure it wasn't lifting in the corners.

I took in a shaky breath but nodded my head. "Alright, lets get this over with," I mumbled before grabbing the edge of the tub.

Aisha was standing at the far end where my head would be, Faye next to her while my blue-clad friends stood behind me. Olen was standing in the doorway, arms crossed. It was like he could never fully enter a room, always needing to be close to the exit. I would tease him about it later. I met his eyes for a second, sending him a wink. I smiled when I noticed his frown lighten up and his lips tug upwards.

I took another breath to calm my nerves before stepping into the water. I hissed at the cold temperature, my skin erupting in goosebumps in a matter of milliseconds.

"Awesome," I groaned, the word coming out as more of a hiss as I lowered myself into the water. My eyebrows furrowed and I had puffed my cheeks out with air trying to get used to the extremely cold water.

Once I sat down with my shoulders resting against the back of the tub, I looked around the room, wanting to remember their worried looks so I could tease them about it later.

"Ready?" Aisha asked me. I tilted my head back to look at her, meeting her eyes before nodding my head softly. I met Olen's eyes from across the room before Aisha's hands wrapped around my shoulders and she pushed me under.

The cold was a shock and I closed my eyes tight.

My hands gripped the edges of the tub as my body felt like it was starting to burn. Not even a second later I felt Aisha send a hot flash of pain through my skull as she started to dig through my memories.

I couldn't help but let out a scream, my mouth immediately filling with water. I tried to take in another breath but was only met with a freezing pain as water rushed into my lungs.

I felt the warmth of a hand grab mine before I started to pass out.

My mind going dark to the pain and my body ceasing its thrashing in the water.

As I faded out, I could feel myself float to the surface, water bubbling up from my lungs and trickling out from my blue lips. There was a warm feeling across my mouth and the pain of warm air being forced into my body as I faded into my memories.

CHAPTER TWENTY-ONE

When I opened my eyes again, I wasn't sitting in the freezing cold tub of water, I wasn't even in the middle of the kitchen. I was back on the mossy, humid planet of Tarkan. Exactly where I had landed after running from my home planet. A humid breeze swept up the dust of the ground and down the alley, pushing me out onto the main street.

I was in the clothes I had been wearing when they submerged me, not the ones I had been wearing when arriving on Tarkan. They were damp and clung to my body, the dust flying around seemed to stick to the fabric making it itchy and uncomfortable. I tried to dust it off but the sun beating down and the slight wind made it impossible.

I looked around for a familiar amber jumpsuit. Searching for the version of me that fit the memory, but I couldn't see a single one, let alone the one I had been wearing.

The breeze wisped around me again, blowing my hair around my face and pushing me forwards, I took that as a sign to follow it, hoping it was a pull from my Song. As I rounded the corner to the main street, I felt the pull, right in the middle of my chest.

I could feel a soft buzz of energy wash through my body, and without thinking I let it pull me in whatever direction it was leading me. The pull let me down a main street before turning around corners and ducking down dark alleys, places I knew I had not been before. I walked down a few more streets before I caught site of a dark helmet, red jacket and bright metal arm.

Olen.

He was leaning against one of the market's stands, talking with a seller behind his table. It looked like he was selling parts and pieces, and a whole lot of junk. A whole bunch of random things littered the table and hung around the canopy above. There were fabrics, beads, carvings, jewellery, I could even see a few weapons scattered across the table. Propped up against the wall behind the stand were parts and boards, sun panels and hovers, from what I could tell. It was a trading hut, it had anything someone could be looking for.

Olen shifted, reaching in his pocket and pulled out a small bag, shaking a few coins into his hand to give the seller. They weren't anything like Prythian currency, they were something found on centre galaxy planets, the Darion's triangle symbol with the panther carved into the gold metal, reminding people of their dark presence.

The man behind the booth looked just as sketchy as the stand around him, but that was Tarkan's aesthetic. You didn't ask on Tarkan, no questions meant no answers, and no getting involved with the people's business. The man had buzzcut hair, a long scar across his eye, the colour of the iris now a milky white. He was hunched over grabbing Olen's coins. As soon as he was paid, he reached behind him and wrapped up something for my pilot.

Olen thanked the man, putting the wrapped piece in a pocket on the inside of his jacket. He turned his back to the stand, leaning his hips back against the table as he secured his purchase. He had pulled out a piece of paper and was reading whatever had been written down, the sun glinting off his helmet.

That's when I noticed it. A small amber gem. The merchant tapped Olen on the shoulder, the bounty hunter turning to get his change. Olen only opened his small bag of coins and the seller dropped his change in. The small amber gem falling in with the rest.

A small gasp left my lips and I took off in Olen's direction. Not even seconds later the past version of me, dressed in a bright amber flight suit, was running down the alley towards him. Olen moved quickly and grabbed past me by the waist, turning and slamming me against the wall.

I ran to turn the corner Olen and past me had disappeared behind, but my surroundings started to change before I made it to follow them.

It was like I was walking through water, the air around me thick and slow as my surroundings melted together. Then slowly, they were made up again and I was standing in another memory.

I was back on the Darion freighter, it was the memory of Olen and I running down the hallway, trying to escape the soldiers. Olen and past me had just rounded a corner, the Darion soldiers hot on our heels. I watched from behind as Olen pulled out his gun, in the process the small amber gem flying from the holster and bouncing on the floor to a corner of the hallway.

I closed my eyes unable to believe it had been right there the whole time. It had been on him, that's why I could access my power, not because I had touched Darious's blade, but because my Song had been right there. It had slipped right through my fingers.

And then my surroundings melted again. I closed my eyes so I wouldn't feel the same thick tug and swirling of colours, not wanting to get dizzy as my environment changed.

I open my eyes, half expecting to be back in the tub. Only I wasn't. I was on Prytha. I was standing in the kitchens, the three Darion soldiers still pounding on the closed door. Past me must have just been here, I had been headed towards the throne room, to save my mother.

Not a second later the soldiers finally kicked the door down, splintering the wood. I ran past them and straight towards the throne room, where I knew I would be. Where Darious and my mother would be. I could hear my heartbeat in my ears as I ran down the hallways, heading to the throne room.

When I burst through the doors the ceiling was already raining down. I was only in the room for a few seconds before I watched the piece of cement fall and hit my head. A slight throb started aching in the back of my head as I watched my body tumble down.

It took me a second to realize that in the memory I had fully blacked out. I had thought I had been awake but dizzy when I had been hit in the head. But I had actually gone unconscious. I was even more surprised when I saw Darious rush across the throne room. He knelt next to me, brushing a few hairs from my face, dabbing the cut on my forehead. Then he pulled something from his pocket. An amber gem held between his fingers as he slipped it into my pocket.

I tried to grasp the memory as it started to fade, but the more I tried to hold onto it, the further it seemed to drift away.

I let out a frustrated yell as I was swept up into another memory. The swirling of my surroundings made my chest tighten, panic flooding my veins as the memories flew around me.

When I felt my surroundings change, I wasn't surprised to see I was back on Olen's ship. Only I couldn't see the stone anywhere. There was no amber gem, no slight glow or sparkle in the air. But I knew it was there, it was somewhere right in front of me. It was telling me to come find it, it was calling me to the ship.

A second later I felt myself getting pulled away from the memory.

I didn't fight the feeling this time, letting it pull me back in waves. The swirling bringing me back to the surface of my consciousness.

Slowly, I could feel water start to fall in around me. My mind swimming through darkness before feeling came back to my body. My fingers being the first thing that I could move, twitching them slowly.

The cold started creeping up my back and shoulders, wrapping around my body and making me shiver. I could feel a warm hand holding mine, their grip tight on my shivering fingers. There was a second of stillness, silence before I was kicked back into the real world.

I forced myself from the trance shooting up in the cold water. I felt my lungs take in a massive amount of air, my skin like ice and my teeth chattering.

Immediately there were arms around me, my vision was a bit blurry so I couldn't exactly make out who was helping me but I was guided out of the tub and to the floor before towels were wrapped around me. I shivered rather harshly, my body flinching with every shiver that pulled across my skin. I could tell my lips and fingers were a soft shade of blue or purple since I could feel the buzzing numb feeling as blood returned to them. A pair of arms wrapped around me and pulled me into a warm chest. I knew right away it was Olen, everything around me smelt like him.

I rubbed my eyes with shaky hands, trying to get the water dripping into my eyes. My hands were shaking so much I thought I might poke my eye out. Olen must have thought the same thing because he grabbed my hands and wiped my face with the towel before pulling my hair back. I met his dark-blue eyes. His eyebrows were furrowed, gaze hard and jaw clenched. A small smirk pulled at my features and I wanted to make a comment about how worried he seemed, but figured I should tell them about what I had learned from my memories first.

Mamarie and Kasian knelt down to my right while Aisha to my left, her snow-white fingers brushing wet hair out of my face, a soft smile on her lips. Faye stood a bit behind, her brows furrowed in worry as well as relief that I was out and fine.

"I saw it," I coughed out lightly. Bringing the towels closer to my body, tucking it under my chin.

"Yes, I saw it too, Olen, you got it on Tarkan, from a trader," Aisha said softly, knowing my chattering teeth were hard to understand. She had lived through the memories I had remembered; she saw what Darious had done.

All that we thought about him meeting me in my dreams was wrong. Everything we had thought up until this point was completely wrong. Darious had a plan of his own, and we hadn't been able to figure it out until now. He didn't think I had my Song; he had given it to me. So why did he seem so surprised by my magic?

I nodded softly, glancing up at Olen above me. I could tell he was confused when she said that, the way his eyebrows furrowed and his arms held me a little tighter.

"Yes, t-then we lo-ost it on th-he Darion shi-ip," I stuttered, pressing my lips together figuring I'd let Aisha continue for me.

"Great so we have to go straight to the evil prince to get it," Kasian said a bit sarcastically. Mamarie was sitting on her knees, back straight as her eyes looked me over to make sure I was okay. She had nudged Kasian a bit at his comment, almost making him loose balance in the low squat he was sitting in.

His comment made a small smirk pull at my lips and I shook my head. Mamarie caught my reaction and looked at me a bit amused. "What? what's *that* look for?" she asked.

"Darious gave her, her Song," Aisha said, wonder and confusion evident in her own voice.

"Darious gave her, her Song?" Faye repeated, not understanding the events that were unfolding.

"Yes. The night her mother passed. He slipped it into her pocket," Aisha explained, standing from her crouched position and hovering over the ground as she thought.

"The dark prince has got some issues he needs to figure out. Starting with picking a side," Olen mumbled from above me.

"Stars, Bennett, how'd you come up with a better name for the bastard then me?" Kasian mumbled at him. Olen only smirked at his friend, his worry falling from his features as the comment stroked his ego. I couldn't help the small laugh that left my lips at their banter.

"Well, that's beside the point. Where is it now?" Mamarie asked, speaking before Olen could retort.

"I saw the ship. I believe it has been left there, somewhere." Aisha answered. I only nodded my head, focusing on getting warmth into my body, not able to use my powers since my core temperature was still too low.

"Well, I guess we better go look," Faye said, her grin stretching up her cheeks. As if she was excited to be apart of the action again. After three hundred years in hiding, I would be excited too.

* * *

It took a couple minutes of warming me up before the six of us piled into the small boat and Kasian drove us back to Olen's ship. I still had a blanket wrapped around my arms as we walked up the ramp of his ship.

"Split up, it has to be here somewhere," Faye instructed, taking Aisha with her as they head towards the med bay.

"Well take the med bay, Mamarie and Kasian can check the cockpit. Olen and Della, go through the bedroom. Then if we still don't find it, well go through the cargo bay together," Aisha said.

The group nodded before heading off in our separate directions. As soon as Olen opened the door in front of him, I could feel the soft hum of electricity. It wasn't the same hum as the soldiers, theirs was silent and dark. This one was singing, light and changing pitches, echoing through my ears. It felt like the more I walked into the room, the warmer I felt, the energy that was coming off my hidden Song was replenishing my magic.

I let the blanket fall from my shoulders and my back straighten a bit as I felt the pull of magic guide me into the room.

"It's here," I said softly, feeling like if I spoke louder than a whisper the singing would stop.

Olen spun to look at me when the words fell from my lips, looking a bit confused before he saw how much more energized, I looked. The colour had returned to my cheeks and I felt like my eyes were brighter. Magic coursing through my veins putting me in a trance. My body was no longer colourless and blue, my skin warming into its tan colour and my lips returning to a light pink instead of the cold purple.

We both moved forward immediately, pulling the blankets from the bed, ruffling through them to find the small gem. Olen started pulling open drawers while I looked behind the minimal furniture.

I shivered as a soft Song-like hum brushed across the shell of my ear like a cold breeze. I immediately turned my head, flinching out of reflex from the cold air. I looked up, spinning around to figure out which direction the call had come from. The small door of the closet was open a crack, the one place we hadn't checked.

I moved across the room and pulled open the closet, pulling the loose clothes out. The last thing sitting in the closet was Olen's dark helmet and shiny silver arm. As I pulled the two pieces out from the floor, I noticed a soft amber glow coming from the hand of his silver armour.

I dropped to my knees with the silver arm in my hands. I noticed Olen move over from across the room, his presence just to my right behind me.

I grabbed the closed fist of his armour and pulled, feeling it slowly start to loosen into an open hand. It took another pull before I finally got the hand open.

Sitting in the palm of the metal hand was my small amber Song. A gem the size of an almond and a bright-yellow colour coming off of it in wisps.

As I picked it up, it left a shimmery gold residue across my fingers.

As soon as my fingers met the cold exterior of the gem, I felt a wave of humming energy to flow through my entire body. I felt the familiar burn in the back of my eyes as they turned a fiery yellow colour, I could even feel a heat rush just under my skin, making me feel like I was glowing from the inside out.

It felt like I was as light as a feather for a few seconds, my hair floated around me and my body feeling suspended in air even though I was still kneeling on the floor. I knew my experience probably looked like a painting. Probably of an angel or demon. I was hovering a few inches from the ground, my skin glittering with sparkles, glowing from just under the surface. Warmth and power radiating from my body, my eyes glowing a fiery amber and my hair floating around my shoulders.

The feeling soon started to subside and I felt my eyes simmer back into their golden-brown colour. I felt energized, like I had just woken up from a good sleep, or had caffeine running through my veins. I knew it was the effect of holding my Song, our powers connected. I turned the stone over in my fingers feeling the residue cover the tips of my fingers. Glittering in the light it looked like I had touched a star.

"That was hot," Olen mumbled. I glanced over my shoulder at him with a small smile. He had his own silly smile on his lips as he looked me over. I couldn't help the warm blush that spread across my cheeks. Or the fact that my eyes had fallen to his lips for a second.

"I guess we were fated then huh?" he said sending me a small wink.

I guess we were. We were meant to meet; our paths were meant to cross. Why else would my Song be passed through him to me. "I guess we were," I answered, rolling the stone into my fist as I held it tightly. I was fresh and full of new power.

Darious didn't stand a chance.

CHAPTER TWENTY-TWO

I was sitting at the table in the kitchen, a zip-up hoodie off one of my shoulders absentmindedly as I worked. Mamarie had been sitting with me earlier, showing me how to wrap a Song in wire. I had wanted to hang it with my sister's necklace. To keep the two of them together. She had liked the idea, saying she had put her own Song on a chain when she had gotten it.

Mamarie had been pulled away by Kasian thirty minutes later, he said he wanted to start a fire, but from the look he was giving her I knew it was more than that. Since Aisha, Faye and Olen had stayed at the ship a little longer, I got a bit of peace and quiet before the fire would actual be built and the group would be pulled together.

I wrapped the gold wire around the small gem. It was hard to believe such a small thing could hold so much power. Every time my fingers wound around the gem; soft gold shimmer stuck to my fingers. It almost reminded me of how Darious had pulled the black stain from his sword and let it climb up his fingers and arm. That colour had been deep, vile. Though it was nothing like the Viridian colour of his magic, the colour of his eyes. Much like his blackened hands, mine were covered in a thin layer of gold.

While working on wrapping the stone, I wondered why he gave it to me. Why did he need help? Where was his Song? Kasian and Mamarie had said a Syron's Song matches their magic, since the colour comes straight from the power of the gem. So where was his? How could he have that power without having his Song on him.

But then again, he had never used his power in front of me. His hands had just turned black, that could have been a power of the enchanted blade itself, having nothing to do with his Song. That still didn't answer where his gem was, and why he didn't keep it on him. You'd think a prince born into the role of the leader of the Darion would want to be powerful and not let his Song fall into the wrong hands.

Faye and Aisha explained that he had been hunting Faye for the past three hundred years, furious about his mother's murder. Just like how I was furious about my own. But even though he had sent his soldiers on a hunt for her, she had only ever seen him once. That was almost two hundred years ago. He had fought against her, their green magic flashing against each other, Faye had overpowered him and sent him broken and battered to the floor. The older Syron had explained how she thought it odd. They had been equal matches, him even winning over her, but then in the middle of their battle he had pulled back. His magic disappearing and hers hit him full force, suffocating him.

Faye had then pulled back and ran, leaving the young lord in the dust.

After that, Darious hid for years, no one saw him, not even a mention of him popping up on a planet with his soldiers. But his symbol shot fear into the galaxy in the absence of his presence.

The symbol, a triangle with the panther circling one of the edges. It would appear on a planet, and days later the planet would be reduced to rubble. Sometimes the Darion would kill everyone, sometimes they would settle for lodgings on the planet's surface.

Occasionally they would take the entire civilization. It had only happened a few times in the galaxy's history. An entire planet's worth of people would disappear, their minds wiped, and turned into cyborg soldiers.

The Darion usually picked their soldiers from a ransacked planet, but sometimes they took everyone. Their army was massive and stretched out across the galaxy, the only way to hit them hard would be to kill their leader. With no one to control the silent soldiers, they would rot into nothing.

That's why we would go straight for the heart, straight for Darious.

We would need help. I hadn't heard of many other Syron. I haven't heard of *any* other Syron since the great war. But I was here, and so were Kasian and Mamarie, that meant there were more. We would have to find them.

Along with the resistance. A myth, but one I would bet my magic on. It was rarely talked about, but there were whispers of insurgents. If we could, we would find them.

I twisted the wire around my gem one more time, bringing fire to my finger tips to melt the edges of the metal together. I made sure it was smooth before taking my chain from my neck and lacing it through the wire. The gem fell right next to my sister's heart pendant.

A soft knock on the door frame to the kitchen made me move my gaze from the chain and up to a pair of piercing blue eyes.

"Hey, Princess," Olen greeted with a grin as he moved into the room. He walked around the table so he was standing next to me, leaning against the edge of the table. He hadn't changed from the ship and was in a pair of dusty black pants and a dirty grey shirt. His hair was even a darker shade, dirt brushed across his face.

"Stars, what were you up to?" I asked with a small chuckle. He moved to lean his hips back against the table, facing the wall behind me, his arms folded across his chest.

He only gave me a goofy grin and shrugged his shoulders. "I had a few things to deal with on the ship," he answered, eyes trailing across my face for my reaction.

I only huffed out a breath of laughter and rolled my eyes. "It looks like you crawled through the engine." I huffed, turning my attention back to my necklace, unclasping it to put it back around my neck.

"Well maybe I did," he said, his hands moving over mine to grab the chain. When I looked up at him, he only sent me a wink. He moved to stand behind my chair, giving me a quick tilt of his head to tell me to lift my hair. I did as he silently asked and bunched my loose hair up and out of the way of my neck.

He looped the chain around my neck, his fingers brushing against my skin. I could feel the smirk forming on his lips when he noticed the shiver under my skin. He clasped the chain together before letting his finger trail across my bare shoulder, where my sweater had fallen. I smiled, closing my eyes at his soft touch. He ran his fingers back up the side of my neck and then I felt him lean down and a wet, warm kiss being pressed to the base of my neck.

I had to bite my lip to stifle a sigh. His other hand trailed the other side of my shoulder, holding the other side of my neck gently. One warm hand holding my left shoulder while he pressed kisses higher up the left side of my neck. His right hand moved and gripped my neck, tilting my chin straight up with his thumb.

I let my eyes flutter open and I met his dark-blue eyes as he looked down at me from over the back of my chair. His eyes turned a deeper blue as he glanced down at my slightly parted lips.

"Are you going to kiss me, or not?" I said quietly with a small grin. He only bit his bottom lip, trying to keep his smile at bay. His head tipped to the left a bit in his action before he leaned down over the back of the chair, pressing his lips to mine.

He kissed me softly, as if I were a glass doll that he didn't want to break. With the hand that held my neck he grazed his thumb across my throat, finding my pulse. Probably feeling how fast it was beating since he smiled against my lips. His other hand trailed over my shoulder, pushing the sweater a bit further down my skin, exposing more of my collarbone.

His kiss became a bit more rushed and excited as I moved my hand up to cup the back of his neck, pulling him closer. A soft groan left his lips and he pulled away slowly, looking down at me with dark eyes as his thumb brushed across my neck.

"Either we stop now or you hop up on the table so I can kiss you properly," he said, his voice low as he brushed his tongue over his bottom lip. I couldn't help the blush that rushed to my cheeks. He must have noticed because he smirked and moved his hands from my neck and shoulders.

In two moves, he had spun my chair around and had grabbed the backs of my thighs, lifting me the short distance from the chair to the table. He dropped me on the edge, stepping between my thighs and moving his hand up to the side of my neck, pulling my lips back to his.

This time a soft sigh did leave my lips and I trailed my hands up his arms before winding my fingers through his hair, tugging on the strands. The action made a groan slip passed his lips and his hand grab my thigh a little tighter.

"And I thought *we* were having fun," Kasian's voice broke out across the kitchen.

I froze in Olen's arms. He groaned as he pulled away from me, dipping his head into the crook of my neck to place a soft kiss there before looking over my shoulder at the Syron who caught us.

"Leave," Olen said, shooing the other man away with a wave of his hand. I only heard Kasian's retreating cackling as it echoed down the hall as he left.

"Bastard," Olen mumbled before turning back to me. He brought his thumb from the side of my neck and to my cheek, brushing across my skin gently.

"Good timing, because you really do need to shower. Never mind the dirt, you kind of smell," I said, pinching my nose as I teased him. He only glared at me playfully and pulled the back of my neck towards him. Kissing me one more time.

This one was short, but much different than our other sweet kisses. This one was hard, probably to shut me up. Not even a second later he pulled away. "You going to join me, Princess?" he asked with a wink as he took a step away from the table. His body's heat leaving with him and sending a cold breeze across my body.

"Not this time, bucket head, maybe next time," I answered, sending him a wink before hoping off the table and heading out of the kitchen. Leaving him standing in the middle of the kitchen.

* * *

The fire was burning bright and big when I made it out to the field. Mamarie and Kasian were cuddled up in the grass, listening intently to something Faye was saying. Kasian lying back in the grass, one arm drawn back behind his head. His eyes closed as he listened to the conversation. Mamarie was sitting up a bit, her hip lined up with his, her elbow resting on his chest as she leaned into him, her attention focused on the Syron and Convoy ahead of her.

The two Syron women sat next to each other on a bench, their hands laced together. I had guessed, but never wanted to assume they were together. It seemed new to the pair anyway, both giddy smiles and their hands linked tight together. Afraid they would lose one another again.

I was sitting back against the bench, my back and shoulders pressed against the wood while I pushed my feet out towards the heat of the fire, savouring its warmth. My eyes were trained on the flames in front of me, barely hearing Faye's story about the war, her voice covered with fog as I focused on the flames.

I could feel it pulling me away, lulling me into a hypnotic state. I could feel the burn of my eyes as they tried to shift colours. And in that small flash of power, my surroundings shifted and I was no longer in front of the fire.

"Don't you dare, you know I need her," a voice growled. I couldn't see anything, as if my eyes were closed. I could no longer feel the warmth of the fire or hear the crackling of the embers with Faye's voice in the background. Instead, it was silent, there was a soft echo of something far off, and it was cold.

"I don't care what she does or doesn't have, you will bring her close. She will have a choice and I hope she chooses wisely," a female voice retorted. I could feel heat grow in my chest, though I knew it wasn't my emotions, I was feeling someone else's. The sound of heels walking off echoed before a door was slammed closed.

Suddenly I opened my eyes, though I wasn't looking down at the fire I knew was in front of me. I was looking down at black dress shoes and black pants, green flames licking at the persons fingers as they brought their hands up.

"You should mind your own business, little dove," the dark voice said.

And then I was shot back into my own reality. My own eyes fluttered open and I was once again gazing at the orange and yellow flames, reaching up into the dark sky.

I had just been in Darious's head. And he had my magic.

CHAPTER TWENTY-THREE

Olen had brought me back from my thoughts when he walked back over to the fire. He was dressed in a black hoodie, and grey sweatpants, his hair still wet and brushed back away from his face. He sent me a wink when he caught my stare and moved to sit next to me. He threw his arm over my shoulders and tucked me into his side.

Despite the unsettling vision, or hallucination, or whatever it was that I had just had, the group's conversation distracted me enough to almost forget about it completely. This would be the second time Darious had somehow gotten into my head. If I had been able to see through his eyes in that moment, has he been able to see through mine?

It was obvious I somehow had his magic; I had slid right into his head. But he also had my magic, Viridian green flames licking at his skin. Was it because our suns shared the same solar system? The same power? I hadn't heard of anything like that from Aisha or Faye before.

The conversation settled to a comfortable silence when I finally decided to voice my thoughts.

"How do sunmates work? There couldn't have been many since the beginning of the galaxy?" I asked, my focus on Faye and Aisha, though I could feel the other three shift their attention to me. The silence had been comfortable but my questions had created a confusion, a tension among the group.

Mostly between Faye and Aisha as they glanced at each other. "Well, consider the rarity of a Syron child being born. Since only one is born every two hundred years or so, save for Kasian and Mamarie who are rarities themselves, the chance that you get two Syron children, born within three hundred years from each other, and from the same solar system, is practically impossible," Faye explained, her eyes shifting between the five of us as she explained. Her focus solely on satisfying my curiosities.

"When I was born, Emila, who had been the Syron child before me, was around four hundred years old already. And before Emila there have only been around three dozen Syron, in the universe's history. Since we become immortal with our Songs, four hundred years is nothing, we are practically still children."

"Darious is practically a baby," Aisha interjected with a small laugh. He was almost four hundred, I think, if he was twenty in the great war, supposedly. He could be older.

Faye only smiled at Aisha's comment before continuing. "I was the youngest Syron for the entirety of the war. Five hundred years of war and it was me against Emila. She had killed most of the Syron that came before her, including Aisha," Faye said softly. Aisha's expression turned dark and her hair floated a bit as a buzz of power rushed through her body.

"However, since the birth of Darious, Kasian and Mamarie were born, along with you, his sunmate. Nothing can stay dark and bad forever. Eventually the scales will tip back in our favour. The scales started tipping back in our favour with Emila's death. Then with three Syron being born within four hundred years. Maybe more, if we're being honest. With this much darkness in the galaxy, its possible Syron children were born to snuff it out. However, you three are the only ones we know of," Faye said, bringing our attention to her story.

"Being his sunmate means you are equals. When your suns were thriving, they shared each other's warmth, circled around each other their entire lives. They pulled from one another and were never without the other. That's how you and Darious's powers are supposed to pull from each other. Though, since you fight on different sides, I'm not to sure how the pulling of magic would work."

"The last pair of twin flames recorded in our history were the first Syron to ever exist. They were born from the first starts of our galaxy. When the stars burnt out, two children were born to a dark planet. One child had the power of light and life, while the other darkness and death. Though they were complete opposites, they loved one another and fed off each other. When their powers intertwined and they pulled from each other like their host suns did, and life was created."

"Light and life sent her magic over the universe, lighting up darkened planets, growing stars and suns, introducing life to the bright planets. But her power of light and life was too much. Life grew to fast and too abundantly, taking over every part of the planets until life was crawling over one another, suffocating each other for eternity. The life that crawled to the top of the pile was burned from the intensity of the light. There was too much. So, darkness and death let her whisps of smoke trail over the galaxy, turning the light around the stars to deep dark eternity. She let her death take those who were suffering, took their immortality and gave them mortality. They created balance."

"And from their union they created the Syron, those with the power of light and dark, life and death. To protect the galaxy until their lives eventually ended. The legend continues to say if twin flames, sunmates, were ever to rise again, the overbearing light or darkness, would be washed from the galaxy and balance would once again return," Faye said, her story coming to a close.

I had never heard an origin tale quite like it, but it stirred something deep in my chest. Like an awakening. I would return balance to the universe, that much was for sure. But would I have to kill my sunmate to do it, or beg him to join my cause. The light.

"And if the twin flames are arch enemies?" Kasian asked. He was now sat up, leaning back against his hands. Mamarie tucked into his shoulder, both watching Faye with intense stares. Though Kasian's was contradicted by his sarcastic comment and smirk.

"There's never been a theory or legend about what might happen. I don't think anyone expected sunmates could take opposing sides," Faye explained.

"I guess there's a first for everything," I said with a huff of a laugh. The tension was cut with my comment, and smiles were pulled around the circle. Olen's hand fell to my shoulder, brushing my sleeve from my shoulder so he could run his fingers over my skin. I glanced up at him with a small smile. He only sent me a wink before looking back at the fire.

"We need to start training you with your magic. Preferably with an opponent better than Kasian," Olen pointed out, a smirk forming on his face when he heard Kasian's offended scoff.

"You're not much better, mortal," Kasian spat back at the pilot. Olen only chuckled at his attempt at an insult.

"Last time I checked, Kacey, you are also mortal," Olen retorted, leaning his head back on the bench a bit as he pulled me closer. Mamarie and I couldn't help but roll our eyes at their banter.

"I'll train with you, Della; these boys aren't as skilled as us. They can go at each other," she told me with a cheeky grin. I couldn't help but laugh at her comment. Both men sending her their own glares. Their egos bruised, even if they wouldn't admit it.

We stayed out by the fire as the moon got brighter, the sun setting and the planet was shadowed in darkness once again. I couldn't stop thinking about the origin story Faye had told. If Darious and I were supposed to be life and death, light and darkness, how would we find balance? I would have to be as bright as the original light Syron to cast out his darkness.

Maybe that was the goal, Darious was drowning in darkness, suffocating the galaxy. Only instead of him asking for help, I would have to force the change, force the balance.

My eyes started to burn from the smoke of the fire, constantly rubbing them to get the stingy feeling to go away. I finally gave up and just let them closed, falling into my thoughts as I did. My head rested on Olen's shoulder and he pulled me a bit closer when he noticed my eyes were closed.

At some point, I must have started drifting to sleep because when I opened my eyes again, Aisha and Faye had disappeared. Olen was shaking my shoulder gently and I turned my attention over to him. Just over his shoulder, I could see Kasian carrying a sleeping Mamarie into the homestead.

"Couldn't carry me, bucket head?" I mumbled, knocking his shoulder a bit as I let him stand up. Lacing my fingers through his as he helped me up.

"No, I like your tired face, especially the drool. It's cute. Especially when it's mixed with your angry face, which is what you're giving me right now," he said with a teasing grin. I only huffed, turning, dragging him along with me back towards the homestead.

"Shut up bucket head, otherwise you're sleeping on the floor," I mumbled. I turned to look at him, just in time to see him zip his lips closed and toss the 'key' over his shoulder, tilting his lips up into a smirk. I rolled my eyes at his antics and pulled him into my room.

I sat on my side of the bed, untying my boots while he just flung his untied shoes at the door. Pulling his shirt over his head and tossing it in the same direction before crawling into my bed behind me.

His hand snaked around my waist and he pulled me back a bit. I couldn't help the small laugh that left my lips as I pushed him off, trying to get my boots untied. I felt him sit up and kiss my shoulders softly. His fingers trailing down my spine to the waistband of my pants.

Though his touch was distracting I couldn't help thinking over the vision, or hallucination I had while staring into the fire.

I pushed Olen's hands from me with a smile when I stood up. He only pouted at me, sticking with the silent act as he rolled to his side of the bed. I pulled on one of his shirts from the small closet, pulling my sports top off along with my bottoms. I clicked the light off before crawling under the covers Olen had opened for me.

He stayed on his back and I cuddled into his side, his arm wrapping around my shoulders, drawing soft patterns on the t shirt.

"I have to tell you something that happened earlier," I said softly into the darkness of the room. He stayed quiet, and I took that as his answer to go ahead. "Before you came to the fire, I was staring at the flames. I think I got sucked into a hypnotic state or something. I felt completely calm, my mind was still. Then the next second I was looking through Darious's eyes. He had green fire coming from his finger tips," I said softly into the darkness, keeping my gazed on the crack under the door, where the light from the hallway leaking into the room.

"Is that why you asked about sunmates?" Olen asked softly, not tensing or flinching at my question, but listening.

I nodded my head against his chest. "I think we're pulling off each other, or starting too. Do you think he gave me my Song so he could steal my fire? Imagine what he could do with both that and his mind magic," I said, voicing my concerns to the darkened room.

"He should be more worried about what you will be able to do with your newfound mind magic," he said softly against the top of my head. Pressing a soft kiss to my forehead, he pulled me closer into his side.

"Get some sleep, Dells, we'll figure everything out tomorrow. No need to waste energy thinking about it now, Princess." I thought about his words for a second, feeling my body relax as I internalized them. I would worry about my training tomorrow. Then I would learn how to master both skills, physical and mental.

CHAPTER TWENTY-FOUR

"Again," Aisha said. Her voice becoming a repetitive loop over the past four hours.

She was standing on the sidelines along with the two, blue-clad Syron and our pilot, watching as I attempted to take on Faye. Like I had been the last few days. An effort to learn as much as I could before the Darion returned, or we found them.

We had expected retaliation for the small battle, any day now. What we didn't expect was to hear Darious's own voice over the radio waves when we had tuned into the galaxy's frequency:

"This message goes out to the last of the Syron. You will not win. I have power you cannot fathom. I have taken what my mother created and turned it into an empire, one that will not fall easily. You acted like gods, but I am a god. I have defeated your immortals and their image, wiped it off the face of the galaxy and created an image of my own. Better, darker, silent."

"However, even with this beautiful darkened, peaceful, world, there are those who defy me, undermined my power. So, let us show them who the real gods are. Let's see just how many planets you can save. In three days, I start picking, planet by planet. I will murder

the ignorant and pathetic. How many little souls can you save? Our game starts now."

I felt my chest tighten as he spoke, his tone nothing like when he spoke in my home. No, his voice was sickening, sticky with sarcasm and insanity. We had all been huddled around the transmitter on Olen's ship. The only way to get messages to or from the planet. Darious had broadcasted this one to the entire galaxy. His message seemed odd; his voice different than the handful of times I had interacted with him. But I believed his threat. Even though something in my gut told me the message seemed off, the threat couldn't be undermined.

"We need to train you, now," Faye said immediately after. I spun a bit in the cockpit to look at her. "His mother was the same, she went planet to planet, killing innocents and smoking us out to slaughter. He will do the same. He is going to murder thousands. We need to face him before he destroys life as we know it," she said, a determined look in her eye.

I nodded my head, my expression hardening as I felt nothing but hate for the dark prince. "He won't know what hit him," I said, my expression dark as I met the eyes of my team, my family.

"Ow! Stars! What hit me?" I mumbled as I was knocked off my train of thought. I looked at what had hit me in the chest. A boot lay limp on the ground at my feet. "You threw a shoe at me?" I said, glaring ay Kasian.

"You weren't paying attention. It's not like the end of the universe is coming," he spat back. The sarcasm seemed to be dripping from his lips, but that didn't stop the tension from filling the air.

"Let's try again," Faye said, grabbing my attention and forcing it back to her.

Ignoring my overly sarcastic friend, I faced her again, imagining building a wall around my mind. The same exercise I had been trying to master for the past few hours. I created the barrier with my magic, a transparent shield of gold and glitter around my mind. Once I had it in place, I opened my eyes and let my power flow through me, my hands lighting up.

I had learned almost everything I could about my physical power from Faye, the struggle now was to fight while guarding my mind. As I fought Faye, Aisha would try to break into my mind, so I would technically be fighting them both. I had only managed to hold it for a few seconds so far.

Faye grinned at me from across the field twirling her staff between in her hands. Then her eyes started glowing a florescent green, a vibrant jungle colour. Small triangles of magic, resembling her face markings, floated around her with a dark almost black mist. It was incredibly intimidating. Where my physical magic took the form of flames and glitter, hers was mist and triangles.

Taking in a small breath, I hardened my features. I wrapped my mind in my magic, feeling it was a better barrier than imagining a brick wall. Not even a second later I could feel Aisha's light scratch on the protective field around my mind. I gritted my teeth a bit but threw myself at Faye.

I pushed my hands out in front of me, sending the amber fire in her direction, her staff blocking it as she spun herself, swiping the staff at my head. I ducked quickly, kicking out my own foot and feeling it collide with her stomach.

She let out a grunt and stumbled back a few steps from the impact. I took a step forward to attack again but a sharp pain pierced through my skull; I could feel Aisha put a crack in the shield around my mind. I hesitated a second and fill in the gap in my mind, but during that second of mental repair Faye had jabbed her staff towards me, the end hitting me in the chest.

I groaned holding my chest as the piercing pain shot though my sternum, taking my breath away. I recovered quickly and with my mental shield repaired I focused back on my fight with the Trilomarnian. Faye came at me again, her staff swiping left and right to try and hit me. I gritted my teeth. With the lack of a weapon, I was only able to dodge her staff. I shot magic at her when her side was exposed but it did little damage as she swung the long staff at me.

Without thinking to much about it, I felt my magic lick at my right hand as gold fire grew from my wrist to the tips of my fingers, leaving gold sparkles all across my skin. My hands were covered in gold much like how Darious's had turned black. The gold grew past my hands and started materializing. The fire grew up, long and skinny, as it formed into a weapon. A gold sword. I swung it in my hand a bit, testing the weight.

That's how Darious had a blackened blade. His magic was such a dark green it had created a pitch-black blade. His Song was his weapon. In the same way, my own magic was now mine.

My eyebrows rose a bit in surprise as it felt decently heavy, like a real weapon.

I smirked a bit as I saw Faye twirl, bringing her staff down hard, only instead of it hitting me, I had lifted my own fiery weapon and countered it. The clang of metal on metal echoed across the field and gold sparks flew from our weapons as they collided.

My eyes met Faye's and she grinned at me, encouraging me to try harder now that I had created a means of defence.

Immediately after she pushed her staff up, throwing my sword to the side. I raised it as fast as I could as her counter came quick, she backed me up a bit as our weapons clashed, her green staff against my amber blade.

I could feel Aisha's scratch on my mind get a bit stronger and I pushed her out, determined to do better this time, to win. I felt my eyes glow brighter and my hair raise as my power rushed through my veins.

With a small battle cry, I flipped Faye's staff out of the way and took the offensive position. I slashed at her weapon, as it was brought up in defence, pushing her back. She blocked my blade and pushed it farther into me. Without thinking too much, I twisted under the block and jabbed my elbow into her side as I slid behind her, taking a stance at her back while she stumbled, and held my blade to the back of her neck, winning the small combat match.

But before I could take the small step to kick her staff out of the way, making sure I held the victory. Aisha's scratching got harder and suddenly the magic barrier in my brain shattered.

I fell to the ground holding my head as I groaned, the searing pain almost familiar after how many times my mind has been invaded. Aisha retreated from my mind as soon as I dropped, making me gasp and close my eyes tightly.

My magic had retreated into my body completely and Faye held the tip of her staff at my neck, the heat from her green Song gem warming the side of my neck.

"That was almost twenty minutes," Mamarie spoke up from the sidelines. Faye smiled from above me at the new number and reached her hand down to help me up.

"That's great, fifteen minutes longer than last time!" Kasian said sarcastically, a teasing smile on his lips. I rolled my eyes at him and dusted the dirt from my pants as I stood up. The two blue-clad warriors were lounging on the grass, completely relaxed while I panted through the pain of my mind barrier and aching limbs.

"Well, considering the first time you tried you dropped in under fifteen seconds, I'd say that's an improvement," Olen added. My three friends were sitting in the grass by the bench, Aisha standing next to it—well, floated next to it.

"I have to admit though, that sword was pretty badass," Kasian added, moving his hands behind his head as he leaned back.

I laughed a bit at his comment and moved over to them, dropping down to my bum in the grass next to them. I fell onto my back, staring up at the sky, I needed a break to get my mind together before trying again. The lack of sun was not helping me recharge as clouds started to cover the entirety of the sky.

I dropped the crook of my elbow over my eyes to try and ease the burning as I listened to my friends chat around me.

"The next thing we need to do is get Kasian's and my Songs back; Della is going to need all the help she can get when she goes up against Darious. He's already picked the place, which gives us a disadvantage, we won't know the terrain." I heard Mamarie say from just over my shoulder.

"How are we supposed to find ours? Della had to basically drown for Aisha to dig around, I don't really want to try that," Kasian muttered. Just listening to his voice, I could tell his arms were folded across his chest, and had a lazy smirk on his face.

"No, we wouldn't have to. You have both already built a connection between yourselves and your Songs, it would be much easier to find them," Faye said. I moved my arm and opened my eyes, propping myself up a bit on my elbow. Listening closer to the conversation.

"What do you mean?" I asked, looking towards Aisha and Faye. They both glanced at each other, sharing a knowing look before turning back to the group.

"Della isn't a Mind Syron, but Darious is," Aisha started for the two. I still hadn't told them about the moment where I had slid into Darious's mind, I didn't want to bring it up either. Something told me I had to keep it to myself.

"A door can be opened two ways; he created a door between both of your minds when he walked into your dreams. Technically, if you were a Mind Syron, you would be able to go through his," Faye continued, looking between the Kasian, Mamarie and I.

That explained the exchange of powers.

"So, what do we have to do to make that work?" Mamarie asked, her eagerness to return to full power, prominent on her face.

Aisha turned to face the brunette, her fingers wringing together where they were clasped in front of her. "I would have to connect Mamarie and Kasian to Aladella's mind."

"Since the two of them are connected to their Songs and they are Mind Syron, they would be able to use the connection between the two of you to search through his memories for their Songs," Aisha continued, giving Faye a hesitant look.

"The only thing is, as soon as we open that door Darious will know what we are looking for, and you won't have much time before he forces that door closed. If you don't get out of his mind before the door closes, there could be severe damage done to your own minds," Faye explained, knowing the risk they would have to take.

"And even if you do come back out unharmed, he would know exactly where we would be headed, and have an army waiting. We would have to get there faster than him," Faye finished. Her brows furrowed a bit as she looked between the four of us.

"Good thing I'm a great pilot then," Olen said, leaning back against the bench, his knee bent and arms crossed over his chest, a cocky smirk on his lips.

"We'll get it done," Mamarie said, a confident smile on her face. I couldn't help but smile myself, a new sense of determination filling my body.

"Alright, this will be much less complicated than what Della had to go through. Faye and I will set up the kitchen in the homestead. We will have to leave as soon as it is done, so Olen grab your ship and land it in the field, be ready for us to board," Faye instructed, a smile on her face as she fell into her leadership role naturally.

"The rest of you, continue sparring, you will need the practice. Della, see if you can take the two of them at once," Aisha said. My eyes widened a bit and I looked over at my friends. I was just getting confident fighting one person not two.

"We'll go easy on you," Kasian said with a wink as he sat up and bounced up to his feet. "Let's show her what Syron can really do," Kasian continued, reaching a hand down to Mamarie to help her up.

I rolled my eyes at the couple in front of me but got up nonetheless.

"You can try," I said, letting my eyes spark at them as a small smirk took over my features.

CHAPTER TWENTY-FIVE

"So how is this going to work again?" I asked, nervously lacing my fingers together. My nerves getting the best of me. I would be in control of my friends lives while poking at Darious's mind. I know Aisha and Faye reassured me there wouldn't be any mind digging pain, but that didn't help in the slightest. I was still scared something might go wrong.

"All you have to focus on is your bond with Darious, think of the connection he created and Mamarie and Kasian will follow the link into his mind. That's when you start searching through his memories," Faye said, her tone, gentle and calm making me feel a bit better. I knew if Aisha tried to reassure me it would have come off as sarcastic and make me even more nervous, she had a tendency to do that.

"Okay, yep got it." I nodded. I fiddled around with the yellow jumpsuit pockets at my thighs, playing with the piece that held my father's dagger to my side. The weapon kept me grounded, I would need it to remember I was in Darious's mind.

It would remind me that he wasn't in mine.

Mamarie had decided we should all change into clothing fit for battle. A war that would inevitably come as soon as we breeched Darious's mind. We had no reinforcements, no back up. We didn't have time to look even if we could. With Darious's three-day deadline before he started murdering innocents, and the need to find Mamarie and Kasian's Songs, it would be just us. The last five Syron and a mortal bounty hunter against the entire Darion army. Or the number of soldiers that could fit on the planet.

Kasian and Mamarie had dressed up in their blue armour, looking just as intimidating as the first day I had met them, their weapons thrown over their shoulders.

Mamarie had pulled her dark hair into a high ponytail, securing it from her face. What made it a bit scarier was the war paint they wore. They said it made them confident and intimidated their enemies, at least that's what Kasian said. I'm pretty sure Mamarie had just done it to appease Kasian's need to match. They had covered their eyes with a dark paint. The black paint was smeared from one temple to the other, across their eyes and nose. The stain then trailed a bit further down their cheeks where they had dragged their fingers. It made their blue eyes pop and definitely made them look more threatening.

Faye had pulled on her armour from the first war as well, something Aisha had disappeared to find last night. She wore an emerald-green one-shouldered wrap that fell between her legs, slit high on her hips for movement. The garment was woven with a mix of vibrant and dark greens, gold and silver threads lacing through, making it sparkle. Her right leg and top of her right thigh were covered with black compression pants but her left leg had a thigh-high silver-armoured boot, protecting her leg from a past injury, and just looked straight-up badass. Her staff was held tightly in her grip and she had black sleeves that protected her wrist up to her bicep on each arm.

The one thing that I noticed all Syron seemed to have was a cloak that matched their Song colour, where Kasian and

Mamarie both had blue fabric over their shoulders, Faye had an emerald green one tucked under her armour, draped off her left shoulder.

Olen had ditched the Syron cloak and instead sported his red jacket, silver arm shining from under the cut sleeve. He had gotten chest armour from Kasian which was shining from under his jacket, a bright silver colour. Held in his metal hand was his helmet, something that he would never have left without. I knew he had programmed it to learn the planet's terrain as soon as we entered the atmosphere. It would help him navigate whatever planet we ended up on.

I had just opted for my trusty flight suit. I had cut it into two pieces, keeping the amber pants but leaving the jacket half in my room. I needed something a bit more protective. So, on top of one of Olen's white long sleeves, my black corset wrapped around my chest and body. The bulletproof fabric protecting everything important.

Mamarie had helped me alter a few things, mostly to help me move better in battle, allow more flexibility, but also be a bit more protected. She had given me black boots, something a bit better than the broken ones I had used for training. Along with that, she had taught me how to use my magic to make a small protective shield that covered my skin, it would act as armour since I had nothing as advanced as the rest of my team.

"Alright, Kasian, Mamarie, each of you take a side next to Aladella. Grab her shoulder or her arm, skin on skin contact," Faye instructed.

The three of us nodded and my blue-clad friends knelt next to me. Mamarie's hand grabbed mine tightly while the other moved my white sleeve from my shoulder and placed her hand on the bare skin. Kasian took my left side and did the same, pushing the sleeve down a bit and grabbing my shoulder, his palm a bit sweaty from nerves. I was about to make a comment about how swampy his hands were when Faye said it was time to begin.

I took a soft breath as I closed my eyes, holding it for a second as I focused my concentration on the link between Darious and I, then let it out.

I fell back into my mind, searching for the door he had created. I felt my surroundings start to melt away and my eyes roll back into my head. With enough concentration, I blocked out the physical realm and sunk into my subconscious.

A hallway formed in my mind, one of the palace hallways from my home on Prytha. The only oddity was the mis-matching doors. Not a single door matched the one across or besides it. There was a tall white and gold door to my left, stretching all the way to the ceiling. Across it to my right was a smaller door, the height of a toddler and painted a soft baby blue. Father down the hallway there were doors of every shape and size. Some metal, some wood, some even cage-like gates. I guessed they led to different sections of my subconscious.

I felt surrounded by my mind as I fell into my subconscious. I searched for the door that would lead me to Darious's mind, and eventually I felt a mental tug in a certain direction. I decided that was as good a sign as any and followed the feeling until I came up on a door.

It was the same door I had seen when in Darious's mind, the giant set of doors that led into the room he had trapped me in. Dark green almost black, double doors that stretched to the ceiling.

This was it.

I took a second, preparing myself, ready to act fast as soon as I entered his mind.

Taking a small breath, I grabbed the handle and pushed it open.

My breath was pulled from my body as I was thrown into the room, I felt my eyes grow bright as the dizzying feeling filled my body. It was like I was being pulled against a magnet. I couldn't get out of the tractor beam as I was dragged into the room. I knew leaving Darious's mind would not be as easy as it was to get in.

The doors slammed behind me and I saw Kasian and Mamarie appear in the room next to me, their own eyes glowing icy blue colours. Their magic shining from beneath their skin. I had never seen them use their magic, but the icy blue glow from their eyes and the black makeup around them was intimidating. They looked like angels of death. They were just missing the wings.

"We don't have much time, lets go," I said softly.

I noticed the other two doors in the room and decided that's where we would start. I opened the door on the left side of the room, but when I did, it only fell off into darkness.

"Not this way I guess," I mumbled, turning to look where Mamarie and Kasian had opened the other door, this one led into a hallway. The three of us took off down the hallway, checking every door we came across. His mind was set up like my own, a long, dark stone hallway with doors of every shape and colour lining the walls.

"It's a bit farther, I can feel a pull from my Song," Mamarie said. I nodded my head and we followed after her quickly, then finally came up on a bigger brown door. Guessing this was the one, I pushed it open.

The door opened to reveal a huge library, shelves going up to a tall ceiling with books filling up every shelf. The room was shaped like a cylinder, the library having three rings of levels, the only way to get to each was by a ladder. The levels seemed to go off in endless directions off of the main ring in the middle of the room. Millions of memories.

"There are four floors, I'm guessing, because he's four hundred years old?" I asked the two, noticing the ladders that led up to two other platforms.

"Four hundred years worth of memories," Kasian muttered.

"Okay, I'll check the top, it's either four hundred up there or four hundred down here."

Without a second thought, I felt my hands burn up and I shot myself up onto the third level, propelling myself like a rocket.

"Sick," Kasian muttered from the lower level before I heard Mamarie nudge him and they followed the trail to their Songs.

I skimmed my fingers across the books, these ones seemed older, this must have been his first hundred years of life. The bookcases were all a dark stained wood and the book covers ranged from a dark green almost black, to a light sage-green, with a few purple spines scattered here and there.

One, I noticed in particular, was a split spine.

The spine of the book was light green then faded to a dark green before it shifted to purple on the bottom, it was the only one on the shelves like it. I gently pulled the book from the shelf, the cover worn and rough around the edges. The book was a mix of purple and greens across the cover, a thin layer of dust across the top.

I wiped the dust I could from the cover before flipping it in my hands and opening to the centre.

It felt like I was being pulled from my reality straight into the book, a nauseous feeling churning in my stomach making me close my eyes as they watered a bit.

When I opened them again, I was standing in the middle of a battle-worn field. The air was filled with smoke and there were bodies littered across the grass.

Ahead of me was a building, well, the remains of one, it looked like it at been bombed to rubble. The ashes were still hot and pieces were still lit in some places. Somewhere in the trees behind the destroyed home I could hear the grunts and wails of battle, meaning it had probably passed through here not long ago.

"Mum?"

The soft voice from behind startled me but I turned quickly to see who had made the noise.

Knelt on the ground was a slightly younger looking Darious, his hair short, almost buzzed. In nothing but a black long sleeve and black cargo pants, nothing compared to the elaborate getups he presented himself in now.

In his arms lay, who I could only guess was Emila, his mother. Her platinum hair was sprawled out around her, tinted a red colour in the places it was matted with blood. She lay limp in his arms, her breaths coming out quickly as she held her stomach, his hand pressing down on the wound as well.

"Darious, sweetie, I-I need your help. Help me," she gasped out, her hand moving from her stomach to grasp the side of his face. I watched as tears fell down his cheeks, his hands shaking as thoughts rushed through his head, trying to figure out what to do.

"I-I can't, Mum there's ... I can't, you're, I can't feel you," he stuttered out, his eyes glowing a soft green as he tried to reach out to his mother. Her soul and magic fading too fast, her body becoming a shell as she started to disappear.

"Darious, please, save me. Save your mother," she whimpered, her hand falling from his face, leaving a bright red hand print of her blood on his cheek.

I watched closely as the soft green of his magic came from his fingers in small shocks of electricity, buzzing against his mother's skin. His eyes closed as he tried to focus, a heart wrenching scream leaving his lips as he focused all his magic into holding onto his mother's mind.

Even though his eyes were closed I could see a small smile pull at Emila's lips before a dark purple magic appeared from her wound, attacking any static Darious's body gave off and turning it purple. The newly turned purple sparks were absorbed into her body and I watched as the colour started coming back to her face and her wound started to close up.

My eyes widened in panic as I realized what was happening. Emila's hand returned to the side of Darious's face as his power transferred to her.

"More." The command came out in a low growl.

Every bit of electricity Darious sent into Emila's body started turning purple.

Darious's eyes opened immediately and looked down at his mother, whose strength was growing. He had a relieved smile on his face, but it changed quickly when he looked down at his magic, first green as it left his body but then quickly turning purple.

A look of panic crossed his face as he looked back at his mother. "What are you doing?" he asked, voice still low but the panic easily recognizable. It was as if he knew exactly what she was doing.

"What are you doing!?" He asked again, this time pushing his mother off of him as he tried to create some distance. Only when he pushed off his body started to tense up awkwardly, a painful groan leaving his lips as he knelt on the ground.

Emila slowly got up from her spot on the ground, weakly pushing herself up into a standing position. "I need it more than you." She said, her tone dark as she held her hands out to absorb the magic coming off of the younger Darious's body. Only instead of it being given by him, being pushed out of his body, it looked like it was being taken, Emila was pulling the magic straight out of him.

I took a step back as I realized what this meant. The severity of the situation playing out in front of me.

Darious let out an agonizing scream as the small shocks now turned into full-on bolts of electricity, leaving his body and being pulled into Emila's hands. She let out a satisfied groan as she looked down at her son. A large smile pulling across her face, thriving off the pain she was creating.

"I still need you; I can't survive without you," she muttered softly.

Another yell left Darious's mouth as his chest was pulled forwards, Emila taking the last bit of magic she needed before releasing him. He fell to the ground, panting from exhaustion. His vision started to go dark and I felt myself start to slip from the memory.

"Now we just need to find her," I heard Emila mutter, her voice distorted as I was pulled out of the memory.

I felt the same gut wrenching feeling as I was pulled from the memory, dropping the book as I was pulled back into my subconscious reality.

I blinked a few times before looking up, wanting to see which one of my friends had found their memory. The figure in front of me picked up the book I had dropped on the ground. Only as I looked up, it wasn't Kasian or Mamarie closing the book and turning it over in their hands a few times.

"Don't you know not to mettle with things you do not understand, Little Dove?" Darious's voice spoke up.

My eyes widened a bit at the man in front of me. He only smirked and patted the cover of the book a few times before pushing it back into its place on the shelf.

"I expected a retaliation, but never this, Aladella. I never thought you would invade my mind; you aren't a Mind Syron, are you darling?" he said taking a step closer to me. Less than a foot separated our chests.

My breath caught in my throat, still not believing he was standing in front of me.

He knew.

We needed to get out of here.

His comment shook my chest as he mentioned my ability to enter his mind. He knew we were growing; he was gaining my power as I somehow gained his. I had thought going into his mind would be easy because he put the door there. But that wasn't the case at all.

I was as much of a Mind Syron as I was an Elemental Syron. Though my strengths would always be physical, I had the ability to use his power. Just like he would have mine.

The smile fell from his face immediately and a dark look took over his expression, he moved quickly and pushed me back into the book shelf. One arm caging me in beside my head while the other held my bicep.

"If you think for a second you thought you managed to stumble over here without my guidance you are very lost, little dove. *I* am in control here; you are in *my* mind. I can keep you here forever if I'd like, keep your body comatose on that sad planet while I blow it to pieces from the sky," he growled out, his heated breath mingling with my frightened pants in the two inches of space between us.

"I could keep both you and your cerulean blue Syron, your bounty hunter wouldn't know what to do with your corpses," he muttered, his voice low and frustrated. His green eyes staring straight into mine once I looked up. His eyes looked back and forth between my own golden-brown ones, a look of frustration across his features as he tried to figure something out. This was more than an interrogation. He had let me in. There was no way me, as a fledgling Mind Syron, could get into his head that easy. The pulling I had felt, that was him pulling me into his mind. How could I have been so foolish?

"You wouldn't, you know I can get out," I spat back, pulling my arm a bit trying to get it out of his grip while also trying to fight the nervous butterflies that erupted in my stomach as I argued with him.

"You cannot kill her. I know, I've tried," he said, his grip on my arm tightening a bit as he leaned closer to me, keeping me still with his body.

"You don't know what I'm capable of," I shot back.

He paused and looked over my face as he thought about my words for a second. My face felt warm from the heated conversation and the close proximity of our faces.

"Remember everything I've shown you, everything, little dove," he said. I stayed completely still, confused as to what his words meant and why my heart was beating so fast at his close proximity. His eyes trailed across my face making me harden my features, trying not to look as startled as I felt. His eyes glanced down for a second and then met my eyes again.

"Remember everything I have shown you; it will be crucial." Without a second of hesitation, his head dipped down and I felt his lips capture my own. I was frozen in shock for a second, trying to ignore the electric buzz I felt when his lips touched mine.

Before I realized what had happened and pushed him away, he pulled back on his own and had disappeared completely. Leaving me with the aching feeling of wanting more.

I heard a faint, "We've got it!" from the bottom floor before my eyes started to close, my body dropped to the floor, eyes closing on the way down, yet I never felt my body hit the ground.

I opened my eyes with a gasp, feeling Kasian and Mamarie's hands leave my shoulders as I hunched over, gasping for breath.

"We've got it, we know where they are," I heard Kasian mumble, gasping for breath just like I was.

"Alright let's go, grab what you need, wings up in five." I heard Olen's voice; a bit muffled from next to me.

I felt like I was stuck in his mind, my vision blurry and my thoughts feeling a light year away. "Della, hey, you okay?" I heard from in front of me. It knocked me back to my senses a bit, the world around me growing a bit clearer. I looked up, meeting Olen's blue eyes right away.

Immediately, I felt guilt rush through my veins and squeezing at my stomach. I know I shouldn't since it was in Darious's mind and he kissed me, but for some reason I did.

I forced a small smile and nodded my head softly.

"Yeah, yeah, I'm fine. I'll meet you on the ship," I said softly, reassuring him gently. He nodded his head, a small smile on his face. He leaned down and pressed a small kiss to my forehead before heading off out of the room, probably to ready the ship.

As soon as he left, the small nagging feeling of guilt clouded my mind and forced me back into my thoughts. Why did Darious do that? What did he mean when he said to remember everything he's said? What kind of backwards game was he playing? Was it psychological? He was showing me the darkest moments of his life to make me sympathize with him, make me forget he murdered my mother?

Shaking my head to rid myself of the worries, I got up from the floor and headed for the ship. Not bothering to grab any of my belongings, I stepped onto Olen's ship empty handed.

I would either come back to get them or die on the battle field. Everything and everyone I needed was already with me.

CHAPTER TWENTY-SIX

"So, tell me again what you saw, I need to get the layout perfect so we can devise an accurate plan," I muttered softly to Mamarie who stood next to me. We were standing around Olen's holomap, trying to create the terrain from Darious's memory so we could figure our way around it.

The rest of our small group was in the cockpit, trying to ascertain how to get to Balcan, the barren planet Darious had hidden the Syron's Songs on. Olen had said it would be a day or two's journey since it was on the other side of the belt. We would have to pass through the centre of the galaxy, the hub, to get there fast enough. He had said we would land on those inner planets to refuel and refill our supplies before continuing. The group had hoped the base would be closer, but, as our luck would have it the Songs were across the galaxy.

I pushed the memory of the conversation aside and looked back at the blue terrain in front of me. From what Mamarie was explaining, she had seen a base built into the side of a mountain. As I built up the dimensions of what she told me I couldn't help but think there was something missing from her story. Not so much that she wasn't telling me something, but as if Darious had intentionally left something out of the memory. Every time I looked over the map something felt out of place, like there was a gaping hole in our information. Something was missing, I just couldn't figure out what.

I sighed running over the layout one more time, running a hand through my now loose hair in frustration. "Go over it one more time, there's something missing," I mumbled softly. I rested my body weight against the table, looking over the holomap as Mamarie sighed next to me.

"I already told you three times, Della," Mamarie mumbled, I nodded my head, knowing I had but needed to hear it one more time.

"The memory starts with him walking off of a transport, a ship, though I couldn't really tell since I was seeing the memory through his eyes," she said closing her eyes to remember it better. "When he looked around, we could see three huge mountains on either side of him, the base entrance was in the small valley in the middle. There are three entrances at the top of the mountains, one going into each peak. He goes into the east facing entrance. When we walked in, there were guards stationed at every doorway. He took the third door to the left. Once he walks in, we see the Songs, there are five stolen ones, and an empty slot for a sixth. Mine and Kasian's are floating in their own glass boxes in the back," she explains.

"Then he takes a green one from his pocket, putting it in the sixth container, then walks out. After that his eyes are on his boots the entire time," she said.

My brows furrow at that last bit of information. He places a green gem in the circle. When Mamarie explained it, she said there were two blue ones, hers and Kasian's, a red, a purple and a black.

The black one intrigued me since I hadn't even heard of someone having black magic before. Faye and Aisha said Syron magic usually came in blue, red, purple, or green, the core magic colours. They had been surprised at the mention of a black gem, saying it was almost as strange as my gold magic.

As I thought about him putting the green gem in the Song stone room, I couldn't help but think it might be his. It wouldn't make a lot of sense since he would be more powerful with it on him. But, something in my gut told me it was his, mostly because the memory he had shown me, about his mother. He would be keeping his true strength far away.

I glance up at Mamarie and nod my head a bit. I shook the thoughts of Darious's Song out of my head before focusing on the task at hand, as I looked over the mountain range one thing stuck out. There was no way you could land a ship there. Not at all.

The valley was incredibly you small and the jagged rocked edges of the mountain were a death trap if someone tried to take off from the valley, the rockets would echo up the peaks and start a rock slide.

"There is no way they are landing a ship in that valley, a ship big enough to hold an army wouldn't fit, and even a small ship would cause the peaks to crumble when it took off," I said, hearing the door to the cockpit slide open as the rest of the group joined us at the table.

"If Darious is meeting us with an army, they will already be inside the mountain. As soon as we landed in that valley, they would surround us completely from the three entrances. They know they can't drop troops there because when the ship would leave it would cause a vibration to echo up the mountain and send the loose boulders from the top down, possibly killing soldiers and blocking their entrances," I explained. Using my hands to point out what I was explaining on the holomap.

"Darious let us see that memory, he wanted us to believe this was the only way in, sending us straight to our deaths," Mamarie said, agreeing with my statement. Her eyes met mine and we shared a small nod. We needed to find another way into the mountain.

"Darious wanted to lead us into a trap? C'mon, he can't think were that stupid," Kasian said, rolling his eyes a bit as if offended by the dark prince's attempt at tricking us.

"I don't think he was trying to fool us, or send us into a trap. I think he was just trying to buy time," I said, glancing over the group.

"That would make sense. He would be buying time to fill his mountain with soldiers while we were looking for an entrance," Faye added, her arms folded over her chest as she thought over the plan we would have to create in the next few days. Sooner rather than later.

Olen looked over the group, rubbing the sides of his arms a bit. His fingers making a soft tapping sound on the outside of his metal arm. I wonder if he could feel it.

"We use his trap to our advantage then," Olen said, looking up at the group around him. His eyes remained a cool tone as he unfolded his arms and held the edge of the table, leaning forwards. "We know what he's doing, we have an edge. We should use it." A slight smirk playing at his features. I could almost feel the cockiness growing on him as he uttered another sentence.

"The dark prince won't know what hit him."

* * *

It had taken a few minutes to get a plan together, a lot of mumbling and our heads down in the map as we devised the best course of action. Olen and I would be on the ship, dropping it down into the centre of the valley. A perfect and big distraction pulling all eyes towards us. I would walk down the ramp gaining Darious's attention and hopefully he would come out expecting a surrender.

While we held their attention, Aisha would take Kasian and Mamarie into the mountain, to search for their Songs and grab them before anyone noticed. All the while Faye would find the other entrance and start breaking down the door, causing a panic within the mountain. That panic would be our signal and we would take off, my pilot taking off fast enough that the rock-slide would miss us and trap their soldiers in the dust.

A good plan—if it worked.

And it would work.

I looked around the table to the group around me, all with their brows furrowed in concentration or worry. Though the more I looked at them, the more the memory I had found in Darious's head kept coming forward. If what I had seen was true, and not another mind game, the plan might not work at all. It might send us to our deaths. That one small piece of information could mean the difference between life and death.

For some reason a small part of me wanted to keep it to myself.

Some small, dark piece of me wanted to keep it locked away. I could feel it eating away at a corner of my heart.

It had started with the dream of my mother. I had pushed it aside as fear, but once it came true, I knew it was something more than that. Then those three dark days I had spent alone on the island I had only let it fester. Fear, sadness and hate. A longing to kill the dark prince that had taken my mother.

That small, dark fleck only seemed to grow every time he entered my mind. I had taken out some of my anger on him in his mind palace, burning him to a crisp. But there was still sticky darkness clinging to my heart. Every time I thought about him, about that memory, him loosing his mother. Only he didn't, he had resurrected her, then killed mine. Mine would not come back.

Then the audacity he had to kiss me.

That small dark part seemed to hum when I thought of the kiss, I guess that dark ruthless part of me liked how brutal he seemed to be. But my bloodlust weighed more. He would die before that piece took over.

I shook my head a bit from the thoughts and looked over the room, my friends, my family, pouring a light over the darkness in my heart. I knew it would eventually go away; they would help with that. But if I ever lost them, that darkness would take over.

"There's something else. I should have said it sooner but I've been trying to figure out if it had been real or not," I said, my voice strained as I looked over the group. I ran my hand through my hair, tugging on the loose knots as they turned their attention to me. "In Darious's mind I pulled on a memory, saw something that I'm not sure I should have or not."

The group around me stilled, their postures straightening a bit as they leaned closer, hooked onto my every word.

"I saw Emila. The day of the last battle," I started, cringing a bit as the next sentence left my lips. "I'm pretty sure she is alive." The entire room stilled for a second, as if they all were holding their breaths, waiting for me to say it was a joke.

"Impossible," Faye said, her eyes wide as her arms dropped to her sides. "Its impossible. She cannot live, be immortal without her Song. It's what extends our lives," the raven-haired Trilomarnian said. I could almost see her replaying that final blow in her mind, her scepter piercing through her gem and then her chest.

"From what I saw, it looked like she was ... feeding from Darious's magic," I explained, not able to find a better word for the pulling of his powers. It had started with him sharing magic to give her strength, then that gratefulness turned to greed and she took everything from him.

Good, bastard deserved it.

"If it was a real memory, and not the mind games Darious enjoys playing, this is a threat we need to talk about now," Mamarie said, her arms folding across her chest defensively as she hardened her look at the group. If I hadn't been looking closely, I would have missed the way she shifted her weight back and forth, a nervous tic.

"We can't focus on that right now. What's important is getting those Songs so we have at least a chance to win this war. Once we get them, we can talk about the possibility of Emila being alive," Aisha said, her tone strained as if she didn't even want to believe the Temptress could be alive. I guess this was something they never expected to hear, Aisha had died during the first war. She never told me the story but based on her reaction, she might have been up against Emila herself.

Realizing your murderer, who you thought dead, has actually been alive for almost three hundred years must have been a shock.

"Aisha is right. Were useless against Darious if we don't have our Songs, Millie. Useless against Emila if we don't have magic," Kasian said, his voice soft as he soothed his partner. I noticed their hands lace together between them, Kasian's thumb brushing across Mamarie's hand.

I couldn't help but look away, my gaze shifting straight to Olen.

His eyes were already on me when I had looked up, trailing over my features. His expression seemed worn and tired and I couldn't help but send him a weak smile, an effort to reassure him.

I was sure it didn't help at all, but he sent me a small smile nonetheless, probably hoping it would have the same soothing effect on me.

It didn't.

CHAPTER TWENTY-SEVEN

"You thought you could spend the entirety of a four-hour space travel avoiding me?" Olen's voice had roused me from my thoughts as he stood in the doorway. Arms folded across his chest and small smirk on his lips.

I smiled a bit and looked back at the small shapes I was making with the magic between my fingers. The tiny flame leapt across my fingers, diving under them and licking at my palm as I moved it around. A trail of gold glitter left in its wake.

"Strange how such a deadly gift can leave such a beautiful trail," he said softly as he nodded down at my hands. Noticing how I had been staring at it.

"Sometimes I wonder if it's a gift at all. Seems like it has caused me a lot of trouble," I said softly, leaning my head back on the wall behind me.

I had moved into Olen's room a little after our plan was solid and we were sent hurtling through space in the direction of Polis, the inner galactical planet we would stop at on our way to Balcan.

I couldn't stop thinking about what could have been if not for this magic. Me and my mother would be safe in our home, coming to an agreement with the Darion. Their shadow would have been cast over our world, but we would have still been together.

The one thing I didn't understand was how I had not been plagued with nightmares since Darious had invaded my mind. I remember having trouble sleeping, waking up in a cold sweat, screaming.

I knew Olen had helped a bit when he slept next to me, calming my nerves. But now I wondered if it was because of the steady sound of his heart beat the lulled me to sleep. Or if I was becoming numb to her death as the stress of Darious clouded my thoughts.

"Hey well you wouldn't have met the lot of us if you didn't have them," Olen said softly. Sliding down the wall to sit next to me, he pulled my hand into his, holding it loosely.

"We're going to get through this. Three hundred years and they haven't seen anything like us." He tilted his head to the side a bit, his brown curls falling across his forehead as he looked at me. His smile was only a slight tug at the corner of his lips, nothing like the genuine ones I had gotten on our island. I think that's why I felt my stomach drop a bit, a weight in the bottom of my stomach.

After today everything would change, if we won or lost.

"I hope two pirates, a master Syron, a ghost, a misfit and a princess are enough," I said, bumping his shoulder a bit as I tilted my own head up to meet his eyes. A small sigh left his lips and he rolled his neck a bit at my words.

We fell into a comfortable silence soon after, both falling onto our thoughts as we dreaded the upcoming battle. This is what we had been preparing for, I would avenge my mother, my sister, my father and fight for the freedom of the universe. No more hiding, not more fear, silence, or darkness.

Freedom.

The universe hadn't seen it in over five hundred years. I knew Prytha had it easy considering we were on the outskirts of the galaxy; it took almost four hundred years for them to even reach our planet. But the inner worlds had been torn to shreds, had seen Emila herself, her brutal violet power.

I had been lucky when considering what had happened in the galaxy's centre, and I wouldn't take that for granted. I grew up comfortably, I was fighting for my mother, for my father, for my sister and Gallio. The family the Darion had taken from me. But I would see the destruction Emila caused when we landed on Polis.

I knew Olen would be fighting for different reasons, freedom of his trade maybe. He had never gone into detail about his upbringing with me before, we just went off of who we were in the moment we met, nothing was expected.

Mamarie and Kasian were fighting for their cause, for their lost Syron soldiers that had fallen throughout the years. Fighting for a freedom they deserved, to be who they are. Their internal need to protect everyone taking over any fear or doubt they might have had.

"Tell me about when you were little," I said softly to Olen. I closed my eyes as I rested my head back on the wall, wanting to listen to something good. Something other than war plans.

I heard him stifle a small chuckle before I heard him move his head a bit, I guessed he was nodding.

"The dirt and grime of my childhood, or my hero stories?" he asked, his tone ever cocky and teasing. I couldn't help the genuine smile that pulled at my features. "All of it," I said. I wanted to take our minds off of the darkness and silence we would soon encounter.

"Well, my parents left me on Tarkan as a child. I was picked up by a couple, two very amazing women. My mums. They raised me on Tarkan, save for when we went off-planet on their raid trips. They were bounty hunters, or pirates ... I never really knew which. They raised me well, Maya and Lady. They taught me how to fly, too. They never told me how I had ended up theirs, but I'm sure it was one hell of a story. I grew up on the backstreets of a rust water planet. Learning to pick pockets when I was five, hot wire a speeder when I was eight, pilot a hover at ten and a ship at fourteen. I guess I learnt all my skills there.

"I ended up joining this rogue group, me my two friends Dee and Jo, and Dee's twin brother Edwyn, we called him Eddy though. We used to go on these stupid 'missions' ... Jo would plan them out. She would find some sketchy job and get some low life to pay too much for us to get it done. That's how we made a living. Surprisingly, we went on some crazy adventures," he said.

When I tilted my head a bit to look up at him, he had a soft smile on his face, his eyes closed and head tilted back against the wall like I had. I could tell all of his adventures were replaying behind his eye lids.

"What happened to them?" I asked. I was hesitant to wonder, not wanting to ruin his small smile with sad memories, if they were that.

He slowly opened his eyes and glanced over at me, his small smile turning into a smirk. "Dee got caught, house arrest for the next twenty years. Pretty shitty if you ask me, she's stuck on her property she shares with Eddy and Jo. Those two ended up getting together, had a kid last year, settled. They're out of the city centre so don't find that much trouble. But they're happy."

I wondered what his life would have turned out like had I not run into him at the market. Would he be settled on Tarkan with his friends, getting a simple job to keep a small house, maybe meet someone and have his own kids. Had I not pulled him into this giant mess maybe he would have found that happiness.

"Stars know what would have happened if I had stayed on that planet. But maybe the universe had this weird twisted plan for me and it was fated I ran into you; I had your Song. We're meant to be in this fight, Della," he said. I could hear the small smile pulling at his lips.

I drop my eyes back to the hand he held loosely in my own, nodding my head. My hair fell around my face as I brought his hand into my lap, playing with his fingers a bit as we fell back into a comfortable silence. Somewhere off into the distance I could hear Mamarie's laugh as Kasian no doubt was saying something stupid to make her blush. Getting her mind off of what we would face, much like Olen and I were doing ourselves.

"Did I ever tell you about my family?" I asked softly.

"Only a little," he said gently, not pushing me for an answer.

"Well, you saw my mother briefly, but she was a fierce woman. She was the one you didn't want to cross when I was younger. She would always be reminding us of what princess were expected to do, how we were expected to act. But she was also the one who made sure we knew how to fight, how to shoot. My father was the kind one, always laughing. He loved throwing these parties where the whole city was invited and he would just joke around and laugh with the entire room until well past midnight. He would pull me and my sister out of our rooms and we would run barefoot to the cliffs to watch the sun come up. It was something special we did as a family.

"My sister, she was two years older than me. She was sixteen when her and my dad went to Diarna. She was everything to me. My best friend honestly," I said sadly. I gently held the necklace around my neck, holding it tightly in my free hand.

"Wherever she is now, I bet she's smiling, proud of the woman you've become." I couldn't help it as my eyes started to burn, my lip wobbling a bit. Olen let go of my hand, putting it around my shoulders and pulling me into his side, his other hand moving to cup my hands.

"We'll get through this, Princess."

I nod my head softly and let the few tears slide down my face.

And I knew somehow, someway, we would make it work.

I felt Olen's lips briefly brush across my forehead before he nuzzled his nose into my hair. His hand moved up my shoulder and he ran his thumb up the side of my neck. I closed my eyes, squeezing them shut as I tried to stop the few tears that squeezed out.

We were going to get through all this pain.

CHAPTER TWENTY-EIGHT

The smooth rock of the ship lulled me from my sleep, a distant alarm sounded. I heard Olen groan as he rolled from his place next to me to silence the alarm. The warmth of his body left my hold and I whined a bit, still under sleep's thick magic as I reached out for his body.

I heard a mumbled laugh fall from his lips, deep from just waking up as he slid back under the covers. His arms wrapped over my shoulders and around my waist, the warmth of his bare arms encasing my body and pulling me back to his chest.

I wrapped my arm around his waist and shifted my body so I was partly over his chest, nuzzling my nose in the crook of his neck as warmth encircled us again.

"We're only a few hours from Polis, Della. You're going to have to get up eventually," he said, his breath warming my ear and shoulder. He dipped his head and pressed his lips to the exposed skin of my shoulder, peppering warm kisses across my skin.

I only groaned softly, tilting my head so he could trail his lips across more of my skin. "Five more minutes," I mumbled softly, wrapping my arms around him tighter. His chuckle warmed my shoulder and his arms tightened around me. Holding me close for another five minutes.

I wished they would have lasted longer, but Olen finally dragged the both of us from the bed after seven minutes, hauling me into the bathroom and leaving me with the shower. Telling me to dress comfortably and in dark colours. That meant no amber jumpsuit.

He returned when I was dressing, giving me a soft kiss on the forehead before hiding away in the bathroom, the shower starting a few minutes later. I had half a mind to join him but shook the thoughts away and dressed, moving to the cargo bay where I would find what little food we had left on the ship.

I was sitting on the steps to the cockpit with a bag of dried fruit and water when Olen walked into the cargo bay. The others had set up in the med bay, taking the few cots and turning them into makeshift beds.

I almost dropped the small bag I was holding. His hair was dripping, he shook it out with a towel before tossing it back into the room. His black combat pants hung loose on his hips, his boots still not laced up entirely. But what took the breath from my lungs was his bare chest, a few drops of water still slid down his tan skin and his shirt was thrown limp over one shoulder.

He noticed my stare and sent me a wink before moving to the med bay, opening the door to wake up our companions. He turned back to me with a big smile on his face. I had to avert my eyes, knowing my cheeks were burning from being caught staring.

"Like what you see?" He teased, leaning down to press a kiss to my forehead. His fingers running across my throat as he continued past me and into the cockpit. My heart was beating so wildly I thought it was about to break out of my chest. I couldn't help the small glare that pulled at my features as I turned to look at the man. He was already smirking, knowing the effect he held over me.

"Shut up," I grumbled and stood, moving to sit in the passenger seat. His smirk only grew when he tossed the shirt into the pilot's seat and stalked over to me, a swagger in his step as he stopped in front of me. He leaned forward, bracing his hands on the arm rests of the chair as he dipped his head down to me level with mine. Water dripped from his curls and onto my lap, but I paid them no mind as I was transfixed by his dark, swirling blue eyes.

His hand moved slowly from the arm rest, his fingers trailing across the bare skin of my arm. My black tank leaving most of my tan skin exposed. With his eyes still locked on mine his warm hand moved to cover my chest, right over my heart. His hand was big enough to stretch over half of my chest, pressing into my skin.

His eyes grew a little darker when he smirked down at me. "I knew I made you weak, Princess. But your heart is trembling," he teased with a grin. I couldn't help the soft gasp that left my lips, his thumb running over the soft skin of my chest a bit.

I kept my eyes locked on his for a second longer and then my lips were on his, my hand sneaking behind his neck and into his hair as I pulled him closer. A soft groan left his lips and he dipped closer to me, taking control of the kiss.

"You know you do have a room. Don't need to fill the rest of the bloody ship with your cooties," Kasian's voice grumbled from the doorway.

Olen pulled back, pressing a small kiss on my cheek before standing straight and glaring at Kasian. "I think you forget this is my ship. And as the captain and only pilot, I can do as I please," he said to the blonde in the doorway.

Kasian stood with his arms crossed, leaning against the doorframe with a wide grin on his lips. Olen only grumbled at his friend before grabbing his black t-shirt and pulling it over his head, wet curls flopping across his forehead.

"We land in twenty. Make sure everyone is in dark clothes. We'll need to cover our heads as well," Olen said to the two of us. He moved back to the pilot seat, dropping us from hyperspace just outside a planet.

Polis.

There wasn't a sliver of green on the entire planet. It was entirely black, black with dots of light spread across entire continents. If there were oceans, they were either concealed by darkness since we had dropped on the dark side, or they were entirely gone. Polis was our founding planet, every bit of our history originated from Polis. It was said to be where the Syron originally emerged. It made me wonder if Faye's story about the first two Syron had any links to the planet as well.

I took one last long glance at the artificially lit up world before leaving Olen in the cockpit. I would need to cover my face, our identities needed to remain hidden. Darious couldn't know where we were.

* * *

I kept adjusting the black fabric that hid my face, the cloak billowing behind me. Mamarie stalked next to me, her own hood pulled down over her features.

The planet was nothing compared to Prytha, but that was because Emila's destruction had torn a deep wound into the solar system. Every single building in the city was a deep obsidian colour, dark enough to be hidden under the blanket of night. I had guessed the buildings had once stood proud and beautiful with their marvellous dark colour. But now the rubble just reminded the people of their past.

The sky remained a hazy grey, clouds and smoke covering the atmosphere and sinking low enough to swallow the tops of the few buildings that still reached the skyline. The cobblestone streets, which had been formed from five hundred years of walking on rubble, were filled with nothing but filth. There were small animals scurrying down every alley, people hidden in the shadows, covered with deep hoods, and locked doors at every corner.

The Darion's symbol still had a strong hold on the planet. Their massive freighters hovering just in the atmosphere, the triangle and panther painted to the bellies of the ships as they loomed in the cloud cover.

Kasian and Olen had stayed at the docking station, refuelling the ship and getting a few parts to ensure our safety on our journey to Balcan. Aisha and Faye had decided to stay inside the ship, fearing someone might notice their recognizable facial markings. That left me and Mamarie. We both had exchanged grins when we said we would hunt for supplies, wanting to go on an adventure ourselves.

We took another turn and finally came up on the market. The stands were the same obsidian colour as the buildings only each one had their own colourful lighting to display their goods. There were signs above the stands, illuminating the name of the vendor. Along with strips of light stuck to the undersides of the tables to brighten up the streets. Instead of the dull and dreary allies we had been slinking around, this market street was teaming with life.

Mamarie and I scoped out every single table. Pulling at some foods, filling our bag with snacks and drinks we would need for the next few days of our journey. We even passed by the weapon tables, grinning at each other like fools from the shadows of our hoods but knew the only weapons we would need were our Songs.

We were making our way back when a hush fell over the entire street.

I glanced at Mamarie, reaching to grab her hand as I pulled her closer. She gripped mine just as tightly and we slipped into the shadows of a doorway. From down the street shouts could be heard, along with an uncomfortable buzz of silence that echoed across the market.

Darion soldiers.

"We need to go," I said to Mamarie, squeezing her hand a little tighter.

"We can't move, if we run now, they'll only chase us. We need to blend in," she muttered to me, pulling me closer into the doorway. I only nodded and wrapped the cloak around my body, hoping to hide anything that might give me away. I watched intently as the soldiers slowed to a stop a few tables away from where I and Mamarie stood. The vendors and shoppers alike all cowered from the three soldiers. Their presence striking fear into their hearts and causing an uncomfortable, unsettling feeling to fall over the market. They poked and picked at a few things around the tables before flipping over the entire stand. The vendor let out a yell as their belongings toppled onto the floor. Weapons made of glass, decorative pieces, all toppled off of the white cloth, shattering as they hit the ground. The blue link of the owner's shop lit up their expression, showing the shock and despair they were feeling.

I felt my magic lick at my fingers as anger flooded my veins. What gave them the right? Four more soldiers pulled up on speeders next to the three who had already been waiting and approached the vendor. They said nothing as they took synced steps towards the individual. The vendor cowered in fear and backed up into the stall.

I felt the magic rush through my veins as I realized the vendor was about to be executed.

I could not let that happen.

I slipped my hand from Mamarie's and we gave each other knowing looks. Olen would have the ship fuelled and repaired by now. We could deal with the seven soldiers and then run to the ship to take off. Easy mission.

Mamarie and I moved in sync, our steps racing silently across the cobblestone street. I heard a gasp from one of the patrons as I reached the first soldier. I jumped up, keeping my magic at bay as I kneed him in the spine, sending the soldier toppling face first into the dirt as I rushed the next. Mamarie had stolen the sword from another and was falling into a duel with another. I grabbed the soldier's fist as he tried to punch me, swinging him down and flipping him into the one who had gotten up behind me, unsheathing his blade in the process.

Three of the soldiers had flocked to me while four had their sights on Mamarie, I couldn't let that happen. The three closest to me unsheathed their blades in sync and ran at me from every angle. I brought up my sword and let my magic finally unfold. My hood was still covering my head, hiding my identity. But if one of these soldiers survived and reported to Darious, he would recognize my magic anywhere.

Magic spilt from my fingers and my golden blade formed from the swirling amber twists. I heard a gasp from the crowd and I took on the soldiers again. My blades countering their attacks as I took the brunt of the fight. I had sliced one down, forcing the fourth that was battling Mamarie to turn their attention on me, leaving us three and three.

My golden blade struck another, forcing him to fall as I ducked around the final two's blades. Mamarie cut her own down, leaving two for herself when a third opponent entered the ring.

Three figures dropped from the roofs of the Obsidian buildings, carrying blades of their own and struck into the soldiers. Killing three and leaving one single soldier left. The last one stood in front of me. The three hooded figures took a step closer and I let my magic fade from my hand.

I took the last soldier out easily enough with his own blade, before dropping the bloody weapon to the ground. When I looked back up the three had removed their hoods.

Before Mamarie and I stood two men and a woman. The two men looked to be twins, both sporting dark hair and tanned skin, the only differences being one had long hair and the other's was cut short to their head. That and they had opposing red irises. Where one eye was a deep chocolate brown, the other simmered with a red rage. They were clad in all black clothing, much like Mamarie and I. The way they stood suggested royalty, though I knew this planet hadn't seen anything like royalty in the last three centuries.

The woman stood between them was tall, maybe even taller than Mamarie. Her hair was a deep red, twisted in knots and locks. Her deep tanned skin marked with pink scars, the biggest being one from the edge of her right eye to the edge of her nose. The trio looked terrifying.

Mamarie and I stilled, unsure weather we were facing friend or foe. It was only when the girl in the middle smiled, that the tension eased from our shoulders. It was genuine.

The two men at her sides dropped the serious exteriors and began chuckling as well, the sound deep in their chests.

"And here I thought you were all but extinct, Syron," the man on the left chuckled. Mamarie and I froze.

"No need to taunt our new friends Ajax, they have much to learn," the woman in the middle said.

"My name is Embry; this is Ajax and Lazarus. We are a part of the resistance. It would be lovely if we could sit and have a chat. That is if you have nowhere you need to be," the woman said, a genuine smile on her face. If anything, she looked excited to see us.

I glanced at Mamarie and could practically feel the curiosity coming off her in waves. We had only heard whispers of the resistance. But to see it right in front of us, to see them right in front of us, it made hope swell in my chest and a new determination form. There were people fighting for the same things we were. Revenge, freedom, love.

"I'm sure we can spare a few minutes," I said softly, a smirk forming on my lips.

Darious wouldn't know what hit him.

Mamarie and I had talked to the three rebels for a lot longer than we thought we would have. So long that Olen had sent Kasian into the market to find us, knowing he and Mamarie had a link he found us immediately. Sitting at a table with the red-eyes twins and their assassin friend.

Embry was an assassin. Or she used to be. She used to work for a woman she would not name. An Aranese under Darious. Embry would be sent on mission to disassemble rebel groups and bring back their heads. Her story wound up getting complicated when she was sent to kill her two friends Ajax and Lazarus and they had outsmarted her, keeping her captive until she eventual broke from Darious's Aranese leader's hold and started fighting with the resistance.

Her story made me smile, realizing many more people were sick and tired of the Darion's mindless soldier's control and wanted out. Wanted him gone. I knew hate for the dark prince ran deep, but his reign had been around for so long it had become normal for anyone born within the last two centuries. It was all we mortals knew. The fight had worn out a long time ago. But to see such young people fighting for a stronger relationships within the galaxy made my heart swell.

Mamarie and Kasian had been around for ages, but they had been only a few years older than me when they started fighting the Darion. I had a lot to learn from them.

We had talked for as long as we could. Kasian just as interested as me and Mamarie were. Though we had to continue our journey to retrieve their Songs so we could end this war once and for all.

The twins had volunteered saying if we ever needed their help all we needed to do was ask and they would be there in the speed of light. Their dedication was true and their story filled with hardships. I knew that if we called, they would answer in a heartbeat.

Though after no more than an hour of talking, we had departed, leaving our new friends on Polis and heading back to Olen's ship.

"If I had a red eye, would you look at me the way you were looking at those twins?" Kasian asked Mamarie as we walked back to the ship.

"I wasn't staring at them like that because they had red eyes Kacey." Mamarie mumbled back, a blush spreading across her cheeks when she realized she had been caught.

"Then why were you looking, sweetheart?" Kasian asked, a teasing smirk on his lips as if he knew the answer. Mamarie's glare hardened as she looked at him, the nickname striking a nerve. Her face grew an even deeper shade of red as she stormed off ahead of her friend and her lover.

I glanced over at Kasian with a raised brow, wondering what Mamarie's deal was. "She has a thing for twins," Kasian said with a small chuckle. My eyes widened and I stared ahead at my friend who was retreating into the ship.

"Oh," was all I managed to get out. Kasian cackled at my answer and followed his lover into the ship.

Olen stood at the base with his arms crossed over his chest. "Do I even want to ask?" he said, glancing up at the retreating couple.

"Nope, no, I don't think you do," I said with a small laugh as we both walked back up the ramp, ready to continue our journey to Balcan. Where we would face the Darion in hopes of retrieving Kasian and Mamarie's stolen Songs.

Then we would have a shot at levelling the playing field.

CHAPTER TWENTY-NINE

"We're entering the atmosphere in three ... two ... one." Olen's voice faded to the back of my mind as my eyes drifted over the planet we had just sped into.

Red.

The planet was red.

The mountain range rose up on the horizon, tall, jagged orange peaks shooting up in every direction. Looking more like towers than the mountains I was familiar with on Prytha. It looked like a bone yard. Some peaks were tilted, shaped to curve inwards, others were jagged and stretched straight up into the sky. The base of the mountain was huge, made up of the rubble of the broken peaks. The tips poking out of the rubble like knives.

It looked like a rib cage, and we were about to land right in the middle of it.

The area surrounding the towering peaks was bone-dry, red desert. No trees, no buildings, just cracked dirt. The occasional thin dry, grass poking from the cracks in the earth.

The three tall peaks we were heading towards surrounded the ribcage of peaks. I could see a glint of metal as we approached, doors on the sides of the mountains. They were at the bottom, hidden behind rubble and jagged mountains, but still reflecting in the heat.

"There, that's where you will have to enter," I said to Aisha, directing her gaze away from the bone-like peaks and to the small glint of a door at the bottom of the mountain. She only nodded her head, a look of slight terror flashing across her eyes before it disappeared. She quickly looked away from the window, glancing at me for a second, a silent understanding between the two of us.

Thank you for everything, stars help you through today.

I nodded my head once, giving her a weak smile. She then turned to Kasian and Mamarie, the slight tilt of her head letting them know it was time.

"This should be fun," Kasian said with a wink. The two of them put their hands on each of Aisha's shoulders. Mamarie rolled her eyes at her partner's comment.

"Yea, it'll be fun dragging you back to the ship when you get a boo boo," Mamarie mumbled, sending a teasing smirk to Kasian. The two only smiled, looking back towards Olen, Faye, and I. Their eyes started to glow a bright blue, their true powers shining through, Aisha's eyes turned a bright white and then they were suddenly gone. A slight dust of blue and white the only trace they were ever even there.

I turned back to my two partners.

"I wonder if Kasian would try tricking a silent soldier to speak?" Olen wondered out loud as we approached the peak of the mountains, lowering down into the cage of peaks.

"He probably has. I wouldn't put it past him if he tried asking a question to see if they answered," I said with a huff of a laugh.

"That kid's stupidity sometimes makes it hard to believe he's a Syron," Faye mumbled beside us. I couldn't help the small chuckle of laughter that left my lips at her joking comment.

The ship slowly touched the ground, stones falling from the peaks and hitting the top of the ship as the rockets shook the earth. There were a few more trickles, almost sounding like rain on a tin roof. The three of us held our breaths, waiting for a peak to come crashing down and through the hull of the ship. But it didn't, we had landed successfully.

We all stayed still, silent for a second, an unspoken agreement that we would spend that extra second together before the battle begun. Honestly, I wished that second could have lasted for an eternity. A moment later, Aisha appeared next to Faye, offering Olen and I a grim smile before she vanished with the other Syron. Before I knew it, I was walking down the ramp of the ship, meeting the Darion soldiers as they rushed from the three entrances to the mountains, surrounding the ship completely.

"What a surprise." Darion's voice drifted across the valley, deep and smooth, as if trying to calm a wild animal. I turned in his direction, almost wanting to roll my eyes at how he held himself.

He was wearing something different from what he did when I saw him in my dreams. He was in all black of course, but instead of the nice coat he had sported when he was in my home. He wore battle gear. All black, of course. Dark pants hung on his hips with his dark blade attached to his side, another smaller blade on the other side. His torso was covered with a black chest plate that almost fit him too perfectly, it looked nothing like Kasian's metal armour but instead resembled a simple thick shirt, though I knew it had to be threaded with something stronger.

One arm adorned a sleeve while the other was bare, showing of the array of dark tattoo's littered across his muscular skin. The part that drew my attention to the marking in his skin the most was the tangle of dark-purple ink that was etched around his arm. It didn't fit, didn't match the look he was effortlessly pulling off.

I was seething at the fact he felt he could stand there, protected and arrogant. His arms lazily at his sides and a small smirk on his features.

"Lovely to see you again, little dove. You look ... stunning," he said sending me a small wink. Though his eyes held a sparkle of mischief, his face remained dark as he held my gaze. I felt my cheeks heat in anger as I wanted nothing more than to race through the soldiers to cut him down. At least make it close enough to see the smirk drop from his lips.

"All that anger in such a small body, I would love to see you take it out on me," he said, knowing it would only rattle me further. Though his tone was teasing, there was something sinister in it.

I was about to storm over there myself and burn him to a crisp when I felt a hand hold my bicep. Faye pulled me back a bit as she took a strong stance beside me. Confidence and power radiating off of her as she observed the soldiers, a neutral expression across her features. She had returned, but why? She was supposed to start a panic in the mountain, that was the plan. Why was she back here?

The look she gave me told me to ask later. The pinch on my arm reminded me to check my emotions. She would never give anything away through her emotions, something I still needed to work on.

"Quite an impressive battalion you've put together, child," Faye said, her own smirk adorning her features. I could see Darious's features harden as he stared her down, obviously offended by the name. "It's a nice effort, do you have more hidden in the mountain? Or is this all of them?"

She was trying to get him to pull more soldiers from the mountain, to give Kasian and Mamarie more of a chance. I let the rage simmer down softly and pulled my own smirk onto my features.

"This is all I need to get rid of the likes of you. Though I wasn't expecting a myth like you, Faye, I think there are more than enough soldiers," he said simply, his tone having some sort of edge beneath it as he gestured to the army around him. He really thought we would be that easy to kill. He thought us weak, even though our magic was tied together.

"Won't take more than a moment," I said to Darious, letting my hands flame as Faye and I took a step down the ramp. If he didn't call more soldiers up right away, we would wipe a few ranks out so he would have to replenish them.

"Little Dove, you haven't even heard what I've had to say," Darious tsked, the edge to his tone dropping. Faye and I paused at the end of the ramp as we looked across the field at the dark prince. He twirled the small blade between his fingers before looking up to meet my eyes.

As soon as our eyes locked, I felt a scratch around my mind. Immediately I brought up the barriers I had created in my mind. He looked almost impressed as he felt around the wall in my mind. "You've been practising," he said with a small chuckle, though I could have sworn for a second, I saw panic flash across his features.

"I have an offer; one I don't think you can pass up, Aladella," he said, my name rolling off his lips. I sharpened my features, hardening them as I heard my name. Nicknames were easy enough to adjust to, but when my name left his lips, I knew he had something actually important to say. Not just mindless flirting and distraction.

"The galaxy belongs to me. It has for three hundred years. A child like you, will not ruin that in a day. If you want your friends to walk out of here with both of their legs, I suggest you try something other than instigating a war you cannot win," he said, tone deadly. "My offer, you come with me, I'll leave your friends and we will loosen our hold on the galaxy. I'll remove some of my troops and allow some freedom." He spoke so casually I didn't know what to make of the offer. I couldn't help but tilt my head a bit in confusion. I go with them and no war, no lost lives and he would lessen the dark hold he had on my galaxy.

I glanced at Faye and saw her features darken. The quick glance she sent me said it all. We would go down fighting for a truly free world. Not half-assed freedom masked by fear.

The era of the Darion would end.

I nodded my head, pretending to agree with his decision. Pursing my lips, a bit I met his eyes, the small smirk pulling at my features. "As lovely as your offer is, Darious. The answer is no," I said simply.

He remained silent for a good second. Without another word he tilted his head slightly, and his soldiers surged forward moving towards the ramp where Faye and I stood.

"They better be quick," I mumbled to Faye, a small laugh leaving her lips before we both pulled at our magic. My hands grew in a yellow flame, my eyes burning a bright amber. Faye's own eyes glowing a bright green from next to me.

We held our position on the ramp, our powers shooting forwards. My yellow glitter brushed across warriors, their metal chest plates melting into their chests from the heat. Their metal visors sinking into their heads as they dropped to the ground. From next to me I could see Faye flipping them around in the air, tripping and being tied up by long dark green vines.

As I fought the silent soldiers, I felt a tap on my mental shields. Not an aggressive push trying to break the walls, but almost a polite knock, asking for permission to send a message. My eyes shifted across the battle field but Darious was nowhere to be found. A feeling of urgency took over my body, almost a panic feeling and I let a sliver of my wall down. Only four words slipped through, Darious's slick voice echoing through my mind.

"Friends Safe. Get out."

Not even a second later the east facing doors burst open, the ground around us shaking. I couldn't help the excitement that flooded my veins as I saw Mamarie and Kasian burst through the doors. Their blue tattoos glowing from the exposed skin on their arms and their eyes shining the bright cerulean colour. They were absolutely ethereal.

Mamarie's hair floated around her and she had a blue aura wisping around her, the dark of her hair contrasting with the blue light around her. With Kasian next to her they looked absolutely terrifying. Kasian's eyes glowed a bright blue like his counter part, only sparks seemed to fall from his body. Bright blue flashes in the form of sparks as he used his magic, axe held tightly in his grip.

Mamarie drew back her bow and let an arrow loose, it twisted and turned in the air, piercing through five soldiers before retuning to its quiver. They only grinned at each other before throwing themselves through the air, flying over the heads of the silent soldiers and onto the ramp. Aisha appearing a second later.

"Go, Olen, now!" Kasian yelled from the ramp once we were all standing on the piece of metal. I noticed the bright-blue gems placed in Kasian's Axe hilt and Mamarie's bow, filling the gap that used to sit there.

They couldn't keep the smiles off their own faces as the ramp closed and we were taking off and out of the ribs of the mountain. The red stones falling down around us and crushing the soldiers below.

"Let's get out of this shit show," Mamarie said, a big grin on her face. I couldn't help the relieved laugh that left my lips as the group moved to the cockpit. We watched as the red stones fell towards the Darion soldiers, sure to crush them all.

Only they didn't.

A soft-purple glow spread across the valley, almost like a shield protecting the soldiers. From under that shield a bright platinum head of hair grinned wickedly up at me. Emila.

"I just have to get to the jump point," Olen said, pointing to the shimmering circle just across the skyline, we would just have to cross a bit more desert to reach it.

"I saw Emila, she's alive." The words tumbled from my lips, almost panicked. The group's relieved expressions dropped immediately, turning into mixed reactions of horror and panic.

Suddenly a giant clang hit the back of the ship and we were spinning towards the ground. A scream filled the cockpit but I couldn't tell if it had come from me or someone else. Olen steadied the ship but didn't have much control as he yelled something about the left engine being on fire.

Another smash sent me into Mamarie and the two of us to the floor, the ship once again on a track to the base of the mountain straight into the cracked ground.

"I can't get us up!" Olen yelled through the alarms going off through the ship.

The smell of smoke filled the cockpit and I heard Olen yell for us to brace and felt Mamarie and Kasian wrap their arms around me as I did to them and we braced for the ship to hit the ground.

And when it did, I was met with darkness.

CHAPTER THIRTY

"Della, c'mon Della, wake up," I could faintly hear Kasian mumbling from above me, a light tapping on my cheek forcing me to open my eyes again.

The cockpit was filled with smoke, my vision hazy and my lungs burning. I took in a gasp of air but the action caused me to cough up whatever had entered my lungs. I pulled my sleeve up to my face to stop me from inhaling the toxic fumes. The window was shattered in front of me and panic swelled in the bottom of my stomach as I started looking around for Olen. Praying to the stars he hadn't gone through the window.

"Faye got him out, its just you lets go," Kasian said, realizing my train of thought. I nodded and he started helping me up, throwing my arm across his shoulders as he helped me from the burning wreckage.

Just outside Mamarie and Olen sat on the red-dusted ground, their faces covered in soot, their clothes covered in a matching ash-grey colour. I figured I came out of the wreckage looking similar. Aisha floated above us, perfectly in one piece as she kept her eyeline on the mountains ahead of us. I looked myself, seeing flashes of silver metal reflecting from the sun as the Darion army flooded out of the mountain, heading straight for our direction.

"And here I thought something was going to turn out easy for once," Kasian mumbled, his arms folded across his chest as he matched my eyeline. He didn't seem to mind one bit his face was covered in ash, discolouring his tan skin.

I couldn't help but shake my head at his humour and look out towards the battle we had been dreading would come eventually. I narrowed my eyes a bit at the challenge, ready for whatever would come at us.

"At this point, I just want to get it over with," I said, joking along with him. His eyes met mine and he gave me a cheeky smile, enjoying the fact I could joke about our seemingly impending doom that was marching in our direction.

"We're going to make them walk the entirety of the desert, right?" Olen mused from where he was lounging on the red dirt. I couldn't help the smirk that pulled at my lips at his comment.

"We are their guests, the least they could do is come to us." The two boys only grinned at my response as my small family rose from their spots. My four Syron companions' eyes glowing their respective colours as we watched the approaching army jump into a sprint towards us.

"You know sometimes it hurts when you guys exclude me from your Syron club," Olen drawled, feigning a pout as he unholstered his guns, spinning them as he did.

"Don't worry, you're an exclusive fragile member," Kasian said, sending his friend a wink.

We watched as the army got closer, our magic mingling together and giving the air around us a buzz of power, the faint smell of smoke mingling in the air from the crash. It didn't take long for the never-tiring soldiers to reach us.

A second later, the firing started.

From above Aisha put up a protective shield, halting any fire the army sent our way, only able to shoot when they entered our vicinity. I felt my eyes glow their familiar amber colour, my Song stone I kept next to my sister's locket warming up my chest as I pulled on its power.

My magic lashed out on the silent soldiers around me, the only sounds across the battlefield being the blasters being fired, the hum of our magic and the soft buzz of silence that came off the army in waves. The sound unnerved me, sending chills up my spine as the sound got closer to me with every soldier. I threw my hands out, my magic wisping across their armour, melting it into their bodies.

The soldiers that made the mistake of getting too close, were taken down by the blade created by my glittering magic, slicing through their armour with a sickening sizzling sound.

I sliced through soldiers, trying to stay out of the way of their blaster fire as I sent my magic around them. To my right, Faye and Olen fought side by side. Olen covering Faye with his blaster fire and Faye using her magic to shield him. She moved effortlessly, taking out twice as many soldiers as I did, though she slowed to make sure Olen stayed safe in her vicinity.

To my left, Kasian and Mamarie fought as if they were a single being, moving and using their own magic around each other as if they knew each move, they would make. Their graceful movements taking out the Darion around them. Kasian's axe turning the bodies of the Darion soldiers to a paper-like ash as he cut through them. Mamarie sending arrows in every direction. The arrow would pierce the skin of a soldier, turning them into the same grey, paper-like ash before the arrow flew back into her quiver, ready to be used again.

Throughout the battlefield I could see blue veins appear on soldiers' bodies as they would start firing on their own army, taking down a few before they themselves would get shot down.

Then, the blue veins would appear on another soldier, and he would do the same. I fought through my own swarm of soldiers, a mist of grey surrounding me as I fought myself further into the sea of soldiers. My eyes on one person.

Darious.

I noticed him immediately, his green eyes piercing from across the battlefield. A different feeling of adrenaline filled my body as I let out a yell of anger. Yellow magic exploded from my body and melted the soldiers around me, clearing a path towards the dark prince.

He just stood there; expression hard as he eyed me down. Feet spread shoulder-width apart and his hands held behind his back. I felt my eye twitch as they turned a darker shade of yellow, the small piece of darkness in my heart growing as I sent the first punch.

I threw my magic down; it raced across the ground, small yellow flames licking at the red ground until it formed a circle around us, a fighting ring. He didn't say a single thing as I sent myself at him, my hands flaming, it would save me from worrying about a soldier sneaking up behind me. There was no sarcastic comment, no relentless flirting, no cocky smirk, just a dark expression across his features. His eyes started glowing a bright green, a soft Viridian green bled around him like an aura.

I sent my fist at him first, his arm moving up to block it, neither of us moving for the weapons we could use easily. This would be a battle I would win with my hands. The green aura around him protected his body from burning and melting from the heat of my magic.

We moved gracefully across the small circle, almost as if we were dancing. Through the ferocity of the punches and kicks I sent towards him were the exact opposite. Yellow met green on the field and my magic bounced off his, we were evenly matched.

Twin suns. Fighting to gain an upper hand on someone who was our equal.

Our power came from the same solar system, two suns who fed off one another for years, that same power flowing through our veins.

I felt his Song pouring energy into my body, I pulled from his power supply along with mine, the two of us using each other as we fought. The dark-green and bright-yellow of our magic moulding together as we dancing through the circle. The colour slowly turning into a bright-lime.

I could feel him pulling at the power of my own Song making me yell out in frustration and finally make contact with his body, with both hands braced in front of me, I sent my power into his chest. As he flew back a few feet, his magic left my system as mine left his. My magic returning to a bright-yellow as his faded into a dark-green.

He groaned from the ground and moved to get up. I didn't let him. The dark corner of my heart grew as I thought of his dark blade ripping through my mother's neck. I felt my own blade grow from my hand, turning into a solid, gold blade.

I held the hot metal to his neck not letting him move.

"Tell me you feel guilty," I spat out, my eyes burning as my hand held my blade, trying to hold back the tremors that wanted to take over my steady grip. I could feel the gold of my heart slowly fading into the dark as it crawled over it, seeping into the organ.

I felt my magic turn a deeper shade of gold, almost looking dirty as my eyes darkened, looking down at the man I held at the tip of my blade.

"I do," he answered, the truth spilling across his features. He wasn't lying. Though his features remained dark and hard, he didn't lie. I held back the sob in the back of my throat the best I could as I realized I wanted to take all of the dark thoughts and feeling out on him, shredding through his skin and let him bleed out on the battle field. But the simple 'I do' made the darkness retreat in the slightest, the gold of my heart shinning a bit from under its veil.

"As touching as this little performance is. We have a lot to catch up on." A sickly-sweet voice said from my left. I turned my head quickly, meeting the dark purple eyes of the platinum blonde witch. Emila.

"Step back from my son or I slit her throat." I moved my eyes down to the girl Emila held in her arms.

"Cerelia." Her name fell from my lips in a whisper.

My sister stood in front of me pale and shivering, her eyes filled with pain and shock. Her frame was thin, starved, and she wore only a thin slip that seemed so large on her small frame, so much smaller than I remember. Though she was two years older than me she looked so young, the fear in her eyes reminding me of a frightened child.

The emotions that ran through my body felt suffocating. I had thought her dead. All this time I thought she was dead but she had been alive and held by the platinum witch. And I hadn't tried to find her.

"Good. Now that I have your attention, move your blade from his neck," Emila snapped. I couldn't take my eyes off my older sister as I let my magic simmer down to a small buzz in my heart. I faintly heard Darious get up from the ground and move over to his mother's side. His head down the entire time until he faced me, then his chin lifted. A proud stance as he stood next to her. Back straight, shoulders back, hands clasped behind his back.

A wicked grin stayed on the evil queen's face as she nodded her head behind me. I turned a bit and noticed my three friends, bound and gagged by Darion soldiers. Kasian and Mamarie's wrists adorned with silver cuffs, purple magic swirling around them. Their eyes didn't meet mine as their gazes were forced to stay on their feet. Their knees were kicked from behind them and the three of them fell to their knees.

My heart quickened and cracked as I realized what was happening. This couldn't be how this ended.

"What a valiant effort the four of you have made today. Impressive really," Emila said, her chaotic gaze sweeping across my line of friends before landing on me. "Aladella, will you surrender or will we carve out your friend's pretty blue eyes? I do love how they change colour," Emila asked. Her purple magic swirling around her fingers as she trailed them across my sister's neck, tears falling from her golden-brown eyes, the eyes that matched mine.

I turned to look back at my friends, all of them now looking up at us. Deadly glares were on Kasian and Mamarie's faces but Olen seemed a little more shocked, his gaze shifting from between me and my sister.

My own eyes burned as I turned back to her, ready to sell my soul for their safety. When I looked up at Emila ready to agree to her terms, a flash of green split through the sky.

My sister was suddenly pushed forward and I immediately dove to grab her. Her fragile body falling into mine and I held her close to my chest, her soft fingers digging into my arms as she sobbed into my shoulders. I held her as close as I could without bruising her pale skin. Looking over her shoulder I saw Faye and Aisha throwing themselves at Emila, giving everything, they could in an effort to bring Emila to her knees.

Right when I saw Emila start to drain, a groan echoed through the desert making me turn my eyes to Darious. The purple tattoo from his arm was glowing purple and crawling up his neck, his eyes glowing a bright purple as he groaned. I furrowed my eye brows and turned my attention to Emila, who was suddenly becoming more powerful.

She was feeding from his power, taking it to make herself stronger.

I glanced down at my sister and quickly pulled her up, moving to Olen, I pushed her gently into his arms. He gave me a small nod, telling me he'd keep her safe. I tried to ignore her yell for me as I felt my eyes glow and I threw myself at Emila.

Only a scream cut me off.

To my right Darious had fallen to his knees, gripping his chest as the purple grew darker, the tattoo crawling further up his neck as he groaned in pain. If the distraction was intentional or not, it took my attention away from the fight, and in that split second a new scream filled the barren desert of Balcan.

I spun my head in her direction but it was too late.

Straight through Faye's abdomen was her own scepter, green gem covered in her own blood. Aisha's scream shook the mountains as her body started glowing a bright white colour, as if all the power she had left was being pushed from her body. My ghost friend dropped next to Faye's body. Her sobbing screams echoing across the desert. My breath caught in my throat as I froze in my spot.

Aisha's glare turned to Emila, and the white magic of the Syron encapsuled Emila. White light surrounding the witch.

I could hear Emila scream from inside the tornado of light, but Aisha did not have enough magic. The light was fading. I hardened my features and shot my hands out, my gold magic mixing with her white light and sent Emila to her knees as we suffocated her power. Aisha was fading and I pulled more of my magic. Intent on ridding the Temptress from the galaxy.

I let out a yell as I pulled more magic, sending the shimmering gold into the mix of white light around Emila. My hair floating and my eyes glowing a bright amber as I suffocated the platinum witch.

But a second later my magic stopped.

Darious grabbed my wrists, pulling them from where I was pushing magic at his mother and clamped gold bands around them. The action was too fast for me to counter.

Needles pricked my skin and suddenly my magic was draining from my body. My skin became dull and I felt a shield go up around my core of magic, unable to access it anymore. Whatever cuffs Darious had clamped around my wrists took my power. My attention turned to Darious, who still held my wrists. His expression not giving up anything, just a hard glare trained on my face.

Without my magic to help Aisha, her magic depleted. From the white magic surrounding Emila, a purple jagged shard pierced trough the white magic, then another. It was like she was growing from within the magic. Another purple shot through the white magic, only it flew through the air, piercing Aisha straight through her chest.

The world slowed, as if suddenly moving through honey. Aisha's gaze shifted to me, and she offered a soft smile. Not a second later her floating body disappeared from the sky. Faye fading along with her, the scepter falling to the ground. The whole galaxy seemed to go silent as the Syron that represented hope was sent to the next realm, by the evil she had killed three hundred years earlier. There were muffled shouts from behind me and tears fell down my cheeks as I realized hope was lost.

Emila's glowing eyes turned to the group of us, her smile only growing as she saw me on my knees. I didn't realize I had fallen, but the weight of my body seemed too heavy with the planet's gravity as my two friends disappeared in front of me. Their souls travelling to the otherworld.

"Do I need to kill them all or can we come to an agreement?" Emila asked, holding Faye's scepter in her hand, the green gem that was once there shattered to pieces on the red sand behind her. I had to swallow a few times before I could answer, my throat dry and cracking from the events of the desert. I tried to reach for my magic as rage flooded my veins, but the damper on my power only groaned in resistance around my wrists. My hands dug into the red dirt beneath me, my frustration building as I filled my hands with the bloodstained sand.

"They go, you don't ever touch any of them and I'll come with you." I managed to crack out, my voice a rough stutter as I glanced back at my family behind me. My sister wrapped up in Olen's arms.

"If only I kept promises." Emila chuckled. True realization sank into the darkness of my heart. She would never let any of us free again, she knew we would fight back, no matter what.

"I think I'm going to enjoy your screams the most," she said, her hand tilting my chin up to see her wicked smirk. The gold cuffs around my wrists swirled with purple magic and I felt her pull at my power, taking some of it for herself.

"Let's go home," Emila said smiling to her son. She twirled the staff between her hands a few times as a ship landed just outside the battle field, where Darion soldiers lay in their own puddles of blood.

And I was pulled to my feet and dragged onto the ship along with my three remaining friends and sister.

My fists relaxed as the hope drained from my chest. The feeling of the red sand slipping from my fingers mimicked perfectly the feeling of loss and anxiety creeping up my throat.

CPSIA information can be obtained
at www.ICGtesting.com
Printed in the USA
LVHW041458091221
705747LV00015B/2379

9 781039 127203